A Subtle Thing

A NOVEL
BY ALICIA HENDLEY

FIVE RIVERS CHAPMANRY
WWW.5RIVERS.ORG

A Subtle Thing, Copyright © 2010 by Alicia Hendley

Edited by Kelly Stephens

Cover photograph Copyright © 2010 by Crystal Andrushko

Published in Canada by Five Rivers Chapmanry, 704 Queen Street, P.O. Box 293, Neustadt, ON Canada www.5rivers.org

First Edition 2010 ISBN 978-0-9865427-0-1

Digital Edition 2010 ISBN 978-0-9866423-2-6

Library and Archives Canada Cataloguing in Publication

Hendley, Alicia, 1970-

    A subtle thing / Alicia Hendley.

ISBN 978-0-9865427-0-1

    I. Title.

PS8615.E533S82 2010   C813'.6   C2010-903866-5

Text set in Perpetua.

Sub-titles, headers and footers set in Copperplate Gothic.

Title and Chapters set in Rage Italic.

To my children, Daniel, Meghan, Maxwell, and Samuel, and to my husband, Joel, with love.

Acknowledgments

I would like to thank my brother, Nate Hendley, for pushing me to always write, even when (especially when) time and energy to do so have been scarce. His ongoing support, input, and belief in me have been invaluable. Here's to you, big brother.

I would like to thank my parents for their love and encouragement over the years and for giving me my first typewriter. I would also like to thank my brother, Matthew Hendley, for modeling the importance of perseverance and good humour when trying to reach goals.

I would like to thank my friends, Alison Beckett and Alisa Sivak, for being early readers of my work and for always reminding me of the importance of writing in my life. I would also like to thank my friends, Christine Kok and Patricia Beck, for listening to me and supporting me in the writing process.

A special thanks to my publisher, Lorina Stephens, and to my editor, Kelly Stephens, for taking a chance on a first-time author and for their work in helping to transform my manuscript into a novel.

Finally, I would like to thank my former clients for teaching me about the courage, strength, and grace required to live on a day-to-day basis with depression. This book is for you.

PROLOGUE

*I*t's subtle at first. You're sitting at your computer one morning when you notice that something, just a little something, is there. The difference is so small, so nothing really, that it almost slips by. Maybe it starts in your stomach, nudging at your ribs. Or maybe you notice it in your fingers, shaking just a bit over the keyboard. If you try and take a deep breath maybe you'll feel it for the first time then, giving your lungs a quick squeeze as they try to fill. This something is so minor, so not anything at all, that you can easily wave it away. Tonight you'll go to bed earlier, maybe have a bath first with the cubes that fizz. Tomorrow you'll skip that third cup of coffee and all will be fine.

And you'll be right. The next morning that something won't be there and you'll forget. Until an afternoon one week later, when a bag of Doritos refuses to fall from the vending machine, *Damn it,* and you burst into tears. The sudden wave of horrific despair will be so hot and wet that it'll shock your eyes dry. *What? …Where?…Why?* You'll demand, as the bottom falls out.

Looking back you'll know it's been there for a while now. Weeks, maybe months, patiently waiting. Anyone could have noticed the signs if they'd been looking *But why would you want to look for this?* Those extra glasses of red wine, the phone calls that went on five minutes too long, the way you'd started looking to the sides of people, not able to deal with anyone or anything head-on.

When the tears come you know that something's different, something's changed. You've cried before, but always as a release, to get something out. Now it feels like the reverse—like you keep taking things in. Whatever blinders you had on before to keep the outside out are gone. Suddenly everything makes you cry. It's the careless bits of kindness that really get to you. A neighbour shoveling out your car just because. The coffee shop lady remembering how you like your coffee (large, two creams, no sugar). Your thesis advisor giving you an extension when you have no solid reason for needing it. Anything, everything makes you cry. Mold threatens to grow on your raw, damp face as the faucet opens up. Your empathy for any living creature that could be experiencing pain also kicks into overdrive. Compassion oozes out of you like sweat, until you're bathed in it. But it's still normal, it's still okay. You've been under stress at school, deadlines are tight. It's just a sign to slow down, to take it easy. You've got too much on your plate.

And so you go into fix-it mode. You replace your caffeine with chamomile, your e-mails with Enya. You sign up for every yoga and mindfulness class you can get your hands on, and pop St. John's Wort with your multivitamin. You start saying no and meaning it. You surround yourself with incense, bubble bath, and essential oils. When that doesn't work, when nothing seems to work, you go see a psychologist. You find yourself temporarily soothed by his reassurances of your sanity, by his pronouncements that all of this, *whatever this is*, can go away if you stop letting in those negative, nasty thoughts. All you need to do is grab those thoughts at the door and strip-search them for their accuracy. No gate-crashers allowed. And for a while you believe him. You learn to identify your thoughts, to evaluate your thoughts, to replace your thoughts with realistic ones.

He preaches earnestly to you about the importance of change, about the *necessity* of moving forward, of *letting go*. He wisely tells you that life is like a river, that you can never step in the same water twice. You go home embracing this as your new ideal, then become paralyzed by the possibility of buying a new brand of toilet paper. Yet you are determined to believe in him, you're desperate for this to work. You convince yourself that with enough effort you too can have a mind that is sanitized and pure. Until that one session, eight weeks in, when your dreams of wells without bottoms and birds flying into mirrors don't fit into his neat, manicured space. When you decide that you want to go beyond what is surface, that you want to show him everything else. When you want him to know the core, with the pulp and the juice and the seeds, with the flesh and the muck. When you hold it all out to him but all he can see is the polished skin, shiny and blemish-free.

So you decide to try the chemical route, to dynamite your brain back into submission. You set a date to see your physician, then sit through the whole appointment silent and weeping. Despite this, or maybe because of this, he hears you, *finally, someone hears you*, and gives you a prescription, your golden ticket. Dutifully you fill it out and put the bottle on your counter, next to the toaster. Your plan is to have it there so that there's no way you can forget to take the pills. No excuses. The medication can't work if you don't consistently take the pills. So why can't you force yourself to take the damn pills? After three weeks spent staring at the bottle (and one desolate night spent envisioning yourself putting its entire contents down your gullet) you dump the pills in the toilet.

And then things get odd. Wet sand fills your veins, weighing you down. Everything feels heavy—the fork in your hand, your lover's gaze, the words in your throat. The world becomes filled with edges that bump against you, bruising you from the outside in. And then the forgetting. Not just simple things like names or dates. *No.* You shampoo your hair and forget to rinse. You put bread in the toaster and forget what comes next. You stare at your lover and forget what the point of it all is. Is there a point? Should there be? *What the hell is the point?* But the remembering is much worse. Every pushed away, shoved down hurt comes bubbling back up. The remembering is not about the wrongs done against you. It's about what you so easily, and so shamelessly, have done to others.

Memories long suppressed start to sprout and bud from that hidden place. You remember tripping a skinny boy on the playground in grade three, just because you could. You remember bribing your whiny cousin fifty cents just so that she wouldn't come to your birthday party and ruin it all. You remember making your little sister sit through the Wizard of Oz and the flying monkeys, just to feel the sweet power of being able to make her cry. You remember ending relationships without explanation and forgetting your parents' anniversary two years in a row. *You remember, you remember, you remember.* All of it, each and every ruthless moment of it, was you. Everything that is callous and brutal at your core starts to rot and you can't get away from the stench.

The funny thing, it's hilarious, really, is that no one seems to know. Not your lover, not your friends, and thankfully not your family. You're walking through your days with parts falling off behind you and no one notices the leper among them. Eyes? Gone. Nose? Gone. Ears? Gone. Brain? Heart? Fingers? All gone. You drift in a sightless, soundless, tasteless void but all's fine with the world.

So you go through the motions (you're great at going through the motions) and try to wait it out.

And then one morning you notice, it's gone. Where it went and why it was here at all becomes irrelevant. The whole thing goes back to that hidden place, where it belongs. Here's what does matter: your hands aren't shaking. You can take a deep breath and fill up the bottom of your lungs. You can hug your friends without splitting in two. You can look at your lover and remember what the point of it all is. It's a subtle thing, really.

CHAPTER ONE

I'm crouched in the bathroom, the whir from the overhead fan almost drowning out the incessant thudding in my head (*idiot, idiot, idiot*). I ball my hands into fists and push my fingernails into my palms. I'd forgotten how this feels. Shame and regret shoot down my throat like a funneled beer. All it takes is one roaring, overpowering rush and I lose my balance.

"Um, hello?" says a voice from outside the door. "Hey? Are you coming out? Is everything okay in there?"

I glance at the door, but don't bother to answer. I can feel my thoughts slipping, unable to find their footing. Fear builds in my stomach, spreading into my lungs. I shut my eyes and try to imagine a stable, peaceful self flickering behind my lids, *Look! Right there!*, but can't forget whose hand is on the projector. Frantically I try to remember the steps that were drilled into me from before—*feelings are not facts, take slow breaths, deep and slow, feelings are not facts*. I slowly stand up again, avoiding the mirror. *Don't think about this right now. Just get out.* I flush the toilet once, twice, then open the door. He (*whoever the hell he might be*) is waiting outside, a concerned look on his face.

"Is everything okay?" he asks again, as I walk past him to the bed and grab a handful of clothes. "You were in there a long time." He smiles, but his grin doesn't quite reach me.

I pull a shirt over my head. "I've got to go," I say. I shove my feet into shoes and head for the stairs. "This was great and everything, but I've got to go." I rush down the stairs and out the front door. The night is black and starless. I walk quickly on the sidewalk, listening to the beat of my footsteps. *Why now? Why now? Why now?* It had been almost two years since the last time. I quicken my pace, heading nowhere. Eventually I start to jog, hoping that somehow, just this once, I can out-run myself. *How could I have been so stupid? When will this go away?* But even as I ask, I know that this will never go away, that nothing will ever change. How do you exorcize your own personality? And if that were even possible, what the hell would be left?

I'm such a fuck-up. I'd become too cavalier, assuming that if I acted normal long enough, I could forget what lay simmering beneath my surface. Completing my undergraduate degree had been a feat and should have satisfied me. But having the taste of success on my tongue had made my stomach lurch for something sweeter. With eyes half-shut, I'd entered graduate school. With eyes half-shut I'd finished my Master's degree. Two terms late, but still. It had been enough of a victory to make me stop looking over my shoulder, to ignore the warning signs, to forget what came next. Going out to celebrate with Patrick and friends after my thesis defense had just been greedy. I'd forgotten how quickly a few drinks could wash away the veneer.

I head away from home, where razors and matches cheerfully

beckon. Instead I enter the nearest twenty-four hour coffee shop, to wait out the night. With slugs of caffeine, I try to blot out the memory of Patrick's confused face and how he continued to give me the benefit of the doubt as I danced with random men. I feel bile begin to rise when I remember how confusion suddenly switched to hurt, like a curtain quickly drawn, as he watched me stick my tongue down the throat of Mr. Hook-up. What adds colour and bite to this particular hell is that I felt justified in humiliating such a kind, gentle soul, that part of me even *enjoyed* it. After all, focusing on being pissed off with Patrick's endless affability had helped me stave off the approaching storm, at least for the night. If that isn't proof that the crazies are back, I don't know what is. I keep glancing at the clock above the counter, cajoling nine o'clock to come already and rescue me. Finally, it's here and in my panic I mess up the long-memorized number three times before finally making the connection.

"Hello, Downtown Community Clinic," a steady voice says, which only serves to increase my anxiety.

"Hi, I'd like to book an appointment with Dr. Miller. As soon as possible."

"I'm sorry, but he no longer works here."

"What? He must! Dr. Peter Miller."

"Dr. Miller retired nine months ago."

"Retired? How could he retire? He's not old enough to retire!"

"Dr. Miller left the practice nine months ago and accepted a teaching position at an American university." The voice pauses. "Perhaps you would like to make an appointment with one of our other psychologists, such as Dr. Green? Many of Dr. Miller's clients have transferred to her and seem quite satisfied."

"You don't understand! I have to see Dr. Miller!" Panic fills my throat, cutting off my air supply. "Please!"

"I'm sorry, but that just isn't possible." Another pause. "Is this a crisis situation?"

"Not if I can see Dr. Miller! Please!"

"I'm truly sorry. Perhaps..."

I hang up, but continue holding the phone in my hand, unwilling to let go of my one buoy. I know I can call any of the friends who were at the bar last night, any of them, that is, but Patrick. There are several messages waiting for me already, voices eager to have me make sense of what happened. But I also know that at this moment, as I am about to be spun face-first into the eye of a crisis, coolly explaining my crazy self would require more mental mettle than I've ever possessed. I need someone from Before, from the past I've tried to out-run, to bare witness to my spiral downward. I begin mentally searching for possible rocks of stability but only come up with a few small pebbles.

I consider calling the one person I'm certain has washed his hands of me. *Adam.* Despite myself, I remember the last time I saw my cousin, almost two years ago. I'd lain slumped and jelly-like on an emergency room bed, while he'd stood rigid against a pulled curtain. I remember feeling Adam's stare push against my cheek, my hair. The weight of it had pinned me in place. I remember trying to turn my head to look at him, to meet the stare, just for a second, but it didn't happen. If I had made a move, if I had even blinked, I would have shattered. Old images now flood my brain unbidden, soft and dreamlike—arriving at Adam's wedding dateless, running into an ex on the dance floor, lurching into the ladies' room to down a bottle of Zoloft, the blissful slide down onto the cold floor and into oblivion. If I could stop the memories there, all would be fine. But the images that follow have jagged edges—being yanked back into consciousness as tubes got pushed down my throat, the absence of my parents at the hospital, Adam instead standing guard by my bed, rigid and brideless, fiddling with his wilting boutonniere.

Not him. I put away my phone and decide I might as well go home. I slowly unfold myself from the booth, my cramped muscles making their voices known. I know I'm safe for now, the razors and matches no longer seeming so inviting. By keeping awake all night I've granted myself a stay of execution—exhaustion envelopes me like a life jacket, helping me to keep afloat.

ℰꙄℛ

I head home on autopilot, the walk from the coffee shop to my apartment never registering in my mind. In my frazzled state, paying the waitress at the restaurant is immediately followed by lying spread eagle on top of my bedspread, with no space in between. No matter. Like a game of hopscotch, the more squares of time I can skip over right now, the better. I stare up at the ceiling, marveling at how quickly I can switch from bright hopefulness to burdensome despair, with no effort involved.

I no longer trust myself. The last time this happened I made a promise to take control of my train wreck of a life before it permanently slipped off the rails. I swore to pay attention, to be more vigilant of the subtle changes that always came first. A slight increase in irritability or a mild decrease in energy and I would be first in line to renew my antidepressant prescription. I might have depression but by God I refused to be a Depressed Person! *What bullshit.* If this were true, why had I ignored what was happening in the last three weeks? Could I really have believed that the unprovoked arguments with Patrick, the sudden belches of tearfulness, and the late nights spent mindlessly watching infomercials were nothing more than jitteriness about my impending thesis defense? Was I really that moronic? I lift my hand to slap myself, but instead cover my eyes with my fingers. Being melodramatically self-loathing will not help me crawl out of the void any quicker.

I don't know how long I am asleep for and when I awaken the

dim, pastel light that fills the room disorients me. Is the sun rising or setting? It's not until I get up off the bed that I notice Patrick for the first time. He is sitting across the room at my desk, a piece of paper in front of him. For the few seconds it takes before he notices me, I stare at his right hand as it grips a pen, white-fisted but unmoving.

"Hey," I say. I watch as he turns his head towards me, the pen still in hand.

"I was going to write you a letter," he says, holding out the pen. "I was going to, but I didn't know what to say." His voice is unfamiliar, broken, and reedy. "What is there to say?"

"Oh, Patrick," I say softly. "I'm so, so sorry." I take a step towards him, but then stop. *Do not pass go.*

"Sorry for what?" he asks, his face closed and tight. He stares at me, his loud breaths filling the room. "Do you have any idea what you're sorry for, Beth? Could it be for humiliating me in front of all of our friends? Or for treating me like shit for no apparent reason? Or maybe for making me worry all night about your safety? Or is there something else you're sorry for?" He grabs the paper on the desk, crumbles it into a ball, and tosses it on the floor, discarded.

"I'm sorry for all of it. For everything." As I look at his face, the ramifications of what I've done crash over me and I feel dizzy from their weight. I take a step backwards and sit down on the bed. "Patrick, please, please, what can I do?"

"Make it so last night never happened. Make this all go away," he says quietly. He glances at me and I can't see myself reflected in his eyes. *Where did I go?* "And make yourself not be such a slut."

I nod repeatedly, trying to buy myself the time I need to change what is happening. Maybe if I can make Patrick *understand* why I acted the way I did, I can slow us down before we reach the end. *I'm not ready for this to end.*

"Did I ever tell you that I suffer from depression?" I ask, looking at the crumbled ball of paper.

"Excuse me?"

"I said, did I ever tell you that I get depressed? That I've been diagnosed with depression?" I force myself to look at his mirror-less eyes once more.

"No."

"Well, I do, Patrick. I have depression. Or depressed episodes. That's what I have. And now I know that another one's starting. That's what last night was all about."

"I have no clue what you're trying to tell me here, Beth."

I take a deep breath, once, twice. "I'm trying to *explain* why I acted like such an idiot last night. Why I hurt you so badly."

"Don't flatter yourself."

"Please! Let me explain!" I say shrilly, moving my empty hands in the air. *Not now. Calm down.* I try again. "Each time I've gotten depressed I've done something really stupid and hurtful, either to myself or someone else." I pause. "This therapist I used to see thought that when I did something dumb I was trying to create a *reason* for why I felt so bad. That it made it easier for me to think my feeling bad was about something."

"And has it?" Patrick asks.

"Has what?"

"Has making out with some random guy and then taking off with him last night made things easier for you?" Patrick stands up, pushes the chair neatly under the desk, and leaves my apartment.

I wait a few minutes and then check myself for bruises. I find nothing. While Patrick was here and I was waist-deep in images from last night, I felt it all—shame, regret, guilt. But since he's left, there's nothing. It's like Patrick was a poker whose presence temporarily stoked some dying flames, but now that he's gone, I'm ash. I lie back down on my bed and surrender to what I know is coming.

CHAPTER TWO

I'm alone. I'm alone. I'm alone. I'm alone. I'm alone. The phrase reverberates through my skull like a dial tone—loud, aggravating, yet impossible to ignore. As I lie on my back, I become acutely aware of the mechanics involved in blinking. Open, close, open, close. The more aware I become, the more panicked I feel. What if my lids stop mid-blink and remain frozen in a perpetual stare? What if I can never shut the world out again? I keep my eyes closed and try to focus on my breathing instead, the thought of having my breath suddenly stop oddly comforting.

The interval that follows becomes a blur of night/day/night. At some point I must get up to use the toilet, grab a handful of cereal, or stick my head under the faucet to wash out the cotton that fills my throat, but when or how, I don't remember. All that stays with me is lying prone on my increasingly sour sheets—too overwhelmed by the relentless monotony of my blinking to deal with the black that has engulfed me. I've heard it said that when a woman is labouring there comes a stage in which the pain and pressure are so intense that she can't imagine what it was like before—that she *becomes* the pain and everything before no longer exists.

As I lie on my rank bed I realize that I've reached that stage. I can no longer recall there ever being a time in which I wasn't in this thick, viscous despair. I *know* that such a time must have existed and that even since first getting depressed ten years ago I've had at least several months between episodes, but I can't *remember* it.

Forget about ever having gone to classes and worked on my thesis, how did I actually get up every morning and plan for the rest of the day? How did I shower, dress, eat, or speak? How did I manage to even walk a few feet away from my bed with these concrete poles for legs? How did I interact with friends, professors, or Patrick, like a normal human being? And how did I summon up the motivation to do unnecessary things like shaving my legs, rolling on deodorant, or checking my eyebrows for stray hairs? What made me believe that the minutiae of life actually mattered, and how can I get that belief back? As I spend an afternoon contemplating whether or not it's worth it to get up and brush my woolly teeth, knowledge of my recent infidelity impresses me, as such actions must have required more energy than I'll likely ever possess again.

As I stare at the ceiling, my thoughts become fixated on all the times I've been depressed, each memory rolling into the next until they become one massive, undulating wave. My mind flips from images of having my teenaged head stroked by my mother as I sobbed across her lap to being told a few years later after one suicide attempt too many that if I wanted to run amok with my life I could no longer expect her or my sister to come along for the ride. Bobbing up and down in this sea of self-incrimination is the image of my cousin Adam, who through it all had been a stalwart ally, until my hurricane-like tendencies caused too much damage in his own life for him to remain standing.

ℰℭ

The son of my mother's sister, Adam, grew up four blocks away from us. In the hazy, dream-like years of very early childhood, my mother and I spent most Saturdays at her sister's house. On warm afternoons my mother and aunt would lay out a platter of crust-less peanut butter and jelly sandwiches and a jug of purple Kool-Aid on the patio table, then leave us kids to our own devices. For Adam and me, Saturdays were spent roaming the neighbourhood together, picking up twigs, stones, and other treasures along the way. Whenever we met an unfamiliar adult they would typically assume that we were siblings. As a child, nothing gave me more pleasure than being told that Adam and I looked alike. The very idea that my skinny, pale, stringy haired self could bare even a passing resemblance to my golden haired, golden skinned cousin made me glow with pride. No matter that he was adopted and that the very idea of us resembling one another was ridiculous. It was clear to me that what the adults were picking up on was the fact that deep inside we were twins, we belonged together. He was mine and I was his.

Even as a child, shy, steady Adam had an inner strength that helped to soothe me at my most frenzied. To impatient adults, my exuberance may have bordered on frenetic, my energy on wildness. I was too full of *antics*, I needed to *settle down*, to *stop asking so many questions*. To Adam, however, I was a free spirit who encouraged him to try new things, who opened up his world to what could be. Whenever one of my ideas crossed some invisible line for adults—and most of my ideas typically did—Adam would always claim that he had been the instigator. Despite what was glaringly obvious—that I had to be the culprit, that any other possibility was laughable—Adam would insist that whatever asinine thing we had just done together was actually his idea. Whether it was pouring vegetable oil all over his mother's kitchen floor so that we could skate across it with sponges tied to our feet, or trying to invent a new kind of soup involving dirt and then leaving on all the burners while we went out to play, Adam took the fall. And I always let him.

In turn, I trusted Adam's opinion about the important things, those things that really mattered. If it wasn't okay with Adam, then it wasn't okay. My opinions about things, while expressed quickly and loudly, often stood on a very weak foundation and could slide away like spring mud. Adam's opinions often took time to take root and thus seemed solid and true. Like whether or not I should trust my mother's new husband enough to accept him as my father. Without ever consciously recognizing it to be so, the fact remained that, even at the age of six, I would never open myself up to Jacob unless he first passed Adam's careful inspection. Adam had my back, Adam was my better half.

"Remember when he ate one of those cookies we made that looked like pieces of rubber and then he wanted another?" Adam asked me, after I demanded he explain why he thought my mother's recent marriage to Jacob was indeed a good thing. I nodded. "That's why."

His logic made sense. Jacob accepted our cookies, no matter their flaws, so I should accept Jacob. With my cousin's stamp of approval I let my guard down and allowed myself the reality of having a father to seep in.

In the midst of this depression, Adam's current absence from my life seems like something tangible, a solid and impenetrable object that I have to somehow navigate around. Too tired to keep dwelling on what I used to have, I take some Gravol and sink thankfully into a dead-like sleep.

8003

A week or an hour goes by and suddenly Patrick is back. The fact that he's here in my apartment makes no sense to me and yet is perfectly reasonable. If my own brain can become my worst enemy, then why wouldn't the man I just betrayed come by for a friendly visit? As I look up at Patrick's face looming above my bed, I attempt a smile.

"Hey," I say, closing my eyes again. "Just napping." I roll over on my side and assume the fetal position beneath my quilt.

"Professor Shields called me into his office yesterday," Patrick says. "You were supposed to start your summer research assistantship last week and never showed. He wanted to know if you were sick."

"Yeah, sick," I say through a mouthful of blanket.

"I told him you had the flu and that he could expect you on Monday, at nine a.m. sharp."

"Hmmmmmm," I answer, snuggling further down on my mattress, my feet sticking out over the edge. Monday is a world away, in a place that might not even exist.

"Your mail slot in the grad office is overflowing with crap," he says. "The secretary told me you haven't signed up for convocation tickets and now the deadline's passed. I tried calling you on your phone about fifty times but you never picked up." He pauses. "After what you told me, I started to get worried."

"Sorry 'bout that," I mutter.

"Enough already. It's time to get up," Patrick says loudly.

"Hmmmmmm. Not right now," I say.

"It's been ten days! Get *up*, Beth."

"Maybe later," I answer, my tongue feeling fat and foreign in my mouth.

"Getting up is non-negotiable," Patrick says, roughly pulling off my blanket. Suddenly the tone of his voice changes from firm to frantic. "What the hell is this in your bed, Beth? And this? And this?"

I keep my eyes shut but can hear a few pill bottles being rattled. "Tylenol? Gravol? Cold medicine? Shit, Beth, have you OD'd?"

Reluctantly I open my eyes and push myself up on an elbow. "Calm down, Patrick. It's fine," I say, pushing a greasy strand of hair off my forehead. I feel as if I'm talking through a giant vat of Jell-o. "I've just been taking a few every day to help me sleep."

"And you keep three bottles with you in bed? Under the covers?"

"I swear, Patrick, it's not what you think." I again attempt a smile, but end up grimacing instead. "I don't want to kill myself," I say unconvincingly. "I just want to sleep until I feel better again. You know, normal."

"Who's your doctor?" he demands, ignoring my explanation entirely. "I'm not dealing with this by myself."

"Patrick, come on. Don't be ridiculous. I just wanted to sleep."

"No longer an option," he says, grabbing at my T-shirt and forcing me out of bed. His fingers graze my bare arm and he quickly lets go, as if burned by my skin. "Now tell me the name of your doctor or we're going to the emergency room."

"This is so unnecessary," I start to say, but Patrick's eyes stop me. "Okay, okay, it's Dr. Nelson," I tell him. "On Bishop Street."

"I'll make the call while you go get dressed," he says, as I slowly stand up. Suddenly dizzy, I use the wall to brace myself.

"Come on, Patrick."

"Come on yourself, Beth. Do you think I'd be here if anyone else was still on campus and could baby-sit you instead? Do you think this is my idea of a good time?" I look at his pale, tense face and hate myself a little more. Only an extreme asshole would make their ex-boyfriend rescue them. I nod, more to myself than to him, and go to the bathroom to change.

As I pull a pair of jeans over my pajama bottoms, I feel an unexpected burst of energy, the experience of letting someone else make all the decisions for me somehow mood-enhancing. Maybe yielding *is* good. For the time being, at least, I don't have to think anymore. *Let him decide.* The trip to the doctor's office is quick and silent. I stare out the passenger window of Patrick's car, the familiar roads seeming foreign and unknown. Patrick parks the car, then walks around to my door and opens it for me. In the face of this chivalrous, yet predictable gesture, I'm jolted by a sudden surge of anger. *Why do you always have to do what's right?* I get out of the car and follow Patrick into the building.

As Patrick sits in the waiting room, I meet with Dr. Nelson in a narrow, windowless office. My appointment with him lasts less than fifteen minutes. We both know the drill, we've been through this enough times before. First there's a superfluous physical exam, followed by a checklist of any possible symptoms. I spit out answers before Dr. Nelson finishes asking each question. How long have you been feeling consistently sad, angry, or numb? *About three weeks.* Under- or over-sleeping? *Over.* Increased or decreased appetite? *What appetite?* Energy level? *Low. Probably why I'm oversleeping.* Thoughts of suicide or self-harm? *Too tired to contemplate either, although rarely eating could be seen as a slow way to go.* Lack of interest in activities? *Yes, unless you count sleeping.* Reduced functioning? *Don't really need to answer, as disheveled appearance and offensive smell probably say it all.* On this test I get a perfect score and together Dr. Nelson and I agree that another trial of antidepressants would be warranted. Just to be on the safe side, a blood test for anemia will be ordered, with the antidepressants started immediately. Also to be on the safe side, a new antidepressant will be tried, as I haven't been so lucky with the last three.

"And maybe now's the time to consider a referral to a psychiatrist as an adjunct to our work together," he says.

"No!" I blurt out. Dr. Nelson raises his eyebrows. "It's just that, I'm done grad school now and will be moving for jobs," I explain.

"Oh? You have a job?" Dr. Nelson puts down my chart and looks at me. "Congratulations!"

"No—well, I mean, I *do* have a position at the university for the summer, doing research for my advisor. I had thought about applying for the Ph.D., but now it's too late for this fall. So pretty soon I'll have to start applying all over the place for jobs and might end up moving far away. I mean, I've lived here for eight years now, I'd like to experience life in other cities," I babble. "That's why a referral isn't such a great idea. I don't want to start with someone and then have to leave." *Anything but a psychiatrist.*

"Why don't we cross that bridge when we come to it, Beth? At the very least, given your history, I'd like to get the wheels in motion for a psychiatric consult, to ensure you're taking the most appropriate psychotropic. Think of it as a preventative measure."

"Preventative," I repeat dully. *How can anyone prevent what's already happening?*

"And I assume you've kept up your appointments with your psychologist?" Dr. Nelson looks at me.

"Of course," I lie, remembering Dr. Miller and his job transfer. *Not my fault he left me too*, I think, suddenly petulant.

"Good. Now back to the Effexor. Beth, I'd like you to make another appointment to see me in four weeks, so we can determine if the medication is working properly," Dr. Nelson says, handing me my prescription. "I'd like you to begin by taking a thirty-seven point five milligram dose for one week and then increase it to seventy-five milligrams until we next meet."

"Okay," I say, suddenly feeling exhausted by so much talking.

"And Beth, when I next see you I'd like us to talk about the possibility of continuing a maintenance dose of Effexor once your mood lifts." Dr. Nelson looks me straight in the eye. "I know how you feel about being permanently medicated, Beth, but when your last episode ended we agreed to consider this if you ever became depressed again, and here we are." I turn my gaze down and shrug. He reaches over and pats my shoulder. "There's nothing shameful about taking care of your mental health," Dr. Nelson says, his tone gentle. He stands up and walks out of the room, leaving me to get dressed again. I remain sitting for a few more minutes, my bare legs dangling like a gawky child's over the edge of the examining table.

The drive home is as silent as the way there. Patrick is meticulous as a driver, always maintaining the appropriate space between vehicles and keeping within the posted speed limits. Now the roads seem overly familiar and in the midst of their sameness I feel claustrophobic. How many times have I ridden to and from Dr. Nelson's office since first starting at the university? In eight years I may have gotten two degrees, but I've also experienced four nose-dives into brain-numbing depression, countless panic attacks, two hospitalizations, and the permanent loss of most family and friends. Not exactly an academic success story.

When we reach my apartment building Patrick keeps the car running. This is so unlike him that I take a risk and break the silence between us.

"You're not coming in?" I ask, turning in my seat to look at him. Patrick's hands remain tight around the steering wheel, frozen in the nine and three o'clock positions.

"My job here is done," he says, staring straight ahead.

"Not even for a minute?" I ask. "It would give us a chance to talk…"

"I think we've talked enough, Beth."

"Can't I even make you a coffee to say thank you for everything you've done?"

"Just make sure to see Professor Shields on Monday, okay? Don't make me look like an ass." Patrick tightens his grip on the steering wheel.

"Patrick…"

"Bye, Beth," he says, shifting into reverse.

"Okay, thanks." I reach over to touch his arm, hesitate, then do it anyway. His flesh feels rigid, unyielding. I have a sudden image of this same arm hugging my naked body bear-close, and experience a fresh wave of shame. "I promise I'll go to campus on Monday, okay?" In the silence that follows, I get out of the car and walk towards my building. Twenty-five steps to the front door. *How many more until I'm forgiven?* When I get to the front door and turn back to look at Patrick, he's already driving away. I walk down the hallway to my basement apartment, unlock the door, and step inside. Just a few hours before, this had been my refuge. Now as I look around, I see it through Patrick's eyes. The curtains are closed, and it takes a few minutes for my eyes to adjust to the dim light. I walk towards the kitchen and notice boxes of cereal knocked over on the kitchen table and the garbage pail overflowing. In the main room, my futon sofa is permanently pulled out into a bed and is covered with blankets, pill bottles, and empty juice boxes. The place looks less like a home and more like a suicide waiting to happen. I quickly turn on the lights and open the curtains. Then I grab a glass of water and take out my new prescription from its paper bag. *Step one.*

CHAPTER THREE

One week goes by, then two, with little change other than I somehow summon the Herculean effort required to go to my campus job each day. I can't let Patrick down again. I walk through the hours like an automaton. The leaden feeling in the bottom of my lungs remains, making each breath seem like a workout. Still, I develop a safe predictability to my days in the hopes that this will harness in my mood and prevent it from impromptu wanderings. Each morning I take my medication, downing a glass of water while standing at my kitchen counter. Mondays through Fridays I spend in a small, temporary office on campus, working for a professor on research that no longer interests me, believing that there's safety in what's known. Every day I take a thirty minute lunch break and sit by myself on a stone bench in a courtyard eating my cheese on rye.

After about three weeks with no end in sight, I begin to see it—the possibility of an end. It comes to me subtly and is almost missed, yet there it is. I'm sitting in the courtyard for another solitary lunch, when I start to notice myself *noticing*—how the sun feels hotter on my scalp than on my back, how the same three birds keep landing near my feet eager for the crusts I inevitably throw them, and how students moving across campus in the summer have this way of loping that I've never seen in the fall or winter. After having experienced false starts in remission before, I'm initially skeptical, but after several days of being able to breathe easily, I'm almost certain that I'm up against the real thing. Another week goes by and then the day of my appointment is here. No longer having a personal savior as my chauffeur, I take three buses to reach Dr. Nelson's office.

"Nice to see you again, Beth," says Dr. Nelson, as he opens the door to the examining room.

"Good to see you too," I say, lifting my chin to give him a full-face smile.

"Have you noticed any changes in your mood since commencing the Effexor?" He asks, settling onto a low stool.

"Definitely," I answer, eager to deliver the good news. "It took about three weeks, I think, but then I noticed myself feeling, I don't know, lighter." I gesture with my hands. "The heaviness started to leave and everything has somehow seemed…easier. The anxiety has gone down, too. I think it's the best antidepressant I've tried yet." I pause, saving the best for last. "I've been thinking more about your maintenance dose idea and think it might be okay for me. At least as something to try."

"Good, good," Dr. Nelson says, returning my smile. "And how have your energy level and appetite been?"

"Energy has still been fairly low," I say. "A bit better than before, I guess, but not the greatest. I'm able to get my work done but I still crash earlier than I probably should. I've also had a lot of nausea, so eating is kind of minimal."

"As you know, both are fairly common when you start an antidepressant and should pass," he says. "Any thoughts of death or self-harm?"

"No, not at all."

"Excellent. Any unusual side effects?"

"Not really," I say, trying to think. "Maybe a few more headaches than before." Suddenly I notice something niggling me in the back of my mind. "And...could not getting my period be a possible side effect?"

"You haven't been menstruating?" Dr. Nelson asks, putting down his pen.

"Not recently," I say. I notice his expression turn from pleasantly professional to concerned and feel my fingers begin to twitch a little. "Is that a problem?"

"Not necessarily," he says, flipping through my chart. "Do you typically have irregular menses, Beth?"

"No. They've been every twenty-nine days for fourteen years, ever since I was thirteen," I say. "I just figured that it was the medication, so I didn't worry about it."

"And what was the first day of your last menstrual cycle?"

"I'd have to look up the exact day, but I know I was supposed to get it just before we last met. I think it was due four or five weeks ago?" I ball my hands into fists to stop the shaking. Within seconds, I feel my whole body start to vibrate. "I guess I've missed two periods. I just assumed it was from not eating enough or from the medication." I look at Dr. Nelson's face and see the doubt reflected in his eyes.

"It's unlikely to be the medication, Beth, but stress and a lack of proper nutrition can definitely affect one's hormonal balance," he says. "Still, to be on the safe side, let's have you do a pregnancy blood test right now and then we can talk more once the results are in."

"I'm sure that's not necessary," I say. "When my ex-boyfriend and I were intimate, we were always doubly protected. Condoms and foam together each time. Always!"

"That's good to hear, Beth. If you did always use that combination, then pregnancy is unlikely. Still, nothing is foolproof."

"I know that's true, but we also weren't really…sexually active in the last few months. My mood was dropping and I guess I just wasn't interested." I notice my hands start to still. *Good.*

"Beth, Effexor has been found to cause difficulties in some infants whose mothers take the medication late in pregnancy. If you *are* pregnant and decide to have the baby, now is the time to discuss your options and your medication. And if you decide to terminate the pregnancy, that's an option we'll need to discuss as soon as possible as well." Dr. Nelson holds the lab requisition out towards me. "Appease me."

As I glance at the extended piece of paper, suddenly I remember Mr. Hook-up. *Shit. Shit. Shit.* Dr. Nelson keeps speaking, but I can longer hear him over the roaring in my ears. I take the paper that he hands me and nod in what I think are the right places. I walk out of his office and into the laboratory on the same floor. Getting my blood drawn takes all of thirty seconds—not long enough for what I assume could be a watershed moment. On the bus ride home I keep covering my mouth to stifle the hiccups of nervous laughter that keep threatening to erupt. No need to frighten innocent strangers. By the time I reach home, the roaring in my ears has ebbed to a low hum. I let myself experience one moment of pure panic, just one, then slam the door shut on it all. *It's just stress or my recent Frosted Flakes depression diet. There's nothing to worry about. Everything will be fine in a week or two.* I have a glass of wine in defiance, then two. *See,* I tell the curtains, raising my glass to the shadows, *it's not happening. I wouldn't be drinking if it were happening.*

But on some level I know. How can I not know? The tight band of skin that's begun straining across my chest, the lurch of nausea as I get out of bed each morning, the way that fatigue fells me every evening, like a shovel to the head. When a phone message is left informing me that the results are back and that Dr. Nelson would like to meet with me ASAP, I don't bother returning the call right away. Instead, I watch hour follow hour and try not to let reality stick. The truth is so ridiculous, so lurid really, that it obviously must be some mistake. Having just reestablished the ability to floss my teeth, it's ludicrous to even consider having to make the mind-bending decision of whether or not to become someone's mother. Before, when it was of course not true, I used to let myself daydream about it, about what it would be like. In my imaginings there was always a house, a career, and a husband. Not a basement apartment with black mold hidden behind a dresser and a coffee table made up of long-forgotten journal articles. Not a diagnosis of Major Depressive Disorder, Recurrent, with no miracle treatment in sight. In my imaginings this news would be like a warm bath I could float in, rather than icy water thrown down my back.

I glance around my apartment, with its makeshift furniture and the futon couches. The former life of a normal graduate student remains in still life, as if to mock my every move. Too late, always too late, I realize that I'm not built to deal with this alone. My recently stabilized mood and I are like two kindergarten children holding hands in a game of Red Rover, our grasp on each other is so light, so tenuous, that it would take something far gentler than this to break us apart. I pick up my phone and call Patrick's number but hang up before he answers. What's left to say?

I decide to get out of the apartment, where a vacuum of loneliness threatens to suck me in. Instead of calling Dr. Nelson back to discuss how to try and right this sinking boat, I head to the movies. The theatre is located next to a mall, in the middle of nowhere. It takes about an hour by bus to get there, which is perfect. More time to zone out and float away from what is. I arrive at the mall with about five minutes to spare and wait in the ticket line with about fifteen others. It's not the first time I've ever gone to a movie by myself, but it is the first time in the middle of a weekday. Standing in front of me are a mother with two kids, two elderly couples, and what looks like a group of undergrads. Everyone seems to have someone, no one else is alone. *I sort of had Patrick,* I think, and my stomach lurches once more.

CHAPTER FOUR

*B*y the time the credits roll, I've made my decision of what to do—I'm going to go through with this pregnancy. It's not that I'm opposed to abortion, in fact, I'm vehemently pro-choice, and it's definitely not that I'm suddenly experiencing baby-lust. My decision isn't predicated on issues of morality or maternity at all. I've decided to have this baby because I know that if I don't, I'll end up using the abortion against myself time and time again whenever I fall into a depression. It might seem like a selfish reason, but it's more a self-protective one. My arsenal is full, I can't afford to have any more ammunition.

Having made my decision, I realize that I have to at least *try* to talk to Patrick. I know it's not fair, but I need to turn to someone right now, someone I trust, even if he no longer trusts me. I get off the bus one stop early and head across campus to the grad pub. At end of term the pub will likely be pretty empty, which is exactly how Patrick likes it. A sudden image flutters across my mind that can't be batted away—Patrick and me sitting away afternoons at a back table in the pub, each nursing a warm beer. Most Wednesdays after class we'd sit there for hours, holding court while friends and colleagues dropped by our table for a few minutes to chat with the golden couple of the Sociology department.

I pull open the pub door and instantly see Patrick at our table. I start to walk towards him, then stop. He's not alone. Sitting with him are two of our friends from the program—Sarah and Claire. Despite the fact that we're no longer together, I feel a twinge of betrayal—*why are they sitting in my place?* As I begin walking towards them, three sets of eyes turn to glance at me, then look away.

"What are you doing here?" asks Claire as I move closer.

"I've come to talk to Patrick," I answer, my cheeks reddening.

"Haven't you done enough?" she asks sarcastically. For a moment I'm startled by her tone, then remember that she hasn't seen me since the night we went out to celebrate my thesis defense, light-years ago. I watch as the two women shift themselves infinitesimally closer to Patrick. *Circling the wagons.*

"Didn't you get my calls?" asks Sarah, her voice gentler, almost kind.

"Yeah, sorry, I've had a lot going on," I say.

"I'll bet you have," Claire says, snorting. I feel her scorn settle on my skin, a dirty film.

"I didn't come here to start anything," I say.

"Maybe next time don't come here at all," Claire answers.

"It's okay," Patrick says, getting up from the table and standing next to me. "I'll see you at convocation, alright, Claire?" Patrick takes my arm and steers me towards the door. "You wanted to talk?" He asks.

"Please," I say.

"Let's go for a walk, then," he says.

"Bye, Beth!" Sarah calls as the door shuts behind us. "I'll see you at the ceremony!"

It's a beautiful, sunny afternoon outside, and a slight breeze ruffles through Patrick's hair. *I wish I could still do that*, I think, my fingers aching.

"So what's this about, Beth?" Patrick asks, as we head down a path towards the campus park.

"I'm sorry to have come to you," I say. "I realize it's probably a mistake. I just didn't know who else to talk to and I really need to at least talk to you."

"Okay. So talk," he says.

"I don't know how to tell you this. I can't believe this is happening," I say, stumbling over my words and my feet at the same time. Patrick catches me by the arm. "I don't think I can say this."

"Beth, what?" he asks. "Are you getting depressed again? Are you planning on hurting yourself?" Patrick continues to hold my arm. For a moment, just this moment, his voice seems to fill with caring.

"I'm pregnant," I blurt. "Not from you! Pregnant from that night of my thesis. From that guy. I've decided that I'm going to have the baby but I don't know what the hell else I'm going to do."

"And what do you expect from me?" Patrick's hand is gone and the caring in his voice has disappeared, replaced by something heavy that I can't name.

"I don't know. I'm an idiot." I sit down in the grass. A minute passes, then two. Finally I force myself to look up at Patrick. "I just needed to tell you."

Patrick nods, but more to himself than to me. "And have you told the…father your big news?"

"I don't even know his name or remember where he lives, Patrick. He was a mistake and now I'm left with the consequences."

"Do you expect me to feel sorry for you?" Patrick asks.

"No." I look across the lawn, at a few students tossing a Frisbee back and forth. "I don't think I expect anything from you."

"Then why are we having this discussion?"

I force myself to look up at him, at this man I used to know. "I wanted to tell you because I knew it would be the hardest thing. Harder than facing you after that night." I turn to look at the students again. "I figured if I could face you, then maybe I'm strong enough to face this." I stand up again and wipe the grass from the back of my jeans. "Now that I've told you, I know that I'm right." I turn and look straight at Patrick's eyes. If I look really closely, I think I can see at least part of myself reflected in them again. "I'm going to make this work somehow," I say. "I'm going to do it right."

"Okay. Good." Patrick exhales loudly. "Look, Beth, I'm not going to judge you right now. I just can't—I can't be a part of this, okay? Not right now. I'm about to start my Ph.D., I just can't deal with this!"

"I'm not telling you so that you'll help me or to make you deal with it. I just really needed you to know."

"Okay," he says again, his voice slowing down. "Okay, then." He nods once more, part of an internal dialogue. "Now I know. I think I need to have some space from all of this for a while."

"Alright," I say. "As I said, I just needed to tell you. You're the first person that I've told."

"Yes, well." Patrick nods once more, then turns to walk back in the direction that we came from. I pause a moment, uncertain of where to go, then head towards the Frisbee players and the path that's laid out in front of me.

ഔറ

After I wake up the next morning, I call back Dr. Nelson's office and agree to meet with him that afternoon. Another physical examination is conducted, with my weight and height recorded and a urine sample taken. Dietary advice is given by the nurse and prenatal vitamins with folic acid are strongly recommended. I agree to begin meeting with Dr. Nelson regularly, until I am referred to an obstetrician. After a brief discussion, it's agreed that I will continue to take Effexor at my current dose until I meet with a psychiatrist. My mood has remained stable during the last several days, despite this crisis. Now is not the time to play guinea pig with it. As the appointment ends, I also agree to continue meeting with my current psychologist on a regular basis. On the bus ride home, I try and convince myself that this white lie is not actually my fault, but is rather the fault of Dr. Miller, who up and left for America when I wasn't looking. Once back home, however, I realize that lying to one's physician isn't a very motherly thing to do, and I try to atone for the white lie by calling Downtown Community Clinic to schedule a session with whichever psychologist will take me. The receptionist is friendly and seems eager to make the process of transferring to a new therapist as painless as possible.

"I think that you'll be quite happy with Dr. Green," she says. "Most of Dr. Miller's clients who have transferred to her have been very satisfied."

I vaguely remember her saying the same thing to me during my panic-stricken phone call several weeks ago, and I find the repetition oddly comforting.

"So, your appointment is for next Thursday at four o'clock. As I mentioned, Dr. Green likes to do an intake of sorts during an initial session, so please be prepared to stay for approximately one and a half hours. Her fees are similar to those of all the psychologists in our practice and are one hundred and twenty dollars per therapy hour. As you might recall, a therapy hour is actually fifty minutes in duration, to allow the psychologist to have the final ten minutes for paperwork. Please remember to bring in any third-party insurance forms that you would like Dr. Green to complete."

"Okay, thanks again," I say, hanging up the phone. I experience a heavy feeling in my stomach, which I don't instantly understand. Then I remember. *Fees. Insurance.* In my quest to undo my lie, I'd forgotten all about the fact that when it comes down to it, a therapeutic relationship is as financial as the one I have with my landlord. Therapy sessions cost money, which I don't have. The numerous times I'd been in therapy before, it was either through an outpatient program at a hospital, through the student counseling clinic at university (although the yearly ten-session limit clearly wasn't created for someone like me), or else through a private practice, the latter sessions paid for by my mother's or her husband's insurance. During my last round of therapy, I would meet regularly with Dr. Miller, and the insurance companies would take turns supplying the cash. Between the two policies I was able to meet with Dr. Miller for close to twenty sessions per year. During the last several years, my main interactions with my mother consisted of me mailing invoices to her and her emailing me to say when the annual coverage limits were about to be surpassed. It was the type of arms-length affection that we had come to prefer. The catch was that her insurance would only consider me a dependent while I was registered in school. No classes, no sessions. While this was no problem before, it is a deal-breaker now. After all, my job as a research assistant can barely cover my rent. How am I supposed to pay the one hundred and twenty dollars needed for each hour of personal growth? Therapeutically speaking, I am screwed.

I spread my fingers around my belly. Somehow, I have to make this work. Someone is counting on me in a way I haven't been counted on before. I've let down many people I've known before, but I can't let down this person I've never met. I realize that if I have any chance of becoming the well-functioning parent I want to be, therapy can no longer be a choice. And so I decide to break a promise I made to myself eight years ago, when I moved out of home for the final time: I will turn to my mother and her husband for help.

CHAPTER FIVE

It takes me two weeks to build up the courage to call my mother and arrange a visit at her house, but I finally do it. I choose convocation weekend as the perfect time to go, as now I'll have a reason for avoiding all of my former friends and acquaintances. Other than a few coffee dates with Sarah, who lives in town and has turned out to be a quietly loyal friend, I haven't heard from anyone and don't expect too. The Master's program was just a pit stop in most people's lives—they don't have time to stick around and get pulled into my drama.

On the morning of my graduation, I take a Greyhound bus back to London, the city I used to know so well. The weather is fair and I decide to skip the taxi and instead walk from the terminal to my old house. I haven't been back since I was nineteen. I try not to think about the chaos that surrounded my leaving for good, but memories flood my mind. It was Reading Week and I'd come home from university for a few days. It was the Saturday evening before my return to school and everyone was supposed to be out for the night. After two hours spent watching reruns, I impulsively went to the upstairs bathroom during a commercial break and downed the contents of whatever prescription bottles I could get my hands on. The overdose was unplanned but somewhere in the recesses of my depressed brain I had counted on it being a weekend when my twelve year old sister was away. What I hadn't known—and what my mother could never forgive me for—was that my sister would come home early, and that when she went upstairs looking for me she would instead be greeted by what she thought was my dead body on the bathroom floor, vomit pooling around my face.

Enough. I stand on the doorstep for several minutes, trying to remember how to breathe. Resisting the temptation to retrieve the key from under the doormat, I ring the doorbell. *The prodigal daughter returns.* My sister opens the door and stands before me, a polite stranger. When did she become an adult?

"Hi," she says, hands at her sides.

"Hi, Heath," I respond. "You look great!"

"It's been a long time." She pauses, rubbing her toe against the edge of the door. "I haven't seen you since Grandma's party at Christmas, and even then you left early."

"I know, I'm sorry. It was kind of awkward because I knew Adam would be showing up. After his wedding fiasco, I didn't think it would be so great for me to stick around and cause more problems. You know…" My face reddens. Two minutes in this house and already I'm talking about my life as a fuck-up.

"Yeah."

"Things have been kind of busy… Have you gotten my e-mails?"

She nods at me, then rubs the door again. "Did you hear that I'm transferring from Western to U of T for September?" she asks. "The plan is to live with Dad for the year, save on rent."

As if to confirm what a lousy sister I am, I change the subject. "Not to be rude, Heath, but can you tell me where Mom is?"

I watch as her face falls—my fault. "Mom and Peter are waiting for you in the living room."

At the mention of Peter, I feel my chest tighten and instinctively cover my belly with both hands. *Just remember to breathe.* I look at my feet as they move forward. Twenty steps to the living room, twenty-one steps if you count walking through the front door. If I just keep staring at the ground, I'll be fine. Following my sister, I enter the living room, brightly lit by the sun. The same tasteful paintings, the same sofa and loveseat, the same coffee table. Even the air smells the same, slightly stale with the scent of furniture polish, window cleaner, and disappointment. My mother and her husband are seated at either side of the sofa like matching bookends. In the moments of silence that follow my entry, I glance at them both. My mother sits on the edge of the sofa, her hands clasped at her knees. How frail she looks! She seems older, almost old. Turning my gaze towards Peter, I feel my chest constrict again. He sits far back into the cushions, his arms crossed in front of his chest, a look of disdain on his face. *The firing squad.*

"Hi Mom," I say, stopping a few feet in front of her. "Thanks for asking me to come." I force myself to turn my head sideways. "Peter."

"Let's save the polite chit-chat for sometime when you're not pregnant, shall we?" he says. "By the by, when are we going to meet the father-to-be?"

"Peter," my mother says, shaking her head.

I turn my eyes back to the carpet, remembering Peter's tendency to incinerate with his white-hot stare.

I take a deep breath, then another. *You are not sixteen. You are not sixteen. You are not sixteen.* "Mom, is there any way we can continue this conversation in private?"

"Not happening," Peter says, answering for her. "This is my house.

And in my house, anything that needs to be said will be said in front of me."

"Mom, please," I say, hating the plaintive tone that has crept into my voice.

My mother looks at Peter, then at me, then back at Peter again. "Beth," she says quietly, "he *is* your stepfather."

I take another deep breath, trying to remain calm. I glance at Peter, who stares back at me in all his smirking glory. *To hell with it.* "With all due respect, mom, *Peter* is not my stepfather. He's just the man you decided to marry after you cheated on my stepfather when I was fifteen. If anyone has a right to be part of this conversation it's Jacob, not *him*." I remind myself of the baby growing inside of me, counting on me. *You can do this.* "You know what? That gives me a great idea. I think I'll give Jacob a call and talk to him, *in private*." I stand up, walk over to where my sister is sitting, and hand her a pen and a crumbled piece of paper from my purse. "Heather, can you give me your dad's new phone number?"

She looks up at me, her eyes telegraphing a message I can't decode. *When did I stop being able to understand my sister?* Eventually she jots down a number and gives me back the paper. It holds the warmth of her hand and I squeeze it tightly, hoping to absorb something, somehow. I quickly say goodbye, making a mental note to start being a better sister, then walk out the door, eager to leave the house before I'm sucked back into its vortex.

CHAPTER SIX

*J*acob. During the last several years I've attempted to block the Jacob from Before out of my mind. Yes, I've exchanged Christmas and birthday cards with him every year, but over time my annual written remarks have dwindled to a quickly scrawled signature. Why would I give him more of myself than that? After all, Jacob was the first of what would become a rooster of people who walked out of my life. More importantly, Jacob was the only one whose leaving was not triggered by anything I had done. Not that I knew this at the time. It took about six months of therapy to come to that intellectual realization and about one year more before I could actually *feel* that I had done nothing wrong. By then it was too late, the damage was already done, mostly by me. Insight cannot change the fact that Jacob's leaving heralded my depression and self-destruction arriving. On the bus ride home from my mother's house, I decide to let the door from Before open, just a little bit, and allow a few memories entry.

ℛℭ

It was Jacob who had done all of the cooking. Roast chicken with mashed potatoes, savoury tofu casserole, thick beef stew, vegetable curry, linguine and garlic bread. Each day after work he'd tune the radio to a 1970s station, then shoo the three females out of the kitchen so he could work on his creations. As I did my homework in my room, the smell of supper would come drifting up, often mixed with the sounds of classic rock and Jacob's slightly tone-deaf warble. I didn't realize how much I associated studying with Jacob's cooking until that first night, at fifteen, when he was suddenly gone. I remember sitting at my desk, staring at my textbook, too distracted by the quiet to concentrate on algebra. It was that same first night that my mother came into my room before bed to discuss plans for the upcoming weekend.

"Since Heather will be with her dad, I thought it would be the perfect opportunity for us to have some quality girl time!" My mother had said, her voice a bit too loud for my small room.

I remember feeling confused. Wasn't I going to spend weekends with Jacob too? Wasn't he also my dad, maybe not in the biological-blood-genetics kind of way, but in the only way that really mattered? Didn't I deserve to keep him too? But as I looked at my mother's red eyes, I knew what I needed to do. And so on that first Friday when Jacob arrived to pick up his two girls, I hung back.

"Aren't you coming too, bear cub?" Jacob had asked in the doorway, as my little sister raced out to the driveway and into his car.

"Nah," I'd answered, shifting from side to side. "Gonna have some girl-time with Mom instead. You know…"

"Are you sure?"

"Yeah…"

"Well, okay," Jacob had said, his voice gentle and low. "Maybe next weekend, then?"

"Well, you know," I'd shrugged, biting the inside of my cheek.

"It's your choice, kiddo. I'd never try and force you to come. Just know the offer is always open, okay?" Jacob reached out to ruffle my hair, then headed back to his car, to his daughter.

I remember that for the next five Fridays, Jacob asked me if I wanted to come too. And then one Friday he stopped. It was as if a line had been drawn in the sand, with Jacob and Heather on one side, and girl weekends on the other. Although I had no clear memory of this, I knew that me and my mother had been a unit before Jacob and would be a unit after, too. To me this felt wrong, but what could I do?

Next comes the worst memory of all. It was almost a year after the separation and Jacob was coming to pick up Heather for a final weekend before he moved to Toronto. For Heather, it marked the beginning of having to sit for two hours on a bus every other weekend. A hassle, a change, and an adjustment, but also an adventure. For me, it marked the beginning of the end. If it had felt too much like a betrayal to say I wanted to spend time with Jacob when he lived in the same town as me, how the hell could I ever commit the ultimate in treachery and ask if I could abandon my mother to Jacob and the bright lights of the big city? A few minutes before Jacob's standard arrival time, however, a sliver of hope began to nudge at my consciousness. I definitely couldn't ask to go to Toronto myself, but maybe, just maybe if Jacob *insisted* I come, it would happen. There was nothing my mother hated more than confrontation. Maybe if Jacob brought up the possibility of court proceedings and the importance of keeping two sisters together, she would back off and I would be free. It could happen! When the doorbell rang, I made sure to be the first to open the door. After greeting Jacob, I closed my eyes and breathed in his familiar scent. *The smell of my father.*

"Hi bear cub," Jacob said, reaching across the threshold to ruffle my hair. "How are things?"

"You know, the same," I said, shrugging.

"Hello, Jacob," my mother said, walking from the living room. "How is the packing going?"

"Not so well," he answered, smiling politely. "You know I've always hated moving."

"Yes, well."

"It'll be worth it, though. It's for an excellent job opportunity," he said, shrugging. *So that's where I got it!* I watched my parents as they performed their weekly dance in the doorway of our house, my mother's crossed arms and downward gaze matching Jacob's forced friendliness and clumsy shuffle. Since separating, they'd perfected the passing of their daughter from one to the other. After over a decade spent sharing a bed, this is what their interchanges came down too: A few minutes of surface conversation, minimal eye contact, and tight, toothless smiles. At all costs, the failure that had been their marriage was politely avoided, neatly folded into a drawer with a perfumed sachet.

I looked at Jacob through my heavy bangs, hoping to convey what I wanted through the intensity of my stare.

"Beth, please tell your sister that her father is waiting," my mother said, turning to me.

"But—"

"Now, Beth."

I left my parents to go find Heather. She was in her room, trying to stuff an extra-large toy rabbit into her knapsack.

"I don't think he'll fit," I said, sitting on her bed.

"He has to come say goodbye to Daddy's place," she answered, not looking at me.

"Here, let me try," I said, grabbing the toy from her. After a few shoves, the rabbit was stuffed into the bag.

"Thanks," Heather said, grabbing me around the neck and squeezing tight. She let go and then looked at me. "You don't think it's too babyish to bring him, do you?"

I looked solemnly into her nine-year-old eyes and shook my head. "I think he'd be disappointed if you didn't," I answered, not sure if I meant Jacob or the rabbit.

"Cool," she said, then jumped off the bed and headed to her door. "Are you coming down, too?"

"Nah, I'll just stay up here for a minute," I answered, pulling at a thread on her quilt.

"Okay! See ya," she said, racing down the stairs, two at a time.

I lay down on my back, staring at the ceiling. I'd give him five minutes to talk to Mom about me going to Toronto. There were lots of arguments he could give, if he just took the time to think about it. For one, it would be good for Heather to have a chaperone on the bus each week. Nine years old was kind of young to be traveling alone. What about stranger-danger? If I was on the bus I could make sure that no one creepy tried to talk to her. I'd even be able to baby-sit if Jacob needed a night out, and I might even be willing to do it for free! My heart started to race as I imagined the conversation that was going on one floor below me. Five minutes passed, then ten. I realized that I should get my own bag ready just in case. I pushed myself up off the mattress and headed to the hallway. Just as I was walking towards my room, I heard my mother's voice.

"Beth? Where did you go? Jacob had wanted to say goodbye to you," she called up. Her words stopped me in my tracks and I felt my cheeks begin to burn. I pressed my fingernails into my palms and pushed as hard as I could. *Goodbye or good riddance?*

₮⇛

With one parent gone forever, I turned my energy onto my mother. Although I had initially felt stifled by her desire to spend every weekend with me, I now found it kind of soothing. At least *she* still wanted me. It was about a month after Jacob moved to Toronto that I began to notice my mother's focus turn away from girl-time and onto self-improvement. She joined Weight Watchers, she joined a co-ed gym, she got plucked and highlighted, she started wearing push-up bras. She wanted to talk all of the time, but about nothing kind of stuff, like fat grams, oat bran, and crunches. She seemed to bubble over with physical energy and good cheer, making my own quiet grief seem somehow like a let-down. Being sad was not what confident, strong women did! Too soon, our twosome became a threesome, with a new guy suddenly in the picture. Smooth, slick, smarmy Peter. *What hole did he crawl out of?* We didn't go out to dinner or to the movies without Peter in tow. Suddenly my mother, who had always seemed an equal partner to Jacob, became passive and fawning when around Peter. She no longer seemed to have a clear opinion of which movies she wanted to see, what appetizer she liked best, or even whether she preferred topping or no topping on her popcorn. As time went on, her tendency to defer to Peter spread to what colour to repaint our kitchen, *Jacob's* kitchen, and where to go during summer vacation. Before long, Peter had moved into our house, his opinion pressed permanently into everything he saw. When I wasn't looking, my mother had been replaced by some Stepford Wife. Hoping to encourage her to see the error of her ways, I tried to act as obnoxious as only a sixteen year old can. Whenever around Peter I whined, I pouted, I exuded adolescent misery. Rather than give Peter the boot, however, my mother turned to him more and more in her new, obsequious way, while I turned to self-cutting and despair.

CHAPTER SEVEN

*F*rom the vantage point of more than ten years, I can now admit that my initial disgust towards Peter had nothing to do with who he actually was or how he acted around me. Even if he'd been the most patient and generous man who had ever existed, my original reaction to him would have been the same. *He* was the reason my parents were no longer together, *he* was the cause of my mother's infidelity, *he* was what would block my mom and Jacob from ever reconciling.

My early feelings of anger and hate were probably unpleasant to be the recipient of, but they weren't personal. At first the actuality of Peter himself was irrelevant. Who the flesh-and-blood Peter was or what he stood for was meaningless to me—he was a cipher, a nobody, a lingering mold that wouldn't go away. It was what came next that I can't, and won't, forgive Peter for—how he stood by the sidelines as my anger turned to wild, attention-seeking desperation, my desperation to depression. Like an unaffected bystander who is in too much of a hurry to get involved when he comes upon a fight, Peter watched me start to fall, then stepped aside rather than even attempt to catch me. As a teenager, nothing reinforces the premise that you are worthless and hopeless more than having an adult in your life see you—truly see you—then choose to turn and walk away.

₮)‒)℟

I remember lying in bed one morning, pretending to be ill. At seventeen the whole act of playing sick felt somewhat embarrassing, shameful even, but I knew that it was necessary. How could I explain to my well-intentioned but frequently clueless mother that I needed a day alone to self-destruct? In the previous few weeks I'd taken to skipping classes, but knew that if I did that more often, Adam would tattle on me. Adam, my guardian. Adam, my albatross. I'd spent those stolen hours wandering in and out of stores that lined a nearby strip mall, aimlessly fingering cheap sweaters and plastic jewelry, while salesclerks eyed me suspiciously. In recent months I'd felt as if the walls of my life were beginning to push in against me at all sides and I knew that if I didn't do something about it soon, I would suffocate.

Before leaving for work, my mother knocked on my open bedroom door. "Mind if I come in?" she asked hesitantly.

"Yeah, sure," I said, pulling the covers up to my chin. I attempted a cough, then another.

"How are you feeling?" she asked, walking over to my bed and sitting down beside my blanketed legs. "Any fever?" She put her hand gently against my forehead. Her palm felt cool and comforting, its temperature something I could always count on.

"Mom, I don't have a fever," I said, shaking away her hand.

"Still." She paused and I watched as uncertainty filled the features of her face. "Maybe I should stay home from work today, just in case."

"No! Don't do that!" My voice sounded shrill and I tried to cover it up with a few sudden coughs. "You see?" I said, speaking now in a hoarse whisper. "It's just my throat."

"Well, if you're sure." She reached over and pushed hair off my face. "You know I'm only a phone call away. And you can reach Peter too, at his office."

"Peter," I said in disgust, rolling over and covering my head with the blanket.

"Yes, Peter," my mother said. "Beth, I really wish you'd give him more of a chance. Your sister seems to like him fine."

"That's because she's ten and doesn't know any better," I muttered into my pillow.

"What did you say?"

"Nothing. I'm fine, okay? I'll call if I get worse. Now will you please just go and leave me alone?"

I kept the blanket over my head until I heard my mother's retreating footsteps. *Finally*. Momentary feelings of guilt washed over me and added to my ocean of self-hate. Why did I always have to end conversations with my mother so badly? Why couldn't I ever be grateful for what she did? Why was I such a horrible daughter? Suddenly fueled by feelings of repugnance and ugliness, I got out of bed and padded downstairs in my bare feet. I glanced quickly at the hall clock as I headed to the living room. It was already 8:50, I was behind schedule. I moved towards the liquor cabinet and opened it. I picked up one bottle, then another. Whiskey, rum, and various liqueurs. Not bad for a family that seldom imbibed. I randomly reached for the whiskey then carried my prize to the kitchen. I took down a large mug and filled it half full. I then headed to the den and turned on the TV as loud as it would go. Time to get soused.

Given that I'd only been tipsy once before in my life and that was when sharing two pilfered wine coolers among four friends, I was startled by the raw, harsh taste of the whiskey and almost gagged. I forced myself to take another sip, then another. I noticed that the alcohol started to slide down easily and provided a comforting warmth as it traveled into my empty stomach. I noticed my mood start to lift a little and briefly thought about whether or not I should reconsider my plans. Then I took another few sips and decided to carry on as expected. The mug empty, I dropped it onto the wooden floor and waited for it to shatter. Instead it did an awkward bounce before lying on its side. I left the TV blaring, then stumbled back towards the stairs.

"Time to get initiated," I said out loud, then laughed. I wasn't sure exactly what I meant, but in my pickled state my words sounded illuminating and wise. On the top stair I tripped and fell. The upper landing was carpeted, so I barely noticed the impact. I stayed sitting for a few moments, suddenly aware that the ceiling seemed to be tilting a bit above me. Weird.

Slowly I got up, using the wall to help guide me. I walked into the bathroom, then stared at my face in the mirror. "You are pissed!" I said loudly, then looked at myself once more. As I stared into my eyes, more feelings of self-loathing bubbled to the surface. "This is your fault," I said, pointing at my reflection. "I blame *you*!" It struck me that I was being melodramatic, that this whole act was a weak imitation of true crazy, but I didn't care. I opened up the medicine cabinet then found what I was looking for—a recently opened box of razors. Peter's razors. I quickly took one out then held it in front of me. It was so small and thin, almost fragile looking. What damage could it do?

I stared at my left wrist, and touched the smooth white skin. My wrist looked bland and unformed, the colour of uncooked bread dough. The only thing interesting about it was a blue-green vein that made a lazy, zig-zag pattern across my wrist. It wasn't just hurt that I wanted to get out, exactly, but more of an itchy sensation that scratched away at the lining of my stomach. It had started as a fairly innocent restlessness, but now the feeling had become unbearable. It just wouldn't leave me alone. It was like drinking five cups of coffee in a row. After that initial flush, you just wanted to crawl out of your skin, to stop the jittering.

I took the razor and pressed its sharpness firmly against my skin. Nothing. I pressed again and moved it back and forth in a slicing motion. Still nothing. In frustration, I looked around the room for something else sharp. I spotted a Diet Coke can in the trash. Someone had crushed it, and there was a jagged edge. It seemed to smile at me. I ran my fingers lightly on top of the coke-drenched spikes. I dragged the edges of the can against my wrist roughly, feeling it catch my skin. I was surprised by the amount of blood such a shallow cut could cause. I felt a tiny *ping* of pressure in my chest, a slight quickening of breath. I was pleased that my own blood could be such a deep-red colour.

I pushed up my shirt higher and tried again just beneath my shoulder. I wanted to also do this in places that couldn't easily be seen. This was to be my secret, just mine. A few cuts later, I suddenly felt dizzy and slid to the floor. I considered trying to cut my other arm, but decided against it. There was such a thing as overdoing it, after all. I was so absorbed with watching my blood bubble up and then congeal, that I didn't notice the footsteps on the stairs.

"Beth?" Peter asked, pushing the door open and hitting me in the leg in the process.

"Ouch!" I said, looking up.

Peter stood a few feet in front of me, surveying the room. He looked down at my arm, then up at my face.

"You must be kidding me," he said, shaking his head. "Cutting yourself? And with a pop can? Are you trying to fit all the stereotypes of the tormented teen?"

"What? No!" I blurted out, too stunned by his words and by my own drunkenness to say anything more clever.

Peter looked at me for another minute in silence, then ran a face cloth under the tap. "Here," he said, tossing me the wet cloth. "Clean yourself up. And don't forget to use the antibiotic lotion. Those cuts could get infected." He took a step out of the bathroom, then another, his job done. "Don't think I didn't notice the whiskey bottle," he said from the doorway. "That was given to me as a gift. I expect you to repay me for that."

I listened to his footfalls down the stairs. A few minutes later I heard the front door slam and a car engine ignite. I stayed sitting on the floor for a few minutes, the wet cloth dripping in my hand. I then stood up wearily and head back to bed.

I slept the rest of the day away and only awakened to the sound of my mother returning home. I rolled over onto my arm and was startled by how much it hurt. As I sat up, the pain in my arm was replaced by a horrible throbbing headache. I got out of bed slowly then headed downstairs for supper. I needed to get this over with. I *knew* that Peter would have called my mother the instant he got back to work and told her what happened. How she'd react or what would happen next was not in my control. All I knew was that something would happen, possibly something big. Nothing could stay the same after this.

I walked into the kitchen and over to where my mother was standing, pulling groceries from a bag.

"I'm here," I said, arms at my sides.

"Hi honey," she said, turning to smile at me. "Feeling any better?"

I nodded once, then twice. I scanned her face for clues but saw nothing but mild concern.

"That's good. I'm making pizza for supper. Any request for toppings?"

"Um, no. Whatever you make is fine," I said, sitting down on a stool. "Can I have some Tylenol?"

"Sure, honey. Just give me a minute," my mother said, putting a carton of milk into the refrigerator.

The back door opened and Heather and Peter walked in, bringing in a blast of cold air with them.

"Hi Beth!" Heather said, running over to give me a hug. "Are you still sick?"

"I have a feeling that she's doing much better now, aren't you Beth?" Peter said, shutting the door. "I have a feeling that this was just a twenty-four hour bug that is now clearing up." He paused, looking at me. "Am I right, Beth?"

"I guess so," I said and shrugged, my shoulder aching.

෨෮෬

In the weeks that followed, I continued cutting myself whenever possible, visualizing Peter's smug face as I tore into my skin. I quickly developed my own technique and rules. I could only use a fresh Coke can, and it had to be diet. I could only use the can in my room, at night. I could only use the can on my left wrist (I'm right-handed, so cutting the right wrist would have been much too awkward). I could only use the can once my sister was safely fast asleep in bed. After a few weeks of scraping away at my skin, a small scar appeared, stubborn in its permanency. I began to cut into the scar. I found it mildly ironic that in scraping away at my flesh I was actually building it up, with scar tissue.

Before falling asleep at night, I'd lift my arm up in front of the mirror to survey the damage. *Look at my war-wounds, my battle scars. Look at my hurt.* Over time, I began to break my rules. I cut myself on Saturday mornings while my sister was downstairs watching cartoons. I cut myself in a washroom cubicle at school during lunch hour. But always with a Diet Coke can. I began to forget my reasons for cutting. I started to wear more long-sleeved shirts.

Caught within a spiral of anger and self-cutting, at first I wasn't aware that Heather seemed to be around me much more than usual. As weeks passed, however, I couldn't help but notice that my little sister kept nipping at the ankles of my misery, forcing me to give her attention. Suddenly, whenever I was alone in my room or half-asleep in the bathtub for more than thirty minutes, she'd be knocking on the door, rattling the knob.

"Beth? Are you in there? I need to talk to you! Can I come in?" Her voice was high and soft, her words always ending in a question.

"I'll be out in a minute," I'd respond, then lapse back into whatever I was doing. Sleeping, cutting, or lying in the tub, ensconced in a thick layer of self-absorption.

"Beth?" She'd ask, moments later, once again rattling the doorknob. "It's been at least two minutes! When are you coming out?"

"I *said* in a minute!" I'd shout back and attempt to return to the task at hand. Eventually I'd hear Heather's footsteps retreating down the hall, away from me. Sometimes I'd later remember to go find her, to see what had been so important that she had felt the need to see me immediately. But usually I'd forget.

One afternoon I was sitting on the floor in the bathroom, about to begin my cutting ritual, when Heather opened the door without her usual rattle.

"Do you mind?" I yelled at her, quickly tossing the pop can in the garbage and pulling down my sleeve. "Have you ever heard of knocking?"

Heather stared at me for a moment, the fragile skin under her eyes looking purple and bruised against her pale face. Why did she look so tired? "Sorry," she said, then quickly turned and walked towards her room.

"Oh, for God's sake," I muttered, pulling myself up to standing.

"Will you wait for a minute?" I headed down the hallway and over to her door. This time she had closed it against me. I knocked once, twice. "Can I come in?"

"Okay," she said in a muffled voice. I opened the door and saw her sitting cross-legged on the bed, holding a pillow against her.

"Sorry I yelled at you," I said, walking over and sitting down next to her. "I just hate it when people barge in on me, you know?"

"It's okay," she said, still holding the pillow.

"So, what's up?"

"I just wanted to ask you about...bras," she said. I looked at her, startled. With her straw-thin arms and legs and her almost concave chest, this was not what I had been expecting.

"But...why?" I asked, trying not to smile. "I mean, you're only ten! Do you really think you need one?"

She shrugged. "It's not that I think I need it," she said, her voice quiet. "I know I'm still flat."

"Of *course* you're still flat! I mean, come on, Heath, you're only in grade five! I didn't get a bra until I was at least twelve! Do all the girls in your class really wear bras already?"

Again the shrug. "Karen and Melanie at school just got them and some of the other girls make fun of me in gym class because of the undershirts Mom makes me wear." She put her head down so that the part in her hair was visible, a perfect straight line down the middle.

"Well, have you talked to Mom about this?"

"She said I don't need a bra yet. And anyway, she's too busy." She looked up at me and again I noticed the purple circles under her eyes. "I just want a training bra, that's all! Just one to wear to school! I'd get it myself if I was allowed to go to the store alone!"

"You don't have to try and get it yourself," I said, reaching out and touching her leg. "I'll take you the next Saturday you're home, okay? We'll take the bus to the mall and maybe even eat at the food court."

"Could we get the sweet and sour chicken balls?" she asked, her face brightening. "They're so good!"

"Yeah, for sure." I patted her knee. "But let's not tell Mom or Peter about it, okay?"

"Never!" She reached out and hugged me, her arms slender as willow branches. "Thanks!"

"It's okay," I said, hesitating for just a moment before hugging her back.

ℰℭ

What I can't remember now is what happened next. My hope is that the following Saturday I woke up bright and early and headed out to the bus stop with Heather in tow for a day of sister bonding. My hope is that we overstuffed ourselves with imitation Chinese food, tried on neon-coloured bracelets and necklaces at a jewelry kiosk, and picked out two or three pretty training bras that would cause an immediate end to any locker-room teasing. My hope is that we ended up staying at the mall much longer than expected and had to run together, out of breath and laughing, to catch the last bus home before dark. My hope is that I was able to step outside of my self-absorbed self for at least a day in order to *do the right thing.*

My fear is that after making a genuine promise to my little sister, I promptly returned to my cocoon of self-hate and forgot the plans we had made. My fear is that Saturday passed with Heather waiting patiently for me at the kitchen table, jacket zipped up and purse in her lap, as I slept the day away in bed. My fear is that at ten years old, my little sister learned that she could not count on me any longer to be there for her. Hope or fear, it doesn't really matter, for the reality is that I truly can't remember, and that I remain too cowardly to ask Heather about what really happened.

CHAPTER EIGHT

*W*hen I get back home from my mother's house, I find an e-mail waiting for me. My mother's message is brief and seems to be full of what she cannot say. She informs me that she has a small inheritance from her deceased uncle that she previously willed to me and my sister. She suggests that she give me my portion now, to be put it in a separate account to use for treatment. She stresses that the amount is not large—ten thousand dollars in total—but could at least pay for periodic therapy sessions for a few years, if needed. She tells me that I am to keep this private and to not let Peter know (as if I might let it slip during one of our many nonexistent conversations). In four short lines, my mother has granted me a reprieve. I e-mail back one word—*thank you*—and hope it conveys in turn what I seem to have become incapable of saying.

I put the piece of paper with Jacob's number on it by the phone. It stays there for the next three weeks, taunting me every time I walk by. I tell myself that now that finances are in place, I no longer need to be in such a rush to call him. I'll get around to it when I'm ready. This phone call has to be on *my* terms, I shouldn't force myself to do anything until *I'm* ready. Will I ever be ready?

As the weeks go by, I become too busy to call. My life becomes punctuated with appointments—the psychiatrist, the psychologist, and now the obstetrician. During my first meeting with the psychiatrist he is direct and gets straight to the point. I am informed that like many antidepressants, Effexor is a Category C medication and could potentially harm my unborn child. I am given a grocery list of possible risks, including feeding and breathing difficulties or seizures. Dr. Reimer stresses, however, that the risk of a mother experiencing a serious depressive episode during pregnancy may be more harmful to a fetus than the medication itself and that he often advises patients to continue taking the antidepressant as a result. He explains that together we will need to regularly assess whether the benefits to me of taking the medicine outweigh the possible risks to the fetus, particularly as my pregnancy progresses. Dr. Reimer stresses the importance of me continuing to take my medication for the time being—major depressive episodes typically last around six months and if I suddenly stop the medication now I will likely be plunged back into mine. He agrees that we can consider gradually weaning me off the medication later in my pregnancy, if my mood remains stable, when the risk to the baby is potentially at its highest. By the end of the appointment I'm shaking and want to immediately dump all of my pills down the toilet. I feel helpless and guilt-ridden with this information, immobilized. How can I risk even potentially harming my baby? Despite the guilt, my depression is still too close to me to even consider the alternative, and so I dutifully continue downing a pill each morning in my kitchen. *What kind of mother am I?*

Between my appointments I spend most of my time on campus and meet with Dr. Shields weekly to discuss progress on his research. While purposely avoiding eye contact with my burgeoning belly, he informs me one afternoon that he has recently received a sizable grant and wants to offer me a guaranteed research assistant position at twenty-five hours per week for the fall semester, with the possibility of continued hours in the months to come. He adds that he has more papers to mark this semester than he can manage and asks if I'd be willing to give him a hand. Whether or not this is a pity offer, I don't care. The job is like manna from the sky. As I agree to the position, I realize that in my quest to acquire funds for therapy I'd never thought much about how I was going to put food in my mouth, let alone get money to raise a baby.

My first appointment with the new psychologist goes much better than my session with Dr. Reimer. I meet with Dr. Green in the same clinic I used to go to see my former psychologist. I had felt some trepidation about entering the same building—what if the absence of Dr. Miller would fill up the room so that there wasn't space for anything else? To my surprise, being in the familiar environment soothes me. *I feel safe here.* Within about five minutes of meeting her, I realize that I like Dr. Green. She's younger than my former psychologist, but not so young that I'd feel like I was her thesis topic. She looks to be in about her mid-thirties and is wearing a wedding ring. A good sign, not because I'm a big believer in the sanctity of marriage, but more that it at least suggests some life experience. What I like best is her smile, which happens unexpectedly and seems natural, rather than rehearsed. I've come to realize that this instant liking, or disliking, is pretty standard in therapy. You click or you don't with a therapist, and there's nothing either of you can do to change this. It's a personality thing, a mixing of selves, and all of the credentials after their name won't make a difference. Luckily for me, Dr. Green seems to be a fit.

Our first session is an intake. Despite having my old file on hand, Dr. Green asks me to describe my entire history, so that she can hear it in my own words. In the past, this type of mindless regurgitation would have annoyed me. *This is costing me one hundred and twenty bucks an hour! If you want to know about my dead father or my absentee stepdad so badly, read the bloody file notes!* This time, however, it makes me feel valued, respected. I like that Dr. Green wants to take the time to truly *know* me, to see me the way I see myself.

Towards the end of the session, Dr. Green asks me what I'd like our goals to be and makes suggestions herself. Again, I feel respected. Maybe what's different is that I never felt ready to be respected before. Now, with motherhood approaching, I am starting to see myself differently. If I'm going to be the nurturer of this baby, I'd better first learn how to nurture myself. Not such an insurmountable obstacle when not depressed.

"To review," says Dr. Green, smiling. "We've decided that given your current mood, prevention will be our primary focus during your pregnancy. You'll be encouraged to practice self-care and self-monitoring until you're blue in the face." She smiles again. "We both know you know this stuff already, so it'll be less me teaching and more us together pin-pointing what areas you need to work on the most." She pauses. "As we talked about, given your history, you are at risk of experiencing a depressed episode following the birth of the baby. This is a risk, not an inevitability." Another smile. "To that end, we'll both work hard to put the pieces in place so that you have adequate support after your baby is born. Ideally, your support team will include professionals, such as myself, and your physician, as well as family or friends."

"Sounds good to me," I say, glad to have a script to follow in the months to come.

"We can do this, Beth," she says, handing me a blank calendar so that I can begin charting shifts in my mood, like changes in the weather. "I know we can do this."

಄ಞ

When I get home, I affix the mood chart to the front of my fridge with a happy face magnet. The chart is made up of columns and rows and creates an instant structure to my days. Each morning and evening I mark down my level of mood from zero (call 911) to ten (Barney-happy). Other information is tallied too, like number of hours slept, whether anxiety is low or high, and if any self-destructive thoughts are happening. After about three weeks of meticulous charting I have proof of my ongoing stability. In mood chart parlance, I'm maintaining a six to eight. As time passes, I start to feel proud, even cheeky about my recovery. *You see?* I silently inform passersby as I walk across campus. *This is how you do it!*

During our fourth session, Dr. Green gives me a CD with mindfulness and relaxation exercises on it and I listen to it religiously. Each day after work I press play and try to turn my attention on my breathing. I focus on what each breath feels like, how my chest rises and falls, rises and falls. Each time I play my CD I notice myself feeling more and more relaxed, comfortable in my skin. And then something happens—suddenly, violently, without even a hint of a warning. It instantly frightens me out of my reverie and away from all that is calm and soothing. I convince myself that it was a fluke, too disturbed to even name what *it* is, but then it happens again a few days later. I call Dr. Green and arrange for an appointment as soon as possible. I walk into her office with trepidation, not knowing what is to become of me or my baby.

"And how have you been feeling during the last two weeks?" Dr. Green asks, taking a sip of her coffee.

"Mood-wise I've been okay," I answer, hoping to butter her up before shocking her completely. "But, um, I've been having these thoughts…"

"Yes?"

"Well, I've never had thoughts like these before and they kind of worry me."

"Are they self-critical thoughts? Or fears about the baby?"

"Not exactly." I pause, wishing Dr. Green would suddenly become telepathic. "They aren't really thoughts, I guess. More images, I'd say."

"Can you be more specific, Beth?" she asks, smiling at me encouragingly. I look back at her for a moment, then cover my face with my hands. *Here goes nothing.*

"In the last few days when using the CD you gave me I've had these images two or three times of stabbing my stomach with a butcher knife," I say through my fingers, feeling the words push harshly against my tongue and teeth. As I mention the images, another one floods my mind, full of colour and shame. I half expect Family and Children's Services to break down the door and take away my belly.

"And do these images upset you?"

"Are you kidding me?" I say, putting down my hands in surprise. "Of *course* they upset me! They horrify me!"

"Do you think you have any real urge to harm your baby?"

"Of course not! But still, these images were awful! What kind of mother am I?"

"A mother who is struggling with anxiety and mood concerns," Dr. Green answers.

"What do you mean?"

"What I mean, Beth, is that these images, while very upsetting for you, are entirely normal for someone with anxiety difficulties. Not merely normal, but predictable." She again smiles.

My eyes suddenly fill with tears. "Normal," I repeat. "Do you realize I've never been called that before?"

"There's a first for everything, Beth."

"But…aren't you concerned that I might hurt the baby?"

"Do you want to hurt the baby?"

"I already answered that! Of course not!"

"Then I'm not concerned." She paused. "Beth, I'm not trying to downplay how distressing these images are for you. Like any anxiety symptom, they feel horrible. What I'm trying to stress is that all these images are anxiety. Just as a panic attack is not a sign that you are about to have a heart attack, these images are not a sign that you could become psychotic or aggressive. They're just a signal that for now we should have you stop using the relaxation CD."

"Why?"

"For some people who are prone to panic attacks, entering a deep state of relaxation can actually trigger intense anxiety symptoms."

"How could a relaxation CD trigger anxiety? Isn't that kind of counter-productive?"

"Well, think of it this way. When you are extremely relaxed, all of your defenses are down, including those that might be keeping your anxiety at bay. Kind of like levees."

"So the solution is to always stay in a state of hyper-alertness?"

"No, but let's stop using that CD for now, okay?"

I nod, looking down at my hands. "That explains why I experienced anxiety. But why didn't I just have a panic attack? Why did it have to come out in such a violent, aggressive way?"

"Unfortunately, violent images can be part and parcel with anxiety. When people have them frequently and try in some way to avoid or diminish them, we call that Obsessive-Compulsive Disorder." She pauses. "Believe it or not, your problem isn't these images you've been having, it's your interpretation of them as somehow bad and your attempts at avoiding them." She leans forward. "Did you know that at least ninety percent of people surveyed admit to having sudden thoughts that are very violent or morally repugnant in nature? Things like swearing in a church, hurting a loved one? It's just that for most of us, these thoughts are viewed as fleeting and silly, nothing to get worked up about. It's when you're struggling with anxiety that they seem to take on a more significant meaning, and therein lies the problem."

"So the problem is what I think about the images, not the images themselves?" I ask doubtfully. I look around the neatly manicured room. When I listen to Dr. Green speak so compellingly, it all makes sense. But what about when I'm alone in my apartment with my crazy self?

"I know you're still scared, Beth. It must have been really frightening when those images came into your head." She pauses. "What might make it tougher for you is what we call thought-action fusion. Many of us have the mistaken belief that thinking about something will actually make it happen. Like if I think about my husband getting in a car accident right now, my thoughts will somehow will it to occur. And that just isn't true. Let's review some techniques that might help if you have these images again." She takes out a cognitive-behavioural workbook from her bookshelf. "I'd like you to borrow this between sessions and begin using some of the worksheets to identify and evaluate certain beliefs."

"Thanks," I answer, putting it on my lap. "What you're saying makes sense, but that's not it, exactly. I mean, I *was* worried at first, but not since you've explained things."

"Then what?"

"Deep down I'm not worried about actually taking a knife and hurting myself or the baby," I say. I look down at my hands. "It's more the thoughts themselves, the fact that they exist at all. I mean, what kind of mother am I going to be if I think such things?"

"The kind of mother who was concerned enough that she immediately took a bus to come see me," she answered. "Now let's take a look at that book together."

CHAPTER NINE

As the months go by, I notice myself feeling weirdly stable. With a few more sessions with Dr. Green, my anxiety goes back to where it came from and the scary images go with it. Even better, my mood remains content, almost happy. On more than one occasion I notice that I'm smiling to myself for no apparent reason. Other than an almost constant case of heartburn, a weird metallic taste in my mouth, and some trouble sleeping, I feel better physically than I ever have before. What's more, with each visit to my obstetrician I learn that everything is going perfectly well with my pregnancy—weight gain is good, there's no protein in my urine, fundal height is as expected, and my blood pressure remains nice and steady. I agree to take various screening blood tests and when the results come in as normal, I feel like I've been given a gold star. With no real effort of my own, I'm finally doing something right.

I'd never really thought much about pregnancy before or what it would be like to become a parent, other than I would never use my mother as a role model. As my belly grows, I realize that maybe *this* is what I was meant to do. Maybe what has been missing in my life was the chance to really nurture another being, to be able to focus my emotional energy on someone other than myself. I find myself caressing my stomach and having conversations with the baby in utero. I just know it will be a girl, all pink limbed and soft-cheeked, and when I go for my eighteen-week ultrasound I learn that I am right. *Kate*. My daughter will be everything that is good in me, but will remain uniquely herself. On weekends I go to the public library and rummage around the shelves for books on pregnancy, childbirth, and parenting. I read up on what to expect in terms of fetal development month to month, week to week. I make a list of things to buy for the baby and decide to give up cable in order to build a nest egg for all that she'll need. Worst-case scenario, I'll have to dip into my therapy fund. Baby comes first.

At twenty weeks, I make the decision to start decreasing my Effexor dosage. Now that I've seen the image of my baby on a screen I just can't keep taking something that could potentially harm her. Or more accurately, I won't do it. It's the first real decision I've made as a mother, and I draw strength from it. I can tell that Dr. Reimer, who has my past suicide attempts and hospitalizations well documented in his file, isn't quite as pleased with my decision, and I don't blame him. Still, it's mine to make. Dr. Reimer agrees to meet with me weekly as I gradually discontinue the medication. I've gone off enough antidepressants before to know that if you stop too quickly, the side effects can be brutal. By twenty-four weeks I'm Effexor-free and other than an increase in anxiety, which I think I can handle, I generally feel okay.

At the beginning of my third trimester I start a nightly ritual of standing naked in front of my bathroom mirror. At first it seems strange to see myself without clothes. In the past I've been too focused on my inner torment to give more than a passing glance at what I actually look like. During the first few nights I try speaking out loud to the baby, but the sound of my voice echoing back at me in the bathroom makes me feel like I'm acting out a play, rather than experiencing a bonding moment. Instead I start to take photos of my growing belly. I want another witness to what's happening. Once a week I turn to the side and hold a camera out awkwardly in front of me. Sometimes I rub lotion across the great expanse of skin, avoiding my new jack-in-the-box belly button. Other times, I just stand and stare. This is happening. This is coming. With no effort on my part, a seismic shift is about to occur.

About once a week after work I meet Sarah at a small coffee shop downtown. She's starting Teacher's College on campus and will be here for the foreseeable future. Without actively meaning to, Sarah's future is planned out—marriage to Alex, her sweet-natured, long-term boyfriend who is also planning to be a teacher, a career in an area that energizes her, and someday a house. Although we were never more than casual friends throughout graduate school, during my first and second trimesters the bond between us slowly solidifies. Not only is Sarah not shocked by my unexpected pregnancy, she is warm and accepting, and goes so far as to express mild jealousy at not having a baby first. In the glow of Sarah's presence, I start to feel proud of my pregnancy, rather than embarrassed and apologetic. When the time comes to find a labour coach, it seems natural to ask Sarah. After all, the only other person that I have even somewhat regular contact with is Patrick through e-mail, in which he checks in bi-weekly to make sure I haven't killed myself yet. During my seventh month prenatal classes start at the local YWCA and Sarah picks me up each Thursday night in her used Toyota. As we sit in a circle on the floor surrounded by female-male dyads, I find myself at peace. Sarah is calm and still. In her presence I notice my tendency to roil emotionally start to subside. During our third class, I watch Sarah focus intently on the instructor as she teaches the coaches how to use stockings filled with rice as back massagers, and I feel myself relax.

ഔരു

At thirty-two weeks, Sarah throws me a baby shower. The invite list is small—just a few former Master's students who are now working on their Ph.D.s, the departmental secretary, and Sarah's own mother, Joyce. Heather is also invited, but declines due to midterms and sends a thoughtful gift and note in her stead. While the reasons for such a small gathering may not be ideal—I've lost friends through the Patrick debacle and have not been able to replace them with new ones—the little group of guests makes the shower feel warm and intimate. As someone who becomes awkward and shy in large settings, this is perfect.

Sarah has decorated her bachelor apartment in pale green, my favourite colour. Streamers adorn the walls and balloons hang from the overhead lights. Despite being the least whimsical person I know, Sarah insists that I wear a crown made of sewn-together baby cloths and forces us all to participate in games like guess the baby food and who can change the doll's diaper the quickest. Nestled in my brightly decorated chair, surrounded by a gaggle of women, I feel normal. The reason they're all here, the reason they've come to celebrate, is because I am to have a baby. Just like generations and generations before me, I am going to give birth, the most basic, natural process in the world. The fact that I struggle with depression or that I've messed up in so many aspects of my life is irrelevant. In this fundamental, biological way, I am normal.

After the games are over and I'm devouring my second piece of cake, Joyce comes over and settles on the arm of my chair.

"Great shower, huh?" she says.

"Yeah, Sarah did an amazing job!"

Joyce smiles at me and I smile back. It's only the third time I've met her and the other two times were in passing. Still, she resembles Sarah (or Sarah resembles her), and this leads to a certain level of familiarity that feels safe to me.

"There's something I wanted to tell you," Joyce says, still balancing next to me. "I'm not sure if Sarah told you this, but I raised her without a father."

"Oh," I say. "No, she didn't tell me that."

"Well, her father did re-enter her life while she was still a young girl, so perhaps she didn't feel it was relevant. The point I wanted to make was that I was only twenty years old when Sarah was born. Her father was still so young, we both were. He just wasn't ready at that time to be involved. And just like you, I didn't have much in the way of family involvement."

I feel my cheeks start to flush. What did Sarah tell her?

"Perhaps I've spoken out of turn, Beth. Sarah mentioned in passing that your mother was invited for today but declined the invitation, and I may have read too much into that."

"She had another commitment," I blurt out, my face burning. I try to forget my mother's half-hearted, overly apologetic message on my answering machine. *You know I'd like to be there, Beth, but Peter has a business function that he's asked me to attend. I'm sure you understand.*

"Of course," Joyce says, patting my hand. "Please don't mind me. I have a tendency of putting my foot in my mouth! What I was trying to say was that having Sarah at twenty was tough. It was incredibly tough. Some days I felt so lonely and I couldn't stop crying. What did I know about babies? I just wasn't sure how I'd get through it as a single mother." She stops. When she speaks again, her voice has changed. It sounds softer, as if she has suddenly become that young girl once more. "My point is that you do, you do get through it. And you more than get through it. What I didn't realize at the time, Beth, was that you don't get through it as a single mother. You get through it as a family, a family of two. And that is a wonderful thing." She pats my hand again, before standing up and gathering plates off of the coffee table. "That's all I wanted to say."

I sit still, staring ahead, the half-eaten piece of cake on my lap forgotten. This is the most motherly advice I've gotten in years. And it came from the parent of someone else.

CHAPTER TEN

It's Monday morning. I'm about to leave my apartment to meet with Dr. Shields to discuss his new survey when I notice a sudden wetness in my underwear. I haven't peed my pants since I was five, but I figure that at thirty-four weeks pregnant, anything goes. As I head to the bedroom to change, I experience another warm trickle. It almost feels like urine, but I'm not sure. I sit bare-assed on my bed, uncertain of what to do. Have I suddenly become incontinent?

As I debate whether to just grab a pad and be done with it, it happens again, a slight trickle. *Please, no.* I feel my arms start to shake, just slightly. I pick up my latest pregnancy book from the library and look up amniotic fluid. The book is reassuring and indicates that often women in their third trimester accidentally void a bit of urine. This seems to fit with what just happened. After all, it was a trickle, not a gush. Still, to be on the safe side, I'm advised to do the sniff test. If it smells like pee, no problem. If it smells sweet, not so great. I awkwardly bend down until I'm kneeling in front of the mattress and put my face near the small wet spot. Sweet. I sniff again, this time my nose touching the sheet. Sweet. *Oh shit.* I suddenly feel faint and nauseous and lie down on my side, holding my belly. I'm acutely aware of my aloneness. *This can't be happening yet. It's too early for this to be happening.* I try and recall all that I've read about the last six weeks of pregnancy. I know that babies are born prematurely all of the time and that by thirty-four weeks they have a good shot at a healthy life. *But what about the lungs? Don't they develop last? Why can't I remember anything about the damn lungs?* As I lie on my side, I notice my own chest start to tighten, as if in sympathy for the baby.

I feel another slight trickle down my leg and force myself to sit up. I reach over to the phone and call Sarah. This time my panic is too strong to be more than momentarily lulled by her calmness. Sarah informs me that she'll be at my apartment within ten minutes and that we can get to the hospital within twenty. While waiting for her to arrive, I stuff my wallet into my purse and grab my contact lenses case, as well as the pregnancy book. At the last minute I also shove in the crumbled piece of paper with Jacob's number on it. I then sit by the door with my legs crossed, as if I have any power at keeping this baby in.

ᎨᏇᏇ

After a few minutes in Emergency, we bypass the wait and head straight for Labour and Delivery. Within half an hour I've been evaluated and told what I already know—I'm leaking amniotic fluid. Thankfully, I'm also told what I didn't know—that I am not experiencing contractions or cervical dilation and that I might not deliver the baby. A physician with a kind face explains that there is a rip, rather than a total rupture of the amniotic sac. She explains that I am to be admitted immediately and that in all likelihood I will go into active labour in the next twelve hours, but that it is possible that I will hold off for several days. I will begin receiving various medications intravenously, including an antibiotic to ideally reduce the risk that the baby develops an infection as a result of the rip. She explains that if I do not commence labour, then the baby and the uterine environment will be monitored regularly, with ultrasounds given as needed. Regardless, I am to remain on complete bed rest, with only brief trips to the bathroom permitted. I suddenly feel any control I have over my life floating out of my reach. Without being asked to do so, Sarah stays at my side, holding my hand, and asks medical personnel to repeat whatever has been said.

While reassured by the news that my baby might have a chance to develop more, I find myself overwhelmed by all of the information that's thrown at me and how quickly things are happening. Within an hour I'm settled into a bed in a ward room with two other women in it. Before leaving for the night, Sarah pulls the curtain around me for a modicum of privacy. Once alone in my fabric cocoon, I notice myself beginning to fill with old feelings of guilt and shame. Somehow, in some way, I have done this to my baby. Regardless of all the milk I drank or the books I read, regardless of all the walks I took or the hot baths I avoided, I did this to her. No matter what anyone tells me, I know this much to be true: while I was busy chattering away to Dr. Green during my therapy sessions or blissfully practicing deep breathing exercises on my living room floor, my depression continued to silently course through my veins and through the placenta, like a toxic sludge.

CHAPTER ELEVEN

I wake up the next morning to see Heather sitting in the small chair next to my bed flipping through an old paperback. Before saying anything I take a moment to breathe her all in, this baby-sister-turned-beautiful-stranger.

"Heath?" I say. "How did you know I was in here?"

"Your friend Sarah called Dad and he called me." She shrugs, my shrug. "We drove down together." She tries to smile. "You look huge!"

"Sarah called Jacob? How did she have his number?"

"She said you asked her to call him last night. Anyway, he's down the hall in the waiting room and wants to see you if that's okay."

"Okay," I nod. I watch my sister as she leaves the room, wishing I knew what I could do or say to change what's happened between us. *Does she still have memories of how it used to be?* A few minutes pass, and there's a knock on the door. The woman in the bed across from me looks up at the same time I do, then quickly turns back to her TV.

"Hey," he says, standing in the doorway. "Can I come in?"

Before answering, I just look at him, at Jacob. It has been years since I've seen him in person. He looks taller than I remember or maybe it is that I've forgotten. His frame fills the doorway, blocks the hall from view.

"Hi. Yes, please do," I say.

Jacob comes near my bed and I gesture for him to pull the curtain. He does, then continues standing. "So," he says. "Congratulations!"

"Congratulations?"

"Not for being in the hospital! For your pregnancy, for the baby-to-be." He looks at me solemnly. "Your friend Sarah filled me in on everything. Do you feel scared?"

"I did last night. But labour never started and they've told me I might be able to keep her inside me for several days or even weeks, as long as there's enough amniotic fluid."

"Her?"

"Yes. It's a she, it's a girl."

"A daughter." He looks at me, then away. "Do you need anything? Anything from home or anything I can buy?"

"I think I'm good for now," I say. "Sarah was planning to bring stuff this afternoon, maybe bring me some work to do to keep me occupied."

"Good, good." Jacob pauses. "At least this hospital visit is going better than our last one," he says, then instantly looks stricken. "Beth, I'm sorry. That was an awful thing to say. I have this horrible tendency of telling jokes when I'm feeling nervous. It used to drive your mother crazy." He reaches down and awkwardly pats my leg.

"What last hospital visit?" I ask.

"Oh God, sweetie, I truly didn't mean to bring it up. That's the last thing you need to think about right now. Please forget that I said anything."

"No, Jacob, I'm serious. I don't know what you're talking about. What hospital visit?"

"You really don't remember?" He asks, lowering himself down in the chair that Heather had been in, his legs long and ungainly in front of him. I shake my head. "Okay. Here goes. I was talking about when I came to visit you during your first hospitalization, after that overdose at your mother's house. First year university, remember?"

I shake my head, suddenly noticing sweat pool on my upper lip. "You came?"

"Of course I came! You're my daughter!" he says gruffly.

"But I thought that you never came when I was hospitalized. Ever. Especially that first time, after what I did to Heather, after what she had to see…" I close my eyes. The lights are too bright.

"Beth, of course I was worried about Heather, but I was *terrified* about you." He pauses. "I was with you until you became conscious."

"Maybe that's why I don't remember. Because you left?"

"Yes, I left. I didn't want to, but when you woke up and saw me, well you became agitated, screaming. You tried to pull out your IV, tried to throw things at me. You wouldn't stop screaming until I left. I was told by staff that my presence wasn't…helpful." He stares down at his open, empty hands. Still like bear paws. "So I never went back to visit, and I stayed away when you were hospitalized the next time. I wanted to help but I didn't know what else to do. I used to call your mother for updates." He looks at me again. "Beth, I'm sorry."

I nod, my eyes still closed. A memory flashes through my mind, all bits of sound and pulsating colour, but my brain refuses to meld them together to form a cohesive whole. "I wish I'd known." I say. "I wish I could remember."

Jacob nods again and looks at the curtain. There's movement behind it and suddenly Heather comes in.

"I got you a few magazines, "she says, placing them on my blanket. "They're all junk but I figured you'd want to be distracted."

"Thanks, Heather," I say. "Better than the journal articles I've asked Sarah to bring me!"

"A nurse just told me that she wants to come check in on you," she says, looking at her father. "We should go, Dad."

"Of course," says Jacob, standing up. He seems too big for the makeshift room. "Can we get you anything?" he asks.

"I think I'm good for now," I answer, suddenly exhausted.

"We'll come back this afternoon, if that's okay," Jacob says and I nod in reply.

I watch as my sister and father leave, each a mirror image of the other. Jacob turns as he reaches the door and comes back to my bed.

"You know what, Beth? I never thought I'd see this day."

"That I'd become a mother?"

"No. That I'd become a grandfather," he says.

I stare at him, not knowing what to say in return. I'm filled with emotions I can't yet name. It's not joy that I feel, exactly, and it's not regret or anger, but yet somehow, it is. It's all of them. Jacob looks at me, his eyes seem wide and pleading.

"Her name will be Kate," I say eventually, giving him a gift.

"Kate," Jacob says, smiling. He pats my leg once more, then lumbers out of the room.

80CR

The days that follow are spent lying on my back, willing my baby to mature just a little more. A strange schism seems to exist between the mind-numbing sameness of each day in hospital and the knowledge that in an instant, everything in my life will change forever. Most afternoons are filled with visits, once by my mother (an exhausting hour for us both), sometimes by Sarah or Heather, but mostly by Jacob. The hole that has existed since my stepfather left my life is now overflowing with his presence and I feel like I'm drowning. Each morning he calls me to make a list over the phone of all the errands that need to be done in preparation for the baby. Just before dinner-time he arrives, to visit while I eat and to fill me in on the day's activities. Any anxiety I might have had about all that was left to be done has been completely assuaged—newspapers are scoured for the best deals on diapers, baby shampoo, and hooded towels, and the merits of bottle feeding versus breast milk are discussed ad nauseam.

At first I feel relief for all that Jacob is doing for me and thank him repeatedly. Rather than slow him down, however, I find that with each expression of gratitude Jacob seems emboldened to outdo himself, to buy bigger and better. Within days a crib is purchased and set up, a change table is built, and a baby swing and a high chair are waiting for me in their boxes. But even these are not enough. No. After touring my basement apartment and judging it unsuitable for his future granddaughter, Jacob speaks to my landlord about the possibility of having me move into a two-bedroom on the third floor. When I protest that the jump in rent will be way too much for a single mother-to-be with no true career prospects to handle, Jacob insists on making up the difference, until I can afford it. After all, he never contributed to my post-secondary education, despite paying the way for Heather. This will make things more even, this will bring him pleasure, this is something that he *really* wants to do. Jacob also insists on organizing the move himself, with Heather and her Toronto friends arm-wrestled into carrying futon sofas and boxes. Now I have one less thing to worry about as I lay on my back, willing my life to become my own again.

In the face of Jacob's generosity, I feel powerless to refuse. How did I get to be so lucky? As time passes, I notice the familiar signs of anxiety returning. Instead of looking forward to Jacob's visits, I begin to feel unmoored right before them. Mixed in with this panic is a sense of self-reproach for not being grateful for what he's doing, for not being grateful for having him back. Isn't this what I'd been wishing for since I was fifteen? Isn't this what I'd missed?

Unfortunately, gratefulness doesn't cut the panic. Instead, I feel sick with indebtedness, a leaden, nauseous feeling with no relief in sight. Following one particularly anxiety-provoking visit, I decide to call Dr. Green from my hospital bed, in the hopes that she'll be able to explain all that is inexplicable to me. The phone call feels different than a therapy session, more personal somehow. I can hear Dr. Green breathing as she listens to what I have to say.

"I think you know what you have to do, Beth," she says, after listening to me prattle on for about twenty minutes.

"And what is that?"

"You need to have this conversation with Jacob," she says. "Explain to him how overwhelmed you're feeling and why."

"I don't know if I can," I say.

"If and when you're ready, you will." Although little advice is actually given, I begin to feel calmer, anchored by her words.

By the time Jacob arrives for his dinner visit, I feel ready for him. He brings in a large bag and takes out what looks like baby pajamas with the feet sewn together.

"This is called a baby sleeping bag!" he announces gleefully, holding it up for all to see. "It's a marvellous invention, really. Do you know how you aren't supposed to have any blankets in a crib with an infant? Well...."

"Stop." I say, holding up my hand. "Jacob, please, just stop for a minute."

"Is something wrong?" he asks, putting the bag on the bed.

"No. Yes." I pause. "Jacob, I'm so grateful for all that you've done.

And I'm so happy that you've come back into my life. I *want* you back in my life." I pause again. "But I need to ask you something."

"Anything, bear cub," he says.

"Why didn't you push to keep seeing me after you and Mom broke up?" I ask, my fingers fiddling with some fringe on my blanket.

Jacob looks at me and sighs heavily. "I've always regretted that," he says, nodding to himself. "At the time I didn't want to rock the boat, make the situation worse than it already was. You didn't seem to want to come with me and I didn't want to push it. Then too much time had passed to fix things." He shrugs. *My shrug.*

"But what if it had been Heather?"

"What do you mean?" Jacob looks at me, then at the curtain.

"What if Heather had said she needed to stay with Mom? Would you have not wanted to rock the boat then? Or would you have tried to fight for her?" My voice sounds harsher than I mean it to be, but I don't try and change it. There's safety in its roughness.

"Beth," he sighs. "You *know* that would have been different."

"But why?" I ask. "Why, Jacob? When I was little you always told me that I was yours, that I was as much your daughter as Heather."

"You were, you are," Jacob says, rattling his plastic bag. "I don't know what else to say, Beth, except that I'm very, very sorry." He pauses. "I screwed up."

I nod once, twice. The words that follow are out of my mouth before I've even thought about them. "If you're going to be in my life now, then I need it to be okay that part of me still hates you," I look into his eyes. "Jacob, I *need* that to be okay."

Jacob looks back at me, wounded. *A direct hit.* "Sure, sure," he says, stuffing the sleeper back into the plastic bag. "I'll talk to you later, okay?" He smiles quickly, a misplaced smile, and then heads to the door. I turn and lie on my side, watching Jacob as he leaves the room, as he leaves me. *Why can't you ever stay when things get hard?*

CHAPTER TWELVE

After almost two weeks spent lying in bed, I'm awakened in the middle of the night by my own screaming. I find myself twisted in soaking wet sheets, my body pulled and contorted from within. One of my roommates has left her bed to stand beside mine and is rubbing my back.

"It's okay," she says softly, as I stare at her unseeing. "I think you've gone into labour." She presses the call button rapidly and continues rubbing my back, her own protruding abdomen pushing against me. "Can I call the dad for you?"

"There's no dad," I whimper. "Have them call Sarah! Please! They have the number for Sarah!"

The hours that follow are a cacophonous mix of noise and colour, too loud and bright for me to shut out. Time seems pulled and twisted into odd contortions like hot taffy. *Together, apart, together, apart.* Contractions last an eternity, while the moments in between barely register in seconds. At some point I'm moved to a different room and my abdomen is strapped to various beeping machines. My outsides are ministered by cool, capable hands, while my insides are left to seethe and roil against themselves, tidal waves of pain. Each time I'm about to draw in a breath, to try and get my bearings, I'm pulled under again. I reach out, I throw out my arms for someone, *anyone*, to save me, but I end up grasping empty air. The worst part is the banality of it all—how procedures continue to be followed and nurses keep bantering back and forth about weekend plans while I scream and writhe in agony. At some point I beg for pain relief but am told that given the age of the baby, the only safe option would be an epidural, but that things are progressing quickly and the anesthesiologist—who is in surgery with another patient— will not be available in time. This information is given to me in a kind, but detached manner, as if they don't understand that they are essentially giving me a death sentence. It makes me want to hurt someone. *We're sorry that you're about to be drawn and quartered, but maybe a few ice chips will make you feel better.* Suddenly, during one of my millisecond respites, I realize that Sarah is not with me.

"Sarah! Sarah!" I yell, all pain and panic. "Please!"

"I'm here, Beth," says Patrick, his face near mine. "Sarah called me to come instead. She has the stomach flu or food poisoning or something and can't be here. She's really, really sorry. But I'm here for you."

"I need Sarah!" I moan. "Go get her! Please!"

"It'll be okay," Patrick soothes, the tone in his voice conveying the opposite. He sounds as if he's calling me from the other end of a narrow tunnel.

"Make it stop!" I beg, rolling side to side on the bed. "Please, somebody! Please, please, make it stop!" Again, I go under.

"Beth, listen to me," says a nurse, putting her face directly in front of mine. "I know this is hard, I know this hurts, but I want you to push out your baby. You need to do this, you can do this!"

"No! I can't! I can't!" I shake my head back and forth.

"You're almost there, Beth, you can do it," Patrick says, rubbing my foot. I kick his hand away from me, his voice and touch an irritation.

"Make it stop!" I yell frantically. "Please, oh please stop!" *Why does it take so long to die?*

"Beth, look at me," says the nurse. "I need you to push out the pain, okay?"

"I can't!" I yell. "I give up!"

"Beth, you cannot give up. You are not going to give up!" Patrick refuses to go away, his grip on me steadfast.

"No more!" I moan, my voice that of a young child's. "I'm done!"

Suddenly, the obstetrician is before me, her nose almost touching mine. "Beth," she says firmly. "This baby isn't moving down. Her heart rate is dropping. We want to avoid doing a C-section at this point if we can help it. We're going to need to use forceps immediately to get her out."

I try to answer but find I cannot. I'm falling down a jagged tunnel that keeps pushing at me from all sides and I can't find a foothold to save me. I continue to thrash and flail, wanting to bite someone. I only hear bits of words as they are flung nearby me. *Back labour. Heart rate dipping. Oxygen. Forceps. Difficult. NICU.* One moment I'm plunged in the burning depths of Hell and the next I'm lying spent on a pillow, Patrick gripping my foot.

"You did it," he says, still holding on. "You actually did it, Beth."

"No."

"She looks great, she really does. They've just moved her to the Intensive Care Unit to get checked out more. You'll be able to see her soon."

"You can go now," I say woodenly, looking at the ceiling. "You don't have to stay."

"Go now?" Patrick moves over to the head of the bed. "Beth, I don't want to go now. This has been…intense for me, but I want to see your baby, with you. Please let me."

"Why?" I ask.

"I've had time to think," he says. "I miss you. I want to be your friend. I realized that for certain the instant Sarah called me for help." He pauses. "After I spoke to her about you, all I could think was, 'Why didn't Beth call me sooner?'"

I close my eyes, my body shivering. A nurse brings a blanket from the warmer to cover me, but I push it away. I don't deserve such comfort. Tears flow down my face, into my ears. I remain on my back, my abdomen like a long-forgotten, deflating balloon, I can't stop thinking about what just happened. *I gave up.* My mind keeps licking at the truth, like a tongue worrying a crumbling tooth, unable to resist the sweet rot of decay. What I now know, what I can now never forget, is that I failed, that as a mother I am breakable, flawed. *I gave up.* Had anyone asked me when pregnant if there could be anything, anything at all that I wouldn't do to save my future child, my answer would have been instantaneous. Jump in front of a truck? No problem! Run into a burning building? In a second! Take a bullet? Without question! I would be a lioness, I would be a mother bear, I would be invincible! But now I know the truth and somewhere, in the deep recesses of her baby brain, so must Kate.

CHAPTER THIRTEEN

A few hours later, after I am all cleaned up, a wheelchair is brought in for Patrick to take me to the NICU. I don't want to go, I see no reason to go, but I can't summon up the energy to argue. Prior to entering the intensive care unit, Patrick and I are told to don hospital gowns and to wash our hands thoroughly. He wheels me through a maze of isolettes until we find her. *Kate.*

She's lying on her back in a plastic-like container, a tiny IV line taped to her left arm. Various wires seem to attach her to an ominous-looking machine that is monitoring data on a moment-by-moment basis. The heels of her feet are covered with bandages. She looks less like a chubby newborn and more like a skinny, plucked chicken. *What did I do to you?*

"She's doing well," says a nurse, coming up behind us. "She just needed a bit of oxygen, but as you can see, she's breathing fine on her own. Sucking reflex seems good, which isn't always a certainty at thirty-six weeks, so we likely won't need to use the gavage tube to feed her." She smiles encouragingly. I give a flat stare back.

"What's wrong with her feet?" I ask.

"Oh, that's nothing to worry about. We needed to take some blood samples and with new babies we usually do that through the heel. Very routine."

"And the IV?"

"They suspect she has an infection. We wanted to start antibiotics as soon as possible." She pauses. "You can touch her, you know. She won't break!" Again the smile. I have an inexplicable urge to smack the nurse, but hold my hands tightly together instead. After a few moments, she and Patrick both move away, to give me and my daughter some privacy. *My daughter. Mine.* I gingerly reach in a hand to touch her foot.

"Did I do this?" I whisper. I experience a sharp kick of guilt, an emotional spur to the kidneys. I wait for the waves of love I've been told to expect to wash over me, for the immediate bonding of mother and child to zap me from above. Nothing. True, I feel protective of this scrawny little thing who seems implausibly vulnerable lying there outside of my body. But actual love? Nothing. *What kind of mother am I?*

The nurse comes back and encourages me to pick Kate up, all wires and tubes, and try and breastfeed her in a nearby room. I'm told that my milk won't come in for a few days but that the colostrum that's awaiting her is liquid gold. If nothing else, it will help us to bond.

Tentatively I pick her up, this baby I'm told is my daughter, and with both the nurse and Patrick in tow, walk carefully to the adjacent room. There's a rocking chair with a nursing pillow on it, as well as teddy bear wallpaper in soothing hues of blue and green. I hand Kate to Patrick as I sit down, the sting from my episiotomy stitches quick and sharp. After I'm settled as best I can, the baby is handed back to me and the nurse begins to instruct me on the art of nursing.

"You want to tickle her lip like this with your nipple," she says, holding my breast like a mound of bread dough. "Wait until she opens wide like this, then move her mouth towards you." She pauses, pointing at Kate's mouth as she begins sucking on my flesh. "You see that? That's a good latch. She has your areola in her mouth, not just the nipple." I glance at Patrick, who appears to be suddenly examining the wallpaper with great concentration.

"Okay," I say.

"It'll take some time to get the hang of it. Don't be surprised if her suck isn't as strong as you'd expect. She is a few weeks early, after all. Our lactation consultant will be here tomorrow afternoon and will be a great help."

"Thanks," I say and watch as the nurse leaves the room. I turn my gaze onto my daughter, who somehow knows how to suck despite coming out four weeks too soon. I again wait for the feelings of love to course through my veins. Other than feeling like a dairy cow, there's nothing.

☙◗◖❧

The next day I sit on my hospital bed, feeling tired and deflated. I try to focus on what it's like to now be a mother, but my thoughts keep being interrupted by images of my cousin Adam. Each time I see his face in my mind I feel unsettled, antsy. Despite the fact that he severed ties with me over two years ago, despite the fact that I ruined everything at his wedding with my last suicide attempt, I need him to be a part of this. Nothing seems real unless Adam knows about it. I can't remember a time that existed without Adam in it. That's how it always was and that's how it was always meant to be.

I can still clearly remember what it was like after Heather was born. Adam and I held a mini-conference underneath his bed to decide whether or not we actually liked the idea of there being a baby in our lives. After agreeing that we did indeed like the baby, we became my mother's little helpers, passing her diapers and talcum powder when the need arose. We took turns pushing Heather back and forth in her stroller around the backyard patio, our seven-year-old selves puffed up with pride at being permitted to carry out so grown-up a task. In secret we agreed that we'd share Heather as a sister, that she belonged to both of us equally. Lying next to each other during sleepovers we talked solemnly about what it would be like to have our own babies. We agreed that despite our children being cousins, they too would call themselves 'the twins.'

Before I can change my mind, I decide to cold-call Adam, to tell him about my new daughter. What other choice do I have? My former child-self would never forgive me if I didn't share this experience in some way with him. I leave three messages within two hours but he doesn't return them. Why am I surprised? On my fourth try, someone picks up. Unfortunately, that someone is Adam's wife, Janice. The same Janice whose wedding I ruined with my dramatic overdose attempt. As I hear her voice, I consider hanging up, but remind myself that doing so would be unseemly as a mother.

"Hi, Janice, it's, um, Beth," I say. "Adam's cousin."

"Hello, Beth."

"I was wondering if you got my messages this morning? I wanted Adam to know that I just had a baby girl. She's in the NICU but I think she's healthy. So, ah, Adam has another cousin, or a second cousin, or maybe it's a first cousin once removed, I can never remember these things."

"Beth." Janice interrupts my babbling. Her voice sounds kind but firm. The voice of a reasonable adult, of someone sane. "We did receive your messages. Let me please tell you congratulations on the birth of your daughter! I'm so pleased for you."

"Thanks. Thanks a lot," I say.

"But I also need to tell you that Adam just isn't ready to speak with you."

"But..."

"He told me that you'd understand." She pauses. "I'm sorry, Beth," she says, then gently hangs up. Even her hang up sounds gracious. Gracious yet final. I hold the receiver in my hand, trying to come up with a way to change what just happened. A wave of shame moves through me, flushing my cheeks and ears. I may be sitting in a hospital bed with breasts beginning to fill, but I feel seventeen again. A screw-up.

Following my parents' separation and Jacob's abrupt departure from his role as father, the one thing I knew I could count on was my friendship with Adam. He had always been my rock and I knew he always would be, if I needed him. As I turned increasingly inward, it was Adam who attempted to pull me out. I depended on him to reach out and grab me and he depended on himself to be able to save me. What neither of us seemed to realize was that when faced with the gale-force wind of depression, Adam was just a boy, just a single, defenseless boy.

℘℃℞

To add to the drama in my life, around the age of seventeen I developed an all-consuming crush on Adam. My change in feelings toward him felt sudden and violent, like a sucker punch to the gut. These weren't frilly, write-his-initials-on-your-binder type feelings. No. What I felt whenever Adam was near me was the fierce pull of desire to be as close to him as possible, to somehow breathe him in. I began to have dreams about him, dreams that would leave me feeling shaken as I woke up in bed with my heart racing and my skin slick with sweat. Somehow, when I wasn't looking, Adam the boy had become a full-fledged man. Without speaking to any of my female friends about it, I knew deep in my gut that I wasn't supposed to notice Adam in this way; he was meant to remain asexual and off-limits. And yet, my feelings were there. Set against the backdrop of our ongoing friendship and cousin-hood, such feelings horrified me and gave me one more reason to find myself disgusting.

I first noticed this change on an unseasonably hot Saturday afternoon in early June. We were lounging in his parents' backyard on big beach towels, a bowl of ketchup chips lying in the grass between us. I'd fallen asleep on my stomach and had woken up to the touch of Adam's hands against my back.

"You're starting to get a burn," he said, as I turned my head to look up at him. "Just trying to undo the damage if I can." He held up his lotion-covered hands briefly, then set back to work.

"Thanks," I said, lowering my head back down. In the moments that followed I became acutely aware of Adam's firm yet gentle touch as he spread the lotion against my skin. I could feel the calluses on his fingers as he rubbed in circles around my back. As his hands brushed against my sides I noticed my breath catch, warmth spreading everywhere. Suddenly all I wanted was for him to stop. Suddenly all I needed was for him to continue. "I think that's good!" I said, suddenly sitting up and knocking the chip bowl over in the process. "Oh, shit!"

"You always were a klutz," Adam said, giving me a good-natured grin. He wiped his hands against his bathing suit, then headed towards the sprinkler. "Want to go to Burger King after I hose myself off and meet up with everybody?"

"Sure," I said, trying not to watch him as he walked away, yet failing miserably. I held my breath, staring at the golden hairs that adorned the back of his tanned thighs. I had the sudden urge to stroke those hairs, to press my legs against his. What was happening to me?

In the days that followed, I tried to protect myself by putting an imperceptible amount of distance within our friendship. Yes, we were still best friends and always would be. But friends at arms length. During the remaining weeks of grade twelve, keeping a bit of distance from Adam was fairly easy to do. At lunchtime I could claim that I needed to study for exams in the library and thus avoided having to sit across from Adam in the cafeteria as he analyzed his latest romance over a large fries and Coke. Weekends weren't so easy, as the tradition of having his family and mine spend Saturdays together had continued since we were children. On the weekends that Heather was not visiting Jacob, I'd encourage her to join in whatever Adam and I were doing. Whether Adam found it odd that I had suddenly developed such an interest in my ten-year-old sister, he didn't say. Trips to the mall, lounging in the backyard, even meeting up with friends, all of it was done with a chirpy chaperone in tow.

As school neared its end, I began counting down the days until Adam and his family would go to their cottage for most of the summer. Normally I dreaded him leaving—nothing was the same without Adam around. That summer everything depended on him being gone. The only way I could get him out of my head and be normal again was to have him go away. Then I could focus on the start of my final year of high school and moving forward in my life. If it meant having to leave Adam behind temporarily, then so be it.

It was one week before the start of finals, and I was pleased to find that my feelings for Adam had lowered in intensity and volume. As background noise, I could deal with liking him. Yes, the feelings were disgusting, yes the feelings were still there, but they were more like a background hum rather than a constant itch that demanded to be scratched. I'd had crushes before, I could deal with this. It would pass. I sat at my desk in my room at midnight, attempting to study. It's not as if I truly cared about my courses that much—since feeling depressed, high school had become a place to pass the time. It was just that I knew if I didn't pass my exams this term then I'd have to redo courses in September, which could tack on yet another year of living at home with my mother's husband. The idea of even one extra minute with Peter beyond my OAC year was enough impetus to motivate a week of all-nighters.

As I was attempting to reread *Macbeth* without success, I heard a strange noise at my window. *Thud, thud, thud*. It sounded as if a bird kept flying straight at the glass, retreating, then flying straight at it again.

At first I tried to ignore it, going with the theory that if you didn't pay attention to something, then it will eventually go away. Unfortunately, this theory didn't seem to be working. *Thud, thud, thud*. I decided to turn off my desk lamp, so I could look out my window without whatever or whoever it was being able to look at me in return. As the light disappeared, so did the familiarity of my room. I could only make out the shapes of things; the substance of my desk or chair seemed to be found in its borders. I headed over to the curtain, and moved an inch or so of the material to the side. I put my face up to the window, then sucked my breath in between my teeth. There was a person on the roof of the garage, throwing stones at the window. I ducked down beneath the window, willing my heart to stop beating so loud.

"Beth!" I heard my name, and for a brief, insane moment I thought that it was my voice that I was hearing. Then I heard it again. That time there was no doubt that it was coming from the other side of the window. On the roof. I took another peek from behind the curtain. Adam's face smiled back at me.

"What the hell!" I shut the curtain once more, and tried to calm down. I glanced quickly at the shadows around my room, hoping for some sudden wisdom about what to do in this situation. Finally, I opened up the curtain, and stared at him.

"Open the window," he mouthed from the other side. I unlocked the window, and then slowly took the screen off the glass. It was heavier then I'd expected, and I stumbled backwards with the bulk of it. A waft of humid air hit my forehead.

"Hi Beth," Adam said from my roof.

"Shhh!" I whispered, then gestured for him to come in. He attempted to climb through the window, and grabbed blindly at my shoulder for support. I could feel Adam's fingers through my thin pajama top. All of my focus was on my left shoulder, and those fingers. For a moment, all I became was this shoulder. *I forgot about this. I forgot.* Suddenly, everything came back, and I was not prepared. Like opening a closet door that you forgot had been crammed to overflowing with things, until the moment that everything falls out on top of you, too late to stop. It all came back, overwhelming me. Adam dropped his hand, and I shivered.

"Adam?" A question.

"Hi," he said again.

"What are you doing here? And why?" I gestured towards the window.

"I just had the impulse to see you before my family takes off for the summer. You haven't been around lately. I know you'll probably be working and won't get to the cottage this year, so I wanted to say goodbye. We've never been away from each other this long before," he said, sitting down on my bed. "Remember how you used to stay with us for two weeks each July and we insisted on sleeping in that leaky tent? Good times!" He smiled. I turned on the desk lamp, then stared at him, trying to memorize his face. He looked the same. Why had I expected anything different?

"But why now? Why aren't you studying for finals?" I remained standing. It was safer.

"I wanted to see you again. Plus I'm burned out from studying. Whatever happens, happens." He patted the bed. "Come sit next to me." I remained standing.

"It's midnight, Adam, and my mom and Peter are home. Asleep, in the other room!"

"I won't stay long. I promise," he said.

"That's not the point. What if you had woken them up?"

"They probably would have been pissed off, but I could have charmed them." He smiled at me, his schoolboy grin.

"No! It would have done more than that. Everything would have been ruined!" I gestured wildly with my empty hands.

"What would have been ruined, Beth?" Adam asked. Again, he patted the blanket next to him. Reluctantly I sat down.

"Well," I said. I looked closer at his face, at his eyes. They seemed glassy. "Wait a minute. Are you drunk?" I asked. *I can't believe this.*

"Just a bit," he shrugged his shoulders. "How else would I ever do something as spontaneous and idiotic as climbing onto someone's roof?" He grinned again. "It was actually Ben's idea. He's had the hots for you since last Christmas and thought that I might be able to make a good case for him." Adam nudged me with his elbow. "Whatcha think?" I moved ever-so-slightly away from him. "Anyway, Ben's somewhere is your backyard right now, almost ready to propose."

"It wasn't even your idea to do this?" I stood up again, crossing my arms. I dug my fingernails into my palms as hard as I could. I needed to feel something that was separate from what was going on in the room.

"Don't be like this," Adam said, leaning back on his elbows. "I know it's stupid that I climbed on your roof, and it's stupid that I listened to Ben, but you're forgetting the main point here."

"Which is?"

"That I've missed you, you moron!" He smiled at me. "If I didn't know any better, I'd think you were avoiding me. Do I smell or something?" He leaned back further on my bed, looking very relaxed. I started to feel panicky again.

"Well, you can't stay," I said, reaching over to grab his arm. "You have to go right away."

"What's the rush?"

"I already told you that my mom and Peter are asleep. And…I have to study!" I waved with my arms until I saw Adam staring at my wrist. I pulled down the sleeves of my pajama top.

"What the hell is that, Beth?" he asked, suddenly sitting up. Gone was the jokey Adam, back was my sentinel. He reached over and grabbed at my arm, roughly pushing the material up to my elbow. "Have you been cutting yourself?"

"That's, it's nothing!" I said, pulling my arm out of his reach.

"You've got scars, Beth! How is that nothing?" His voice was loud and bounced off each wall.

"Shhh," I whispered, "You're going to wake up my mom and Peter!"

"Maybe they need to be woken up. What the hell are you doing to yourself?" I saw his forehead furrow, and wanted to reach over and smooth it out. Instead, I stood taller.

"I just was stupid, okay? I got upset one night and I did this. It's no big deal. It's over." I paused, and took a step backwards. "I don't have to tell you everything, you know. You might not realize it, Adam, but we're not exactly twelve anymore!"

"Since when did you stop telling me things?" Adam asked.

"Since I grew up a little and realized that I could make decisions without running everything by you first," I said. "You might think you're so perfect, but here's a news flash for you—you're not!"

I'm not sure why I said this, other than to make him stop caring. And maybe to hurt him a little bit. Hurt him for not feeling the same. Adam snorted, and began to head towards my bedroom door.

"You haven't exactly acted like a best friend either, Adam!" I said, then stopped, uncertain of what to say next. I needed to figure out a way to make all of this *his* fault, his mistake. I needed him to admit to something, to anything, to help take some of the pressure away. "A best friend would have noticed that I was getting...upset over a year ago!" I watched as my words spilled out over him. "I guess I figured that you didn't care about all the crap that's been happening in my life!"

"And what exactly is happening in your life?"

"Just stuff with Peter," I said. "Just never mind."

"Beth." The way he said my name killed me. I knew that I could be eighty years old, and if I heard my name said that way, I would instantly remember. Adam walked over to me, and put his arm around my shoulders. For a moment, I moved into his hold, safe. Then the disgusting feelings came back and I abruptly moved away again.

"No, Adam. Forget about what I said. Forget about everything. My life is great! Life is wonderful."

"Fine." He moved away, too. "If you want to act this way, then go ahead. Obviously I can't stop you from being an idiot. I mean, as long as those cuts were a one time thing, I won't freak out about them." He paused, looking around my room, the same one he had sleepovers in until he was eleven. "Maybe it *is* time to get our own lives. I mean, a year from now we could be at universities across the country from each other, right? We better get used to it. Maybe you have the right idea after all." This time when he looked at me there was distance in his eyes. He was already walking across the grass in my backyard towards Ben, shrugging his shoulders.

"Oh," I said. "Yeah." I walked towards my bedroom door, then led him down the darkened stairs. We made it to the backdoor without waking anyone up.

"I guess this is goodbye," I said, sticking out my hand.

"Look, Beth," Adam sighed. "Even though we won't see each other much this summer, you know you'll always be my best friend.

We'll talk once I get back from the cottage, okay? Maybe hang out on Labour Day?"

"Fine. Okay," I tried to smile. Adam reached over and gave me a rough hug. Then he let go, and looked me in the eyes. The distance seemed to be gone.

"Things never come easy to you, do they?" He asked, not waiting for an answer.

He opened the back door, then walked outside. I could see Ben leaning against the porch, smoking a cigarette. Adam gave him the thumbs-down.

"See you," Adam said, shutting the door behind him. I stood by the window for a few more minutes, shivering.

CHAPTER FOURTEEN

In the weeks that followed Adam's impromptu visit, I became focused on one goal—to get over my crush before he returned from the cottage. With that end in mind, I forced myself to socialize as much as possible, pushing my black mood down into the bottom of my lungs. As long as I didn't try to breathe too deeply, I would be okay. One night in early July I slept over at a friend's house. Although not necessarily my best friend, Lucy was someone I felt safe with. For reasons I couldn't put words to, I trusted her. Maybe it was her eyes. She had one of those heavy stares that pushed against you, burrowing into what's hidden. While I never shared with Lucy how I'd been feeling lately, I knew that if I did, she wouldn't judge me. Lucy was the type of person who seemed to accept whatever people threw at her. The fact that Lucy was different than me in many ways never seemed to matter, as whenever I spent time with her I would end up feeling less hollow. With Lucy, there was no void to be filled. Somehow, despite all odds, she had come out complete. Lucy had an air of serenity to her that I tried to imitate whenever she was near. Maybe if I tried hard enough, I would no longer feel so broken.

Our night together was supposed to be one of wild, spontaneous freedom. It was all planned. We set up a two-person tent in her backyard, and told her unsuspecting parents that we wanted to experience the outdoors. Our plan was brilliant! After watching TV inside with her little brother, we headed out to the tent with a bag of chips and our sleeping bags for an early night. At midnight, we sneaked out of the tent, fully clothed, to conquer the world. Unfortunately, the world seemed to have gone to sleep a few hours before.

Without discussing it first, we eventually wandered over to the Grove, a small circle of trees at the edge of the local park where teenagers liked to herd together on Saturday nights, passing around bottles of whiskey and wet cigarettes. We neared the Grove hoping to see the light of a fire or the noise of many drunken voices mixing together. Instead as we approached the trees it remained blue-black and quiet.

"This sucks," Lucy said. Her voice seemed to get caught in the darkness.

"Maybe we should head back to your place," I said. "We could always see if there's a good movie on TV."

"In a minute, I'm tired." Lucy sat down on a nearby log and stretched her legs out in front of her. "Do you miss Adam?" she asked suddenly.

I felt my face redden and was relieved that I remained in shadow. "He's gone every summer, so I'm used to it," I said. "You know." I shrugged, more for my benefit than for hers.

"Yeah," she said. "You guys are so close, though. Kind of like a brother and sister, except that you get along!"

"I guess so," I said. I remained standing and hugged my arms against my chest. It was cool for a July night, an unexpected breeze making me shiver. Suddenly I heard the crunching of branches on the ground nearby.

"Anybody here?" A young male voice called out. I shivered again.

"We're over here," Lucy answered. "Who are you?"

The voice didn't respond but in a moment the beam of a flashlight shone in my face and I was blinded. "Can you please move that away?" I asked, covering my eyes.

"Hey, Dave, I know these girls," a familiar voice said. "It's Adam's cousin Beth and her friend." I looked up and saw myself looking at a smirking Ben, the same Ben who had convinced Adam to climb on my roof. *He's had the hots for you since last Christmas.*

"Hey," Lucy said, standing up and walking over to the two boys. "Is anybody else coming?"

"Nah, just us," the other boy said. He was someone I barely recognized, a friend of Adam's who went to a rival high school. He kicked his foot against the grass. "I'm Dave, by the way." He smiled at Lucy.

Ben held out a knapsack and pulled out a bottle of rum. "Sorry that I don't have anything to chase this with," he said. He unscrewed the top, then handed the bottle to me. "Ladies first."

I took a small sip, not having drunk any alcohol since Peter caught me bleeding in the bathroom. I felt my throat burn and started to choke, spitting most of the liquid out into the dirt.

"God, Beth!" Lucy said. "What an amateur!" I tried again, this time imagining my throat as a huge, open tunnel. *You can do this.* I gulped down the rum, feeling the warm sensation enter my stomach.

"Easy, girl!" Ben said, taking the bottle from me. I felt my muscles start to loosen.

Lucy grabbed the bottle and tipped it into her mouth. "Just what I needed," she said, wiping her mouth.

I looked at Ben. I'd never really noticed him before. He was attractive, but in a pleasant, forgettable way. In school, whenever he had stood next to Adam, his looks had always faded. I stared at his mouth. His face was clearly a boy's, with slightly rounded, milk-fed cheeks, and unfocused eyes. My gaze kept being drawn back to his lips. They were fully formed, finished. *Maybe this will get me over my crush.*

"Beth?" Lucy poked me. "Are we going to stay here with them, or what?"

"Um," I said. *Please leave us alone,* I thought, not knowing exactly whom I was referring to. *Something could happen.*

Lucy squatted down by the fire pit, a pile of old twigs encircled by stones. "I forgot about this," she said. She grabbed a handful of sticks, then threw them into the pit. "Anyone got a light?"

"Yeah," Dave said, handing her a lighter.

"Um, should we really do this, guys?" I asked. "I mean, won't we get caught if we light a fire?"

"Live a little, Beth," Lucy said, as she tried to make a teepee with the branches.

"Here, let me do it. You're doing it wrong," Dave said, pushing her out of the way. After a few minutes, a small fire was started.

'Show-off," Lucy said, but she looked pleased.

Lucy and I sat down cross-legged in front of the fire. Ben remained standing as he took a few swigs from the bottle.

"Hey, come sit down," I said, feeling brave. He looked over at me, then flopped down onto the dirt. I noticed that heavy bangs were hanging in his eyes. I reached over and pushed them away.

"Hey," he said. I left my hand on his forehead for a moment. His skin was so pale, you could almost see through it. I didn't think that I'd ever touched a boy's face before. Ben's skin felt just like my skin, which kind of surprised me.

"You're so pale," I said.

"I know, I know. That's what being Irish does to you," he said. "You should see how I look when I'm around your cousin! Like a ghost!"

"Yeah, I know. It's not fair that Adam has a year-round tan," I said. I grabbed the bottle from him and took another big swig of rum, eager to wash the image of Adam out of my mind.

"So, ladies, why haven't I seen you before?" Dave asked.

"Because we weren't looking," Lucy answered.

"Well, now that we *have* met, what do you want to do next?"

"Next?" I asked, taking another swallow of rum. "I kind of thought that this was it."

"Well, I must admit that getting sloshed by a fire is okay, but what are the plans for after the bottle is empty?" Dave nudged Ben. "We don't have an unlimited supply of booze here, and the bugs are killing me."

"We could go back to Lucy's place," I said, looking at Ben's forehead.

"Are your folks gone?" Dave asked, turning to Lucy.

"No—but we've got this tent set up in my backyard. I guess we could head there, and maybe I could sneak in and get some more to drink."

"A tent? Sounds promising," said Dave.

Lucy stood up, and began to push dirt onto the fire. "Down, boy."

Ben took the empty bottle, and tossed it into the trees. I watched it get trapped in the moonlight, then disappear into the blue-black. I never heard it hit the ground. We all pushed dirt onto the fire with our sneakers, then crossed a soccer field. As we walked under a line of streetlights, I glanced down at my watch. It was after three o'clock. I couldn't remember the last time that I was awake this late. And never with a boy.

Ben walked with his right foot on the curb and his left on the road. Every few steps, he kept falling off of the curb. "Shit!" he said. I liked how he kept getting back on, despite himself.

The tree-lined streets seemed to be in a state of hibernation, asleep for everyone but us. I felt light, airy. I was so alive that I could hardly bear it. I couldn't keep walking at this pace, I wouldn't! I started to run down the street.

"Wait, Beth!" Lucy hissed behind me. I entered into a sprint. Maybe I'd join the track team this year at school! I could feel my feet pound against the asphalt, but I couldn't feel my legs beneath me. I was running away from Peter, running away from the ghost of Jacob, running away from my disturbing crush on Adam. I could do it! I was the champion! I reached Lucy's house and ran into her backyard. Then I fell backwards onto the ground, the grass wet against my back. I put my arms straight out at either side and let the ground support me. I looked up at the sky, which seemed empty of stars. The darkness was comforting and safe; you could lose yourself in its shadows.

"Damn it, Beth!" Lucy said, as the others collapsed onto the grass nearby. "You almost killed us all!" I ignored her, and kept looking up at the sky.

Ben lay down next to me, his hair stuffed into the hood of his sweatshirt. We both looked up. I could feel the warmth of his body next to mine. My skin started to vibrate, and I noticed that I was breathing loudly.

"So—what about those drinks?" Dave asked.

"I'll be right back," Lucy whispered, slowly getting up. I continued lying on my back, content.

A few minutes later, Lucy returned, a bottle in her hand. "I got this," she said, handing it to Dave. He pulled out his lighter, to read the label.

"This looks like some weird liqueur from Germany or something."

Ben looked at the label. "That's Russian," he said.

"It must be from when my parents went there during one of my dad's sabbaticals. I think it's a couple of years old." Lucy said. She walked over to the tent and unzipped the door. "Anyone coming in?"

I crawled over and moved onto a sleeping bag. Ben followed and sat next to me. Lucy wedged herself into one corner of the tent, Dave in the other.

"Let's try it," she said. We started to hand the bottle around. The liqueur was thick; it tasted sweet at first, with a nasty kick as you swallowed. After a few swigs, I started to lean against Ben. He leaned back.

Lucy yawned and grabbed a blanket. "I feel pretty wiped," she said. "I think I'll head onto the porch for a while. Care to join me, Dave?"

Dave quickly got up, heading after her. "Have fun, kiddies!" he said, zipping the tent up after him.

"So," Ben said. "Do you often invite strange guys into your tent in the middle of the night?"

"It's not my tent. It's Lucy's," I said, suddenly shy.

"You know what I meant," he said, elbowing me gently. "Is this what you typically do for fun?"

"Nope. This is a first."

"I'm glad." We sat in silence for a few seconds. "Well," he said. We both moved closer together, and suddenly we were kissing. Kissing and touching, a mess of arms and legs. I moved my face away for a moment, and looked at Ben. His eyes were closed.

"I'm attracted to you," I blurted out. "But I'm not looking for a boyfriend right now."

"No?" He opened his eyes.

"Yeah. I mean, Adam told me before that you kind of liked me, and I don't want you to get the wrong idea about tonight. Tonight's about fun, you know?" I paused, feeling foolish. "I just don't want you to get hurt."

"Fun's good, Beth. I'll take fun," he said.

We went back to kissing again, lying on top of the sleeping bags. We were like two puppies that had just caught the scent of each other. My lips became swollen and sore, but I couldn't seem to stop. Tongues, teeth, hands.

The zipper of the tent opened behind us. Dave reached in and grabbed at Ben's ankles, trying to pull him away from me.

"Come on, lover boy," he said. Ben kicked at Dave and moved back onto the sleeping bags. More kissing.

"Beth!" Lucy poked her head inside the front of the tent. She was covered in a blanket. "Let's wrap this up, okay?" Between the two of them, they were able to force Ben and me away from each other. I stumbled out of the tent, surprised that the sky was now grey-pink. I looked at Ben. In the dawn light, I suddenly felt suddenly nervous. *What am I doing, exactly?*

"Um," I said, shuffling my feet in the wet grass. Ben walked over to me, and took my hand.

"This was nice," he said. "And very unexpected."

"So," I said.

"I'll call you tomorrow," he said, pulling up his hood. "It would be good to hang out with you sometimes." He looked directly at me. "Don't worry, I know that this was about fun. I like fun."

"Come on, man!" Dave said, already halfway across the yard. Ben gave my hand a strong shake, then loped after his friend.

"Tomorrow," he called back. Dave slapped him on the back, and they started to jog away. Lucy and I watched the boys until they'd rounded the corner. I kept looking in the same direction for awhile.

"You owe me, Beth." Lucy took part of the blanket, and wrapped me up with her. "You really owe me."

I turned and kissed her on the cheek. We headed into the house, and crept upstairs to her bedroom. We planned to crash in her bed until noon, if possible. Lucy fell asleep almost instantly, her breathing becoming deep and even. I lay on top of her comforter, staring at the ceiling. I needed time and quiet to figure out how I felt. I gave myself an internal check and realized that my feelings for Adam had faded, just a bit. I knew I didn't like Ben in a substantial way, but I *had* liked kissing him, and maybe for now that was enough.

CHAPTER FIFTEEN

A few nights later, Lucy and I agreed to meet up with Ben and Dave again. This time we headed to Dave's house, empty for the weekend of any parents. Within minutes of arriving I was sitting next to Ben on a sofa in the den, while Dave took Lucy on a grand tour of the remaining rooms. Despite having intimate knowledge of his lips, tongue, and hands, I felt awkward around Ben. After all, it was already clear to me that he was someone I was attracted to but didn't really like, at least not with the previous hurricane-intensity of my feelings toward Adam. In agreeing to come over that night, I had hoped to be so drawn into the reality of another person that I could forget myself for a while. Unfortunately, my plan was failing. Although I'd succeeded in rising my body temperature, my messed-up self was still dominating my thoughts. *Why do I put myself into these situations?* Instead of feeling closer to Ben, I felt like he was more of a stranger than before.

"Beth?" Ben asked, his arm around me. "Is everything okay?"

"Huh? Yeah." I moved my mouth closer to his.

"No, really." Ben pushed me back. "You just don't seem into this."

"I'm into this, I swear I am." I attempted to nibble his lower lip, while simultaneously reaching my hand down to rub his upper leg. *This isn't working.*

"Why don't we slow down for a minute?" Ben asked, gently taking my hand away from his leg.

"Am I doing something wrong?"

"No. It's just that I was hoping to get to know you a bit. You know, talk for awhile." He paused. "I mean, the other night in the tent was a lot of fun, but it would be cool to find out who you are as a person." He let out a low laugh. "Please don't tell Dave or Adam I just said that!"

"I won't," I said. I stood up and readjusted my shirt. Then I walked over to Dave's stereo and flipped through a collection of CDs. "This one is cool," I said, holding up a cover by The Black Crowes.

"Beth, what are you doing?" Ben asked, still sitting on the sofa.

"I just want to change the mood around here a bit with some music. Is that okay?"

"Of course it's okay."

"Fine." I kept moving through the albums, wishing that this night were over already. My lips felt sore and uncomfortable, as if I'd been sucking on limes. Where the hell was Lucy?

"Dave and your friend must be having a good time. They've been in his room for over an hour."

"Yeah. Well. What do you think of the Foo Fighters?" I held up a CD in front of my face, avoiding all eye contact.

"Put on whatever you want. I'm going to go outside for a smoke."

"Have a good time," I said. I kept looking through the albums, finally settling on something old—Substance by New Order. I put in the CD to the song Perfect Kiss, and turned up the volume. Then I grabbed my jacket, and headed outside to join Ben. At least he was someone to hang out with, to talk to. At least he was here.

"Hey," I said, sitting next to Ben on the back steps. He turned to look at me, then blew smoke in the other direction.

"So our little DJ has decided to take a break, eh?"

"Yeah. I got bored."

"Thanks a hell of a lot," Ben said, pushing his heavy bangs out of his eyes.

"No. I didn't mean bored with you. I meant, bored with looking at the CDs."

"Which you were doing because you were bored with me."

"No. I don't know." I stared out at the trees in Ben's backyard. A few leaves had started to fall already, an omen of what was to come.

"Why did you agree to come over tonight, anyway?" Ben asked. "If the tent night was a one-time thing, fine, but why come here in the first place?" He blew out more smoke.

"I guess to fill my time," I said, watching as the smoke quickly disappeared in the hot night air.

"Once again, thanks a hell of a lot." Ben tossed his cigarette onto the patio and stood up. He looked at me for a moment, then slid open the door and went inside.

"That's not what I mean! Jesus!" I stood up as well and headed after him. The difference between the humid outside air and the overly cool air conditioning inside was startling. I grabbed a nearby blanket and wrapped it around my shoulders. I could sense that my hair had gone all crazy with static. Very attractive. Ben was lying sprawled across the sofa, with no room made for me.

"Ben?" I said loudly above the music, pushing his feet off of the sofa.

"What?"

"All that I meant was that I wanted to do something to fill my time this summer until school starts. I just want to get the year started and be done with high school already. I want to move on, be in university, you know?"

"I guess so." He shoved himself over on the sofa. A good sign. "What's so great about university?"

"It's not here," I said, gesturing around the room. "It's got to be better than here."

"Well, I'm not holding out any great expectations about it," he said. "My sister flunked out her first semester at McGill. I don't even know if I'm applying this fall for next year or not. I might take a year off, travel in South America or something." He nudged my arm. "What are you trying to run away from anyway?"

I looked at his face, his eyes. They were dark brown and reminded me of Lucy's eyes. Not the colour (hers were blue), but the intensity of them. I couldn't look at his eyes for long because being caught in their stare was like being caught in a lie. You didn't feel like you could get out of it, so you eventually just gave in. Ben seemed fairly honest, but what the hell did I know.

"What makes you think I'm trying to run away?" I asked. He stared at me. "Okay, maybe it *is* kind of running away. But it's for a good thing. I'm so sick of high school. I want to have a new experience."

"You have to leave town to have a new experience? Why not go to university here?"

"I don't have to go away, I want to. My stepfather's an idiot. And besides, I want to go to a place where no one has some preconceived image of who I am. Everyone here knows me."

"I don't know you," he said. "Until a few days ago, you were just Adam's cute cousin."

I noticed myself flush at the word cute. No one had called me that before. "Well the people who do know me expect certain things." Peter's face suddenly entered my mind and I felt nauseous. "They expect that I'll act a certain way. And I do. I act exactly how people think I will. I've become a routine. I'm predictable. I'm sick of it."

"Why do you have to move to get away from that image? I mean, I'm just getting to know you and I have no idea who you really are or what to expect from you," Ben said.

"Well I expected certain things from you," I said, picking at a thread on the side of my jeans. *Ben's somewhere is your backyard right now, almost ready to propose.*

"And what did you expect?" Ben leaned back into the sofa.

"I kind of expected what happened. That if we ever met we might end up fooling around." I looked at him. "I mean, come on, Adam *did* say you were interested in me."

"So, I'm that predictable?"

"Of course you are. So am I. That's my point." I reached over and touched his arm. Suddenly the CD ended, and there was silence in the room. I noticed myself feeling completely alert. Alert, lonely, and depressed. What was the point of any of this? I was sitting next to a near-stranger, going on and on about the philosophy of my life, making it up as I went. With every word that came out of my mouth, I could feel myself moving further and further away. I was already on a bus headed to university, and I hadn't even lifted my ass off of the sofa.

Ben stared in front of him. "Beth, I saw your arm," he said quietly. His words bounced off the ceiling and fell across the top of my head like water balloons, leaving me feeling drenched.

"What do you mean?" I asked, crossing my arms in a feeble attempt to hide what was visible.

"I saw it the other night, in the tent." He paused. "I saw the scars."

"They're nothing," I answered. "They're just stupid."

"I used to put out cigarettes on myself last year," he said, not looking at me. "On my arms and legs. I did it after my girlfriend broke up with me, probably for a few weeks. I never told her about it but I think I wanted her to somehow find out, to see what shit she'd put me through. Make her feel guilty, you know? When I think about it now, it seems so stupid. It kind of helped me at the time, though."

"That's too bad," I said. "But I'm not like that."

"If you say so." He stopped. "I just wanted to tell you so you'd feel like you could talk to me about stuff, you know? Now you have something on me, so you don't have to worry about me telling anyone about what I saw."

"Um, thanks, but I'm really okay."

"Good to know," Ben said. He stood up and headed to the kitchen. I looked down at my lap, my throat tight and aching. I felt an odd mix of shame and relief flood my veins. *He saw and he wasn't repulsed.* Then another thought entered my mind, a thought that refused to leave me alone. *How could it be that the only people who really noticed I needed help were young and stupid like me?*

I heard the fridge door open and then the sound of beer bottles banging together. Ben reappeared in the den, holding two bottles in front of him. He walked back to the sofa and handed me a beer, already opened.

"Friends?" he asked, settling down next to me. I looked at his eyes, then hit his bottle with mine.

"Friends are good," I said, taking a swallow.

"And don't worry about us not working out," he said, shoving his hair off his forehead. "I'm not exactly great boyfriend material." He grinned. "If you asked Adam, he'd tell you I've got what they call a roving eye."

"Thanks for the warning," I said.

$$\infty\heartsuit$$

In the weeks that followed, Ben seemed content to share a casual friendship with me, our mutual self-injuries never mentioned again. Over time I began to trust that he wouldn't tell anyone about my scars, to believe that life would remain as it was, at status quo. Having come to the realization that time spent by myself meant being tempted by self-destructiveness, I tried to be out of the house whenever possible. I accepted every shift that was offered to me at the ice cream store job I had gotten for the summer and snatched up every request from neighbours to baby-sit. Time off from work usually meant hanging out with Ben and his friends. Lucy often tagged along with me, having developed a sudden interest in Dave. I found that my strategy of keeping as busy as possible seemed to be working. Both my mood and my feelings toward Adam had gotten lighter, which meant less for me to carry around. By the end of August, I had not cut myself in almost two months and felt confident about starting my final year of high school and of seeing Adam again.

The end of the summer was capped off by a toga party at Dave's house. It was my first experience partying in a sheet, and I didn't want to screw up. Lucy and I arrived at the party early, in shorts and T-shirts. We were ushered upstairs to get ready with the other girls in Dave's bedroom. A girl I vaguely recognized from school offered to help me put together my toga.

"So, you're Adam's cousin, eh?" she asked, helping to pin the sheet across my shoulder. "When is he coming back?"

"Next weekend, I think," I said, stiffening at the mention of Adam.

"You know Adam?" Asked a girl who was getting dressed next to me. "He's so hot!"

The first girl ignored this interruption and continued speaking. "Can you let him know that Dianne has been asking about him?" She smiled, shoving a pin deeper in the cloth.

"Okay, sure," I said.

"You don't think he's going out with anyone, do you?" she asked, uncertainty filling her voice. "I mean, I know he was going out with that Sandy from track in May but I thought they'd broken up in June, so…"

"They definitely broke up," chimed in the other girl.

"I haven't heard from him in weeks," I said. "Your guess is as good as mine." I searched my mind for a way to change the topic. I was so tired of everyone noticing the Greek God that was Adam. Why couldn't people get over him already? The fact that throngs of silly girls seemed to swoon in his presence made my own recent crush all the more predictable and humiliating. Couldn't I even be original in who I liked? And was this the way that my final year of high school would be, with girls who'd never bothered to speak to me before suddenly falling over themselves to be my best friend in order to get that much closer to Adam? I noticed the familiar leaden feeling begin to fill up the bottom of my stomach, weighing me down. *Was this how it was always going to feel?* I was so tired of not being able to depend on feeling stable for more than a few weeks at a time.

"Thanks for your help," I said, moving away from the girl's hands.

"But I didn't even finish pinning you," she said.

"It's fine, it's great." I looked in the mirror, and watched as the left side of my toga started to droop, revealing my not-so-significant chest. "It'll do."

I went down the main stairs and headed into the kitchen. It was already filled with about twenty people dressed in sheets. As I stared at the girls, I noticed that I didn't recognize most of them. Any of them could be interchangeable, replaceable. *Just like me.*

"Hey, sexy Greek lady," Ben said from behind, grabbing my waist. "Where did you get your keen fashion-sense?"

"Where's the beer?" I asked, moving away from him. I needed to get drunk as quickly as possible.

"Did someone say beer?" Dave asked, pushing a large plastic cup toward me. He was wearing a weird looking crown on top of his head, covered in leaves. "Before you partake, however, I must insist that you get marked."

"Marked?"

"Give me your wrist," he said, grabbing my left arm. I quickly pulled away, before he could see my scars.

"That's the one I use to tell time," I explained lamely. "Use my right one."

"Whatever, give it here," Dave said, pulling my right wrist in front of him. Carefully, he took a marker and drew a thick black line across the skin. "Each time you have another one, you get marked. The person with the most marks without puking is the Greek God of the night!"

"Or Goddess, right?" I asked loudly, taking a long chug of my beer.

"Yeah, yeah," said Dave, moving onto someone else's arm. "Just remember that it's permanent marker!"

As quickly as possible, I emptied my glass, and got my wrist marked again. And again. Sometimes I talked to Lucy, sometimes I flirted inanely with boys, but mostly I focused on getting drunk. Around midnight, I accidentally bumped into someone on my way back from the bathroom. "Esh-cuse me," I said.

"Beth! There you are!" It was Adam, his shorts and tanned legs standing out in a sea of white togas. As I stared at him, it hit me that my crush was over. He was just my beautiful, smart cousin that everyone adored once again—no more and no less. With this realization came knowledge that was darker, more desperate. Suddenly I knew that my feelings toward Adam hadn't been such a negative in my life. If anything, they had helped to distract me from my depression, and had reassured me that I was *normal*—after all, what girl hadn't been upset by an unrequited crush? Now that those feelings had faded, there was nothing to disguise the harsh fact that I was seriously messed up. Maybe what I needed to do was to stop fighting this upstream battle already and to give in to my fate of being mentally unbalanced.

"When'd you come back?" I asked, my drink sloshing onto his sandals.

"We came back a few hours ago," he said, smiling. "I heard that Dave's parents were out of town, so I assumed there was a party going on, and I was right." He touched my arms. "It's really great to see you! I missed you!"

"Yeah, me too." I attempted to smile back, but my cheek muscles didn't seem entirely in my control. "Did you hear that I've become friends with Ben?"

"I did. I think that's great. No love connection, I take it?"

I shrugged. "You know me. Destined to be alone." I shrugged again. "Whatever. I need to get another drink. I think I could win!" I pushed my wrist under his face. "Check out the marks!"

"You've had eight beers so far," he said, touching each black line. "Isn't it time to slow down?"

"Not until I've got a match," I said, shoving my other arm at him. "See! Now my wrists can be twins again!" I stared down at my ink-covered skin. "Oh no! My right one now has double the number of my left! That can't be good!"

"What's going on, Beth? Have you been cutting yourself again?" Adam frowned at me. Suddenly I hated that look, that concerned, I-really-care-about-you-and-will-always-be-there-for-you   look. Adam and his look could both go to hell.

"I need some fresh air," I said, heading toward the sliding back door. I stepped out onto the deck, and looked up into the August sky. The dark was blue-black, just like the first night I hung out with Ben, eons ago. I heard the door open behind me, and felt Adam take a few steps outside.

"What are you doing?" he asked.

"It's amazing out here," I said, twirling around. My foot caught onto my sheet and I tripped across the deck. "This thing's got to go," I said, tearing at the cloth. I pushed the toga off of my shoulder, and shimmied out of it. "Here, catch!" I said, throwing the sheet at Adam. Then I went back to twirling, this time only wearing my underpants. *This is what truly crazy must feel like.* I jumped down the steps off the porch and began to twirl on the wet grass.

"Beth!" Adam hissed from the deck. "Get back here! The neighbours will call the cops!"

"It's okay! I feel great!" I said, still twirling. "Don't worry about me!" I twirled so fast that the earth started to spin. I tripped again, and fell onto the ground. "Shit!"

Adam headed over to me, and tried to cover me with my sheet. He rubbed my back through the cloth, slowly painting circles onto my shoulder blades.

"What's going on with you?" He asked softly. "Really, I mean."

"I don't know," I said. "I guess I'm just," I paused.

"You're just what?" *I'm just scared.*

"I'm just…sick," I whimpered, and turned my head to the side to throw up. My stomach emptied beer after beer onto the grass. Tears and vomit poured out of me. Through the whole process, Adam held my hair back. For a few hours, I felt safe again.

∽⃝℃

Adam called me repeatedly the next day but I avoided his phone calls. It wasn't that I didn't want to see him exactly. It was that all of my energy was focused upon lying in bed not moving, in an attempt to prevent my pounding head from exploding. Heather kept answering the phone downstairs and then walking all the way up to my bedroom to try to coax me to get up.

"Adam said to tell you that he's worried about you," she said from my doorway late afternoon, following the fourth call. "Why would he be worried?"

Slowly I turned my head towards my little sister. Heather stood leaning against the door, her skinny legs making up most of her body. Her body had yet to develop any curves and reminded me of a gazelle. She began biting her lip in concern, a too-adult look crossing her face.

"I'm fine, Heath. Just feeling sick." I slowly reached over to a nearby table and picked up a glass of water. "I'll be better tomorrow."

"He said he needs to talk to you now or else he's gonna talk to Mom. Why would he want to talk to her?" Again the middle of her bottom lip slipped into her mouth to be chewed.

I forced myself to sit up, willing myself not to throw up. The bed seemed to spin, just a little, and I braced myself against the mattress.

"Maybe he wants to tell her about the cottage," I said inanely.

"I doubt it," Heather said. "Come on, what should I tell him?"

"Can you maybe ask him to come over a bit later? Like around nine tonight?" I asked. "Tell him I'll talk to him then."

"Okay!" Heather's face lit up with a clear direction to follow and she skipped out of my room. I groaned and sank back into the mattress.

By eight o'clock the room no longer seemed to be tilting and I slowly got out of bed and took a shower. If Adam was getting worried enough to consider talking to my mother then I needed to head him off at the pass. The last thing I could deal with was to have Peter fed anymore information about my screwed-up self. I just needed to get through the next year and then I'd be free. I grabbed a piece of paper from under my pillow and then headed down the stairs as the doorbell rang.

"It's for me," I called out and slowly went to answer it. Adam stood on the front step, a clear container of pebbles in his hands.

"I picked these up on the beach for Heather," he said. "I know she likes collecting rocks."

"I'll give them to her later," I said, grabbing the container from him and putting it down on a shelf. "Let's go for a walk to the park, okay?" I slipped on a pair of flip-flops and then headed out of the house, shutting the door behind me.

"So," Adam said, as we walked down my driveway. "Do you want to really tell me what's happening with you or do I need to have some adults involved?"

I held up my hand. "Can we get to some neutral territory first?" I asked. "Let's just go to the park, okay?"

Adam nodded and fell into step beside me. Our walk to the park was in silence, the quiet broken by the sound of my flip-flops hitting the sidewalk. I walked with my arms crossed in front of my chest, still fearful that in my hangover parts of me might break apart. When we reached the park, I sat down on a bench. After Adam had joined me, I reached into my pocket, and pulled out the piece of paper.

"Read this," I said. "Read it out loud." I handed him the paper. "It's a poem I wrote this summer when you were gone. It's about me and what's been going on lately. It kind of sums up how I've been feeling, I guess." I shoved my hands between my knees and rocked from left to right.

Adam unfolded the page and began to read out loud:

"The sky is blue like a baby's eye,
the breeze is slowly tumbling by,
young robins in nests are learning to fly,
yet all I see is grey.
The lilacs have begun to bloom,
spring weddings for each bride and groom,
yet when I'm locked inside my room,
all I feel is grey.
The grasshopper has begun to play
a song that the wind will carry away,

no voice can touch, no words can say,
for all I hear is grey.
The sky is crimson like a lover's cheek,
for a moment even the birds can speak,
in such brightness my world has become so bleak,
for all I want is grey.
The sun will set, why I don't know,
the stars will come out to whisper hello
to the ancient moon of so long ago,
it's too dark and how I shiver so,
in my world, which has turned grey."

Adam finished the poem, then looked at me. "It's…ah, it's nice," he said.

"Nice?"

"Well, it's kind of dark, actually. It's…I'm not used to poems, Beth."

"It's supposed to be dark! It's about me feeling upset all of the time!" I stood up and walked over to the pond. "It's about how everything has affected me." I picked up a rock and threw it in the water. "How can you not get that?"

"I get that you're angry at me, and that I haven't done anything," he said.

"I'm well aware of that."

"What the hell is that supposed to mean?"

"It means that…I don't know what it means." I sank down into the grass, suddenly exhausted at even attempting to explain what was happening to me. *This is futile.*

"Beth…" Adam walked over to me and sat down. "This is all getting so complicated. I'm really worried about you. Why don't we maybe talk to your mom about this? We could go together."

"You can't do that!" I said, my voice high and tight.

"But why not?"

"She'll tell Peter." I started pulling up pieces of grass and shredding them.

"So what if she does? At least then maybe you'll get the right kind of help."

"Peter can never know about this," I said, shaking my head vigorously. "It would be so much worse if you said anything to my mom."

"Well, then who?"

"Just…nobody," I said. *Just Jacob.* I pulled up more grass. "I've done a lot of thinking today and I have a plan." I tried to force conviction into my voice. "I'm just going to focus on getting through this year, getting good marks. Then I can get away from everything and start over." I turned to look at Adam. "I think university is really going to help."

"But that's a year away, Beth. And if you keep hurting yourself, I can't just hang around acting like everything's fine."

"What if I promise not to cut myself?" I asked. "I mean, I haven't done anything for a few months. What if I promise never to do it again? Can you then keep all this a secret?" I tossed a handful of grass into the air, letting it land on my lap.

Adam sighed. "You're asking a lot from me, you know," he said. "I don't know if I can handle you on my own."

"I'm not asking you to *handle me*! I'm asking you to try and trust that I want to get my life together so I can get out of here and start over! Can't you trust that?"

Adam pulled up a few pieces of grass and gently placed them on my pile. "I guess I can." He shook his head. "We learned about depression in health class last year, remember? Maybe that's what's happening to you."

"I'm not *depressed*, okay? I've just had some trouble with my parents breaking up and then my mom marrying Peter. I hate living in my house. I'm just having a hard time…adjusting."

"I don't know, Beth." Adam looked at me, a hint of exasperation in his voice. "I hope I'm not making a mistake in trusting you."

"You aren't. I swear!"

"But no more drinking so much, okay? You and beer don't seem to mix well."

"Yeah, okay." I walked over to a picnic table and sat on top. Adam stood beside it, kicking at the ground.

"Can you at least try to not be so dramatic, though?" He asked. "I kind of want to focus on other things this year, without being so worried about you, you know?"

"I know," I said. I sighed. Suddenly I was so tired. I didn't want to try and cover up my craziness anymore. I just wanted to go home. Home to my mom and Jacob, to a place that no longer existed. I wanted to get tucked in at night by my parents and find comfort in having my door left open two inches.

"I'm not going to stop caring about you, Beth," Adam said, reaching over to give me a one-armed hug. "You know that."

"Yeah."

"We'll always be friends, even when we're old and thirty."

"I guess so."

"Thanks for showing me that poem, even if it is totally obscure," he said. "No one has ever let me read their poems before."

"You're welcome," I said. Suddenly images of all that we used to do together as kids and how simple things seemed then entered my mind. I thought for a moment. "You know how you just said that you'll always care about me?"

"Yeah?"

"Prove it."

"What?"

"I want you to prove it." I stood on top of the table. "If you really, honestly care about me, then you'll meet me tomorrow morning for a picnic."

"No problem."

"A sunrise picnic," I said, spreading my arms out wide. Standing up on the picnic table made me feel like king-of-the-castle.

"A what?"

"A sunrise picnic. You know, getting together to watch the sun rise. It would be fun, kind of like old times." I looked at Adam. "Don't you remember all those times we'd force ourselves to stay awake at sleep-overs until we could see the sun come up? It would be like that again!"

"It would be pretty damn early is what it would be!"

"It would mean a lot to me, Adam."

"Okay, okay. What do I have to do?"

"Just meet me on the hill behind your house by six o'clock. I'll bring the food and the blanket. It will be great!" I took a flying leap onto Adam's back, causing him to fall on the grass. For a moment I felt like a child again, life simple and predictable once more.

ℰↃ∁ℛ

After I got home, I decided to start planning my picnic ahead of time. You could never be too prepared for that kind of thing. Luckily my mother and Peter tended to sleep in on weekends, so I didn't have to worry about explaining my plan to them. As long as I tried to be as quiet as possible, everything would be fine. I started baking muffins at 1:00 a.m., careful not to rattle pans or drop any ingredients. As I stirred the batter and filled the pans, I noticed a calm pass through me. Toga parties were not what I needed to feel grounded. What I needed was unstructured time with Adam, just like when we were kids. By two o'clock, I was starting to fall asleep at the counter, so I headed up to my room, and set my clock for five. I could always sleep after the picnic. Too soon, I was awakened by the alarm and had one of those highly disturbing moments when you don't remember who you are or what the hell is going on. Then I remembered, and felt instantly energized. I got dressed quickly and headed back downstairs to cut the oranges and soft boil the eggs. I wasn't quite sure how we'd manage the eggs, but I knew they'd look amazing in the little blue and white egg cups I'd found shoved in the back of a cupboard. I vaguely remembered being told by my mother that she and Jacob had bought them on their honeymoon, eons ago. I tried to brew some coffee for the first time in my life and improvised a bit on the number of scoops. I decided that it was better to err on the side of generosity, as Adam was likely to be tired. I found a basket and filled it with a white cloth. Then I packed up the breakfast and grabbed a blanket to lay out on the grass.

By the time I left my house, the sky was already turning a grey colour. I took a shortcut, so that I could make it to the park on time. I couldn't wait to greet the morning with Adam and was confident that he'd be waiting for me when I reached the pond. After all, he only needed to show up. How hard was that? *He wasn't there.* I set the basket down on the top of a hill, and looked all around the park. The sky continued to lighten.

Feeling increasingly irritated, I made my way down the hill and jogged two blocks over to Adam's house. My sneakers were getting soggy from the damp grass. I headed over to his first-floor window. I tried to open it, but it was locked. Shit! How was Adam going to prove that he cared about me if he was still asleep? I wondered if I should risk waking everyone up by knocking on the window and then figured what the hell. It was Adam's fault if my aunt and uncle got upset about this. I first gently tapped on the window, but quickly proceeded to hitting it with my fist.

"Adam!" I hissed, hitting it some more. "Adam!" After about ten hits, the window opened.

"Huh?" Adam's blond curls were messed up and he was wearing boxers and an old T-shirt. *If only the girls at school could see him now, they'd lose their minds.*

"Get out here!"

"Is that you, Beth?" Adam pushed his head further out the window and yawned in my face. "Why are you here so early?"

"Think, my little friend, think!"

"It's only six o'clock, Beth."

"Just in time for a picnic, isn't it?"

"Oh shit, I forgot."

"That's not all you forgot." I stared at him a moment, then started to walk away. *So much for childhood memories.*

"Damn it, Beth!" Adam stepped back into his room and shut the window. A few moments later, I heard his footsteps behind me, stumbling down the sidewalk. I didn't turn my head until I reached the park. I laid out the blanket and started to put containers upon it. The dew seeped through the cloth.

"Okay, I'm here!" Adam sat down on the blanket. He was still wearing his boxers, but had pulled a sweatshirt over his T-shirt. It wasn't fair that he could look so good just after wakening and that no matter what I did, I always looked so ordinary. Adam stretched out his legs and moved his bare toes toward the early morning sun. I sat down next to him, and took off my shoes.

"You almost didn't make it," I said.

"But I did make it," he said, sitting closer to me.

"But you almost didn't," I paused. "Soon we'll be living different lives and won't be able to do things like this."

"No more picnics? How will I live?" Adam said.

"I'm serious," I elbowed him. "This is important." An image suddenly entered my mind of picnics that Jacob used to organize on our front lawn. The picnics started the spring after Heather was born and she was in that perfect stage of babyhood where she could sit up but not yet move from where you put her. Jacob would spread an old quilt out on the lawn and would carefully help my mother sit down before handing her the baby. While my mother sat nursing,

Jacob and I would head to the kitchen and grab whatever odds and ends we could find to make the perfect feast. Cold spaghetti, old bread toasted and spread thickly with garlic butter, broken pieces of gingerbread, whole tomatoes that we'd eat like apples, chunks of cheddar cheese, thin slices of pear. Anything, everything tasted wonderful when eaten on our front lawn as a family, lazily watching cars and people that sped by.

I looked at Adam. "Seriously," I said. "We're almost adults. Do you realize that?"

"Okay, okay, this is important. But remember, you promised no more drama."

"Okay," I said. I rested my head on his shoulder, just like I had since I was a little girl. *Twins*. In silence, we watched the sky change colour. Our quiet was broken only by a few birds that were waking up and Adam's occasional yawns. We forgot to eat.

CHAPTER SIXTEEN

*M*y thoughts are interrupted by a knock at my hospital room door. "Special delivery," says a young girl carrying a bouquet of helium balloons. "Where do you want me to put this?"

"Right here is good," I answer. She ties the balloons onto a chair next to me then quietly leaves. I reach over and grab the small card that's attached to the strings.

"Congratulations, Beth! We're all thinking of you! Love, the gang." I put the card down on my lap. The gang—my four female friends throughout high school, including Lucy. The same four friends who were with me the night before my first suicide attempt at nineteen. I messed with their lives, yet they're still here for me, if only on the periphery. *See, Adam? See, Mom? People can forgive.*

I stare at the garishly bright balloons and remember that night before the bottom fell out. It was the last Friday of Reading Week and my return to university was looming. University hadn't turned out to be all that I'd hoped. I'd begun the year convinced that it would be a fresh start for me, that the black, suffocating mood that had followed me since I was sixteen was going to be a part of my high school past. University was different—a place for new friends, new experiences, a place to finally be my own person, separate from Adam. It would be a chance to throw away my uncomfortable old identity and try on other ones, until I finally found one that felt like it fit.

And I tried, I really tried. All throughout the fall semester I pumped endless energy and hope into making university work. I went to every Frosh Week activity, forced myself to talk to every student on my dorm floor, and became friends with my quiet but pleasant roommate. I got up early for each morning class and feverishly took notes in even the most boring of courses. I ignored the darkening clouds that always seemed to follow me wherever I went. I was certain that with enough time and enough effort I could make this go away. I just hadn't tried hard enough before. I just needed to be fast enough, determined enough to beat this thing. September to December became a frenetic blur.

And it half-worked. My days became so filled with endless activities that I didn't have time to think about what I was feeling. I was so focused on *doing* that emotions took a back seat. Yes, I became ever so slightly out of kilter, but so what? No one seemed to notice if my voice was just a bit too sharp, my laugh just a bit too loud. Who but me could tell if the colours of my life were being scribbled outside of the lines? What I didn't realize was that depression is patient. Depression waits. By the start of the winter term, I began to slow down. I started to sleep through morning classes. I could feel my mood pull me in, underneath the covers. It was a familiar pull, almost comforting, like the firm tug of a parent's hand. It wasn't so bad and it required a lot less energy to maintain.

I went home for Reading Week determined to spend my days

hibernating and thus keep my mood at least at a functional level. Lucy had other ideas, however, and insisted I come out with her and my other high school friends for at least one night. I agreed, knowing that with enough alcohol I could drink my way into temporary giddiness. The knowledge that over-drinking inevitably led my mood to nose-dive even further during the next day's hangover wasn't enough to stop me from going out. As I stare at the balloons, I want to stop the next memory from flooding my mind, but it refuses to leave, like an unwanted house guest.

ℰᗞᏣᏉ

There were four of us in the backseat. Sandy was the skinniest one, a mess of elbows and knees that poked across our laps. Lucy was riding shotgun, but kept turning around in her seat to take a swig from my Peach Schnapps bottle. We didn't know where we were going, but that was irrelevant. Fortified on alcohol and bravado, we owned any destination. Lucy's boyfriend, Dave, made a sudden right into a driveway, spilling Schnapps and Sandy in the process.

"Shit!" Sandy giggled from the floor of the car. "Could you be any smoother?"

"He is in *some* ways," Lucy said from the front, rubbing her fist against her boyfriend's cheek. We all found this hilarious and laughed hysterically. More Schnapps spilled.

"We're here," said Dave, turning off the engine. He glanced at the backseat. "Can you guys at least *try* not to embarrass me tonight?" Without waiting for an answer, he opened his door and started walking towards the house, his long, basketball legs resembling that of a grasshopper.

For a few minutes we remained where we were, just us five. In the car we were a gang, a gaggle, a unit. We sat in silence a bit longer, until Sandy started shifting on the floor.

"If I don't get up, I'm gonna piss myself!"

As if released from a trance, our voices suddenly tumbled over each other as we attempted to disentangle ourselves and get out of the car.

"Shit, Beth, that's my boob!" Rachel said, as I pushed my way into the winter night.

"Sorry!" I answered, standing up and stretching. The air was cold and heavy with the memory of snow. I took a deep breath, then let it out. I *did* feel better, going out with my old friends. Maybe the problem was university and not me. I looked around and felt my confidence grow. *As long as we stick together, it will be fine.*

"Don't forget the beer!" I said to Lucy, as she rummaged in the trunk.

"Got it," she answered, balancing a box between her hands. "Shit, Beth, I'm going to miss you when you go back."

"Me too," I said.

"Lucy, can you hurry it up?" Her boyfriend called from the front door. Lucy glanced at him, then back at us. It was no contest. She waited until we were all out of the car, then loped to the house with the rest of us.

A guy answered the door. He looked a bit older than we were, maybe twenty-one or twenty-two. "Finally!" he said to Dave, clapping him across the back. "What the hell took you so long?"

"I had to wait until they got ready," he answered, jerking his thumb in our direction. A look of recognition passed between the two boys which annoyed me.

"Some people are in the kitchen, but the rest of us are hanging out downstairs," the guy said, walking into the house.

Lucy stepped into the hallway and headed to the kitchen with the beer. We all followed, Sandy clutching the empty Schnapps bottle. We stumbled into the kitchen, giggling loudly. Sitting around the table were six girls deep in conversation. They immediately stopped talking and turned their eyes in our direction. Under the glare of the overhead light, I felt myself start to sober up.

"Yes?" One girl said, looking at Lucy.

"Just putting this in the fridge," she said, stuffing the box next to some wine coolers. She grabbed several beers and handed them to the rest of us. "Let's check out what's happening downstairs."

"Bye," I said to the group at the table. They continued staring. I quickly swallowed about half of my beer, eager to wash away the kitchen from my otherwise perfect night.

❧❦

Downstairs there were about ten or twelve guys, all former students from a rival high school. Some were playing pool and the others were playing a drinking game, sitting on the floor in a haphazard circle.

"Can we join?" Lucy asked, finding Dave and falling into his lap.

"You can if you're good," he said back, touching her hair. She whispered something in his ear and he whispered back. I looked away, embarrassed. *I wonder what it's like to have that.*

I sat down cross-legged next to Lindsay, with Rachel and Sandy across from me. The game involved dice and a bottle of Canadian Club. If you rolled doubles, you took a drink. If your dice added up to ten or six, you took a drink. In-between turns, I took slugs from my beer. I liked the way that it was just the five of us girls, surrounded by guys. It felt much safer here than it did upstairs. I also liked the way the whiskey warmed my throat going down, like hot chocolate. A boy next to Lindsay kept putting his hand on her leg, but she carelessly swatted him away.

Eventually the bottle was empty and most of the guys drifted away from our cozy circle on the floor. Lucy remained on her boyfriend's lap, creating a circle of their own. *And then there were four.* I felt a familiar ping of desperation in my chest, just a little one. I wanted to make sure that the rest of us remained a pack, just for that night. I didn't want us to start to drift off into our own separate corners.

❧

What happened next was not planned and was barely discussed, but seemed completely natural in my alcohol-fueled haze. The four of us decided to try and make out with each of the boys, other than Lucy's boyfriend, and then compare notes at the end of the night. After all, we knew that boys always rated us on things that shouldn't matter. Now it was our turn.

And so the game started. With a strong sense of social justice, I began things by grabbing the most unattractive boy of the bunch, pushing him against a wall, and pressing my lips against his. He was caught by surprise, but began to respond within a few seconds and open his mouth.

"Who are you?" He asked, coming up for air.

"Does it really matter?" I answered, turning my face away and primly wiping my lips with my sleeve. "See ya!" I stumbled over to a nearby table and grabbed a half-empty beer. I finished it in one swallow. *One down, eleven to go.* Next, I headed towards a boy who was sitting cross-legged on the floor, sorting through album covers. I grabbed at his shirt and pushed him under the table.

"Come'ere," I slurred, pushing my mouth against his. After a few minutes I got up and stumbled around for another conquest.

After three more guys and another pilfered beer, the room started to tilt a bit. Despite my dizziness, I could feel a strange new power coursing through my veins. Secretly still a virgin, I'd made out with more boys that night than I had since starting university. In truth, my only romantic experiences had been with Ben. Normally I was shy around guys, my awkwardness when in their presence almost tangible. But that night? That night my friends and I *owned* the room and had become capable of rendering the males around us helpless.

I looked around for Lindsay. She was lying on a couch on top of a boy, her face against his.

"My turn," I said, pushing her off him and climbing aboard. Without so much as a hello, I began kissing the guy's bruised lips. It was the guy who had opened the door when we'd arrived. The only one in the room who seemed more like a man than a boy. He looked at me through startled eyes, but quickly obliged. His kiss felt softer, gentler than any of the others. We kept kissing and I didn't resist when his hand touched the back of my jeans. After a few more minutes, I decided to take a break from my kissing expedition to pursue things a bit more. "Come with me," I urged, pulling at his hands.

"Where are we going?" He asked, following.

"Just come on!" I opened a nearby door and pulled him into a dark bathroom. Once inside, I locked the door.

"What's your name? Did you come with Lucy?" He asked me.

"Doesn't matter," I answered. I stroked his cheek.

"Let's turn on a light and talk a minute," he said, trying to reach around me. Suddenly it was bright, too bright, and I was back to being an invisible girl. "That's better," he said, smiling down at me.

"No! I want the lights out!" The familiar desperation began to fill my throat.

"Let's at least talk, okay? It would be cool to get to know you a bit." His voice sounded far away in the blackness.

Back in darkness, my confidence returned. I reached my hands out to touch his face, his neck, his shoulders. Carefully I examined his arms with my fingertips.

"This is too weird," he said, reaching around me and turning back on a light. In the sudden brightness I felt awkward, de-robed.

"Just stay," I said, grabbing at his hands.

"Why don't you drag some other guy in here?" He asked, a hint of distance in his voice. He gently pushed me out of the way and unlocked the door.

"Fine!" I said, stumbling back into the main room. I walked over to the first guy I saw and grabbed him from behind. "Let's get to know each other!" I slurred, pushing his face towards me and trying to stick my tongue in his mouth.

"Beth? What the hell are you doing?" he said, pushing me roughly away.

I looked up, my vision double. I saw two Adams staring back at me. I blinked a few times, hoping to make the image alter. *Please, please, anything but Adam.* My vision cleared and I looked up at one Adam, still staring.

"What the hell was that?" He asked me again, grabbing me by the elbow and leading me into a corner. "Do you realize you just tried to make out with me?"

"I didn't mean to," I said.

"Then what were you doing?"

I stared at Adam, not knowing what to say. He looked so righteous, so certain of himself. I couldn't explain what I was doing in a way that made sense, that would make him not judge me. And so, sodden with alcohol, I did what would become almost habitual for me—I made a somewhat bad, somewhat embarrassing situation much, much worse.

"Come here, you," I said, pushing Adam against the wall and shoving my body against his. "You know you want this!" I attempted to kiss him, while rubbing my hands across his body. If he'd just respond, then he'd be just as culpable for this situation as I was. I needed him to take the fall for me, as he always had. *Just play along.* I tried to reach my hand under his shirt but he grabbed me by both wrists and pushed me to the floor.

"What the fuck do you think you're doing? Did you somehow forget that you're my cousin?"

I glanced up at his face and saw something worse than hurt or disappointment. I saw disgust. Suddenly sober, I stared down at my hands.

"That's your cousin? That's twisted, man!" I heard one of my previous conquests say. "Did you know that she's been making out with every guy in this place? How much does she charge for an hour?"

"Beth! What did you just do?" I heard Lucy nearby, rushing to where I sat. I kept looking down, anchored to the rug by the weight of my self-hate.

I don't remember what happened next. Self-preservation has allowed me to forget how I got from sitting on a stranger's rug with my "twin's" saliva drying around my mouth to shoving a bottle of pills down my throat the next night. In a way, not remembering the steps that led from A to B is irrelevant, as the suicide attempt seemed apt and inevitable.

∞)(ଓ

Following my suicide attempt and a night in the ER, I was transferred to the inpatient psychiatric unit, where I remained for a few weeks. During that time I ate grey food on grey trays, while trying to participate as little as possible in various therapy groups. I knew that becoming active in the group and expressing both regret and keen insight about my over-dose were the keys to being discharged, but I was too tired to bother. It wasn't that I wanted to stay in the psychiatric ward, it's that *where* I was had become irrelevant. I'd eventually fade away anyway, so what was the difference? Once my antidepressant medication began to kick in, however, things started to shift, and I began to notice just how tedious and dull it was being a psychiatric patient. The days were structured around meals, group, or talking to the nurses. The hours in-between were spent walking up and down the corridors, slumped on a chair in the common room, watching a TV that was bolted to the floor, or having visitors. In the first few days following my overdose, I had the bulk of my visitors, people in my life who seemed anxious to get a glimpse of me, to make sure I was still alive. Lindsay and Lucy came to visit twice, both times talking about the latest gossip among our high school friends, as if there was any gossip bigger or juicer than my suicide attempt. They spoke in loud, clear voices, their words bouncing of the walls of my room and falling heavily into my lap. I was glad that they wanted to visit, but felt incredibly relieved each time they left. Following their second visit, they each had to return to their respective university, Reading Week over.

Adam came several times throughout the two weeks, usually sitting quietly and holding my hand. The fact that he too was supposed to be resuming classes was irrelevant, not worth mentioning. It was understood that he would not leave to go restart his university life until it was also safe for me to do so. Adam's near-constant presence during visiting hours showed me in ways that words never could that he had chosen to forgive me for my obnoxious behaviour at the party. Why he gave me another chance, I'll never know. Whether it was the fact that our history together at that time still held more weight for him than a one night screw-up or whether the drama of my overdose reignited his desire to somehow protect me, I don't know. What I do know is that by my fourth day in hospital, we had become friends again. The friendship was predicated on a promise I made to him while sitting side by side in the empty common room. I promised to never, ever do something as stupid as taking pills again. I would always call him first if I was even considering killing myself, no matter if we were in a fight or if I had done something as stupid as kissing him (the kiss of course was never actually mentioned and never would be). As long as I kept to my promise, we were okay.

Adam had me sign a piece of paper with this promise, which he then carefully folded and placed in his pocket.

"There," he said solemnly. "You can't change your mind now."

While in hospital, visits from other family members were nonexistent. I held out hope that Jacob would rush to my side, but as far as I knew, that never happened. To me, it was as if our father-daughter relationship had hung by a thread and I had chosen to make the final cut with two handfuls of pills. My mother rode with me in the ambulance to the hospital following my overdose, but then did not return until she was asked to come for a family meeting to discuss my discharge. The meeting took place in a large room that I had never noticed before, just past the doors leading into Unit 1A. Around a narrow rectangular table sat the psychiatrist, a nurse I'd been assigned to, the social worker who ran group, and me. The meeting was set for ten o'clock, but it was fifteen minutes past and my mother was nowhere to be seen. I stared down at the table and attempted to avoid eye contact with the health professionals who surrounded me.

"I know she's coming," said the social worker suddenly. "She confirmed it with me yesterday." I lowered my head further.

Suddenly there was a commotion at the door and I turned to see my mother and Peter involved in a heated, whispered discussion.

"Sorry we're late," my mother said, rushing into the room.

"No problem. Have a seat, have a seat," the psychiatrist said.

My mother quickly sat down, while Peter walked around the room slowly, taking his time to sit.

"Now that everyone has arrived, why don't we begin?" The psychiatrist paused and opened a file in front of him. "We're here to discuss the imminent discharge of Beth and what discharge plans are set in place for her." He pushed the bridge of his glasses higher up on his nose. "Beth has been taking Prozac now for a little over two weeks and has begun to notice some improvement in her mood. Is that right?"

I opened my mouth to answer, but was beaten to the punch by the nurse. "That's right," she said. "Beth has spoken to me about feeling less hopeless and about sleeping better."

"Good, good," said the psychiatrist. He turned to look at the social worker. "Any concerns from group?"

"No," she answered, smiling encouragingly at me. "During the last few days Beth has been participating more and more in group, which is quite a change from when she first arrived." She looked around the room. "I would ideally like to see Beth transfer into my bi-weekly cognitive-behavioural group. I run this group on an out-patient basis for young people who were recently hospitalized. I think Beth would truly benefit from such a group, in conjunction with personal counselling, of course." She paused. "Does that sound good to you, Beth?"

"Um, sure," I said. "I mean, that does make sense, but what about my school?"

"Your mental health must come first," she answered. "I'm sure that your parents would agree with me on this."

"Actually, I don't agree," Peter said, his voice loud and strong. All eyes turned to look at him, including those of the psychiatrist.

"Please, tell us what you mean," said the social worker.

"I know Beth quite well and both her mother and I feel that what would be best for Beth is a return to her normal routine, as soon as possible. I've spoken to the university and there is still a chance for her to catch up on her missed classes." He looked at me as he spoke, his voice warm and his eyes cold. "Beth is normally quite a happy, well-adjusted girl. Whether this overdose was related to a romantic disappointment or to a poor grade in school or to an argument with a friend, I don't know. What I do know is that if we all drag this out and have her miss the semester at school, what was an impulsive, adolescent incident could turn into something much, much worse."

'Thank you for your thoughts, Mr....." the psychiatrist looked down at his notes.

"Mr. Curtis," Peter said, arms folded.

"Thank you for your comments, Mr. Curtis. What concerns us here today, however, is that Beth's overdose did not appear to be an impulsive, adolescent incident. In fact, it seems as if she's been struggling with a fairly significant major depression for quite some time." He cleared his throat and pushed up his glasses once more.

"Well, what about services for her on campus?" Peter asked. "The people I spoke with said that there are counselors on site that she can meet with, plus a psychiatrist at their health clinic." He looked around the table. "I want what's best for our daughter and I truly, truly believe that going back to university is what is best."

"And what do you think, Mrs. Curtis?" The psychiatrist cleared his throat again.

"I think...I think that my husband is right," my mother said, her voice soft and uncertain.

"And what about you, Beth? Is this what you want?"

I kept staring at the table, feeling an equal mix of rage and impotence. *A happy, well-adjusted girl? The same girl who has scars running up and down her arm? And wanting what's best for your daughter? The same daughter you've ignored or ridiculed since entering the family and basically destroying it? Are you serious?* Unable to channel my emotions into words that would make sense, that would express even an iota of the pain of the last few years, I simply nodded.

Within a week I was back at university, preparing for the mid-terms I had missed. Being plunged back into campus life had its advantages. Other than having to remember to take my medicine every morning and to make weekly visits to the on-campus counselling clinic, my life resumed as normal. Few people seemed to have noticed my absence and even fewer people seemed to care. Other than my roommate Ella, three random girls on my floor, and the resident advisor, no one stopped to ask why exactly I had been gone for three weeks. I felt disappointment mixed with relief at not having to use the lengthy explanation I had concocted about a bout of pneumonia. My long-distance friendship with Adam also continued as if nothing unusual had occurred. Throughout the rest of the semester, and the semesters that followed, I continued to write him lengthy letters on a weekly basis and he continued to send me brief emails regularly. While no longer twins, necessarily, our alliance remained. It would take more than a drunken kiss or an impulsive suicide attempt to topple what we had. Until that day a few years ago, when watching Adam get married and start a new life that wouldn't always include me was too much to handle, and I broke our contract.

ಬಿಡಿ

The next day a small plant is brought to my hospital room. There's a small card, tasteful and simple, congratulating me formally on the birth of Kate. The card is signed Adam and Janice, but his signature is in her writing. I toss the plant into the garbage can and roughly cover it with an empty juice box and some candy wrappers. A few minutes later I reach through the garbage to retrieve it, but it's too late. Most of the soil has fallen out of the pot and the most of the leaves are bent. *Ruined.*

CHAPTER SEVENTEEN

The next forty-eight hours in hospital are a blur of family visits, breastfeeding lessons, and self-loathing. Images from my past collide against one another in my mind, blurring my baby's face. I receive confirmation from NICU staff that Kate does indeed have an infection and that her IV must remain in place. I'm discharged from the hospital but ignore Jacob and Patrick's encouragement to go home for a night and have a good sleep, choosing instead to lie motionless and greasy-haired on a couch in the NICU's family room between feedings. On the third day I'm told by the neonatologist that Kate's bilirubin levels are high, that she has developed physiologic jaundice, and that she needs to be placed under fluorescent lights until the levels diminish. I'm reassured that jaundice is normal, to be expected, and that many babies—particularly those who are premature—develop the condition. When I look around the NICU and see babies so much smaller and more fragile than my own, babies who might not ever leave the hospital, I know that I'm lucky, that Kate is strong and fairly healthy, and that this experience will be a mere pit stop in our lives. But as I stare down at her lying so still and yellow on a blanket, wearing nothing more than a diaper and a visor to cover her eyes, with the IV still snaking over her arm, it is not luck that I subscribe to myself, but failure. As a mother I have failed in the most fundamental way possible—when giving this little being life, I gave up, I tried to protect myself more than her. Plain and simple, I failed.

On the fourth day I call Dr. Green. In hesitant whispers, I speak to her about my feelings of numbness, my intense guilt, my lack of love towards my daughter. Dr. Green asks standard questions about my mood, sleep patterns, appetite, and thoughts of self-harm. She then reassures me that bonding is often not instantaneous, particularly when a birth is premature or traumatic. I discuss the tears that are flowing faster than my breast milk, and am reminded by the psychologist about the baby blues, a temporary experience that occurs to many women. I promise to contact her immediately if my mood worsens further and we agree to meet again the following week. I hang up the phone, relieved. *This is normal. This is fine.*

On the sixth day, instead of the highly anticipated feelings of love, thoughts of suicide arrive, as strong and fierce as before. It is as if the last several months haven't happened, as if the confident, capable creature I've been learning how to become never existed. *Ha. Fooled you. We're back.*

Instead of thinking about my new daughter, images fill my mind of climbing onto the hospital's roof and jumping to the parking lot below or of breaking off a piece of a bathroom mirror and dragging its jagged edge down my inner arm (vertically, the *right* way) until I'm swimming in a pool of red hurt. The images calm me down in a way that nothing has since Kate's birth. It's that calmness that jump-starts me into action. I know how lethal such calm can be. Having first-hand experience of a parent dying before I ever had a chance to know him, I cannot leave that legacy to Kate. I contact Dr. Green, who agrees to meet with me for a same-day appointment. Fueled by anger at both the psychologist and myself, I ask Jacob to stay at the hospital with Kate and Patrick to drive me to my therapy session.

As Dr. Green opens the door to her office, my fury breaks through any social niceties. "You lied to me!" I yell at her. "You said that if I did everything right that this wouldn't happen!"

The psychologist motions me to enter the room, then shuts the door gently. "Beth, what I said was that it wasn't inevitable. We both knew that there was a risk, and unfortunately it was a strong risk, that you would become depressed postpartum."

"Then what was the point of all those sessions and all of the work I've done?" I shout, my voice ending in a sob. "What the hell was the point?" For some reason my fury seems to trigger letdown and two large wet circles begin to spread across my shirt. *How appropriate.*

"I know you're angry and frustrated right now, Beth, and you have every right to be. It definitely *isn't* fair that you experience recurrent depression, especially given all of the hard work you do. But let's use that anger to get energized to keep working."

"Please don't patronize me," I whisper through my hands. "Not now."

"I would never patronize you, Beth. I'm being serious. I'm on your side and am frustrated too. But I'm confident that you can once again fight this and get stabilized."

"How can you be so confident when I'm like this?"

"Because I know you," she says simply.

෫ාஐ

While I sit weeping beside her, I agree to let Dr. Green contact the psychiatrist. Patrick and I arrive at his office an hour later. I let Patrick do most of the talking and sit limply beside him. The anger has coursed through my veins like a cocaine fix, and I feel spent. Dr. Reiner asks me the standard questions, with a particular emphasis upon whether or not I am about to go run in front of oncoming traffic. The fact that I sought help seems to reassure him, and me, that I'm not in imminent danger to harm myself. While I wait in hope that Dr. Reimer can somehow wave a magic wand and all will be back to normal again, he advises that I am to immediately commence Effexor, this time at a higher dose.

"The good news is that we know you quickly responded to the medication during your last episode," he says.

"But what about breastfeeding?" I ask quietly. *Liquid gold. The one good thing I can give my daughter.*

"I would encourage you to discontinue breastfeeding immediately," he says. "Effexor is passed through the breast milk and could potentially cause side effects to your daughter."

"But…"

"I would like your permission to contact the neonatologist myself, so that we are all on-board."

I nod in defeat. "Do you have any idea when the baby is expected to be discharged?" He asks Patrick.

"They mentioned possibly next week, if the jaundice improves."

"I'm sure that the hospital would agree that a plan needs to first be in place to ensure that both Beth and her daughter have adequate support within the home and the community until her mood stabilizes."

"There's already a plan," Patrick says.

"There is?" I turn to look at him. *Since when?*

"We were going to suggest all of us meeting in the next few days to discuss how to make this work for you," he says, a hint of apology in his voice. "We weren't trying to cut you out of the plans. You've just had a lot on your plate to deal with." He takes my hand and squeezes it. "I thought you needed someone else to take over for a bit."

"And what is the plan?" Dr. Reimer interrupts.

"We've agreed that between a few of us, someone can stay in Beth's apartment for the next few weeks, until she's...back on her feet."

"Good, good," says the psychiatrist. I push my fingernails into my palms, the only experience that feels within my control. *This is for Kate. This is for Kate.*

ഔരഃ

One of Jacob's many purchases is a car seat, which he brings proudly up to the NICU on Kate's discharge day, one week later.

"We're all ready," he says, smiling at me. I look at the seat, wondering how Kate, who barely weighs six pounds, won't be dwarfed within it. Jacob begins to help pack things up for me as I finish final paperwork. Since my outburst, Jacob and I haven't spoken about us. Anything, everything, but us. As we get Kate ready to go, Jacob begins reviewing the "plan" with me. He reminds me that he will stay at my apartment, an apartment I have yet to see, for the next two weeks, with Patrick and Sarah relieving him for a few hours at a time. *The safety brigade.* After two weeks, the situation will be reassessed (meaning: I will be reassessed). If I need help for much longer, my mother is on standby to come and stay with me after Jacob returns to work in Toronto. Normally the possible involvement of my mother in this scenario would have triggered instant panic, but instead it takes all my energy to just follow what Jacob is saying. *This is too complicated.* What is emphasized to me is that I am not to worry about anything, that everything will be taken care of, and that my job is to take my medication, get adequate rest, and to start to feel better.

And so the plan begins. The first week passes in a surreal blur, with me feeling like a guest in my new, unfamiliar apartment. Jacob has arranged my furniture how he imagined I would like it, taking his cues from his knowledge of me as a young adolescent. It's not that anything is in the wrong place, exactly, but more that it isn't quite right. As a result, a mild feeling of disorientation follows me as I walk from room to room. Jacob stores an air mattress in the second bedroom, so that he can be with the baby at night. Kate is still jaundice-sleepy and needs to be awakened frequently for feedings. But instead of me stumbling around in the dark for a bottle, it's Jacob. I'm advised to shut my door, to get the sleep I need in order to be a mom. Each afternoon Jacob takes a nap. Rather than leave me with Kate for a few hours, however, Patrick or Sarah inevitably swoop in to take the baby for a long walk. I'm to put my feet up, take a bath, read a book. I know I should be grateful for so much support, but the reality of not having Kate settled against my skin after having her inside for so many months makes me feel even more off-kilter. *I am the mother, a noun. But I seem incapable of mothering, a verb.*

After about twelve days at home, and almost three weeks on the medication, I notice my mood begin to stabilize. My first indication of a mood shift comes when I start caring enough to rearrange my furniture. The waves of love have yet to come and wash me clean, but I do start to experience strong feelings of protectiveness towards my daughter. With those emotions to back me, I begin to insist that the others let me start to parent my daughter.

"I'd like to take Kate for a walk today," I tell Patrick one afternoon when he arrives at my door. "Why don't you come by tomorrow?" I experience a jolt of satisfaction as I gently shut the door in his face.

Towards the end of the second week, I sit Jacob down and inform him that I will be the one in charge of night-time feedings from now on. If all goes well, he can probably move back to Toronto within a few more days. After all, if I don't start doing things on my own now, when will I learn? Jacob listens as I talk and nods to himself. I can tell that it will be tough for him. He's become so used to being Mr. Mom (and, if truth be told, is someone who *has* bonded with Kate), that he seems to find it difficult to let go of any responsibilities. With a heavy sigh, he agrees to give me a chance to mother my daughter.

That night I wake up at the sound of the first cry. I tiptoe into the kitchen to warm a bottle, testing the formula on my wrist before heading into the nursery. The feeding goes well and soon Kate is slumped against my shoulder, her body heavy and boneless. Instead of putting her back in the crib, I rock her back and forth in the chair, letting myself become lulled by the movement. The room is silent, except for her quick intakes of breath. Thirty minutes pass, then an hour. I keep rocking. Never before have I known what it was like to become a part of stillness. I have never sat silently for such a long period of time. I have not thought myself capable of such stillness, such quiet. And yet, as minute follows minute, I find myself enveloped in my daughter's rhythmic breathing, ensconced by the rise and falls of her chest. It's then that I notice the feelings starting to come, a slight flutter at first, like a ripple from a gentle breeze, but definitely there. I silently weep with relief. I don't speak, I don't apologize with lullabies. I just rock with my daughter, quiet.

After about ninety minutes I decide to place her back in her crib. As I stand up I feel a moment of confusion, experiencing the forgotten cramps in my feet, my back. After placing her gently down, I settle back into the rocking chair and I look intently at the baby before me. My daughter. I reach out hesitantly into the crib and touch Kate's cheek. My fingers burn as they graze against her cool skin.

"Kate," I whisper. "It's me." I gently take her small hand in mine and rub it. It has more weight than I would have expected, more substance. This is not my two-dimensional daughter, the pink-cheeked fairy-child of my dreams. I hear footsteps behind me and feel the presence of Jacob. I turn my eyes to him.

"Thank you," I say. He gives me a look of recognition, then settles in a chair beside me. Together we watch. I gaze at my daughter, then at my stepfather, and know that we're going to be okay. We're not perfect, we may never be perfect, but we are mending.

CHAPTER EIGHTEEN

After my mood has stabilized and Jacob has moved back to his home, Kate loses her sleepiness and instead develops a tendency towards crying. Not just-pick-me-up-please-because-I'm-hungry crying, but almost endless bouts of shrieking that no amount of rocking can assuage. *What am I now doing wrong?* After a visit to Dr. Nelson, I'm told that this is colic and that other than try and comfort my baby, I'm going to need to be patient and wait it out. During my second week on my own, the outside buzzer rings. I scoop up a screaming Kate and head to my door. "Who is it?" I ask, pushing the call button.

"It's Mom," my mother says tentatively. "May I come in?" She pauses. "Peter's not with me."

"Okay," I say, surprised. I press the buzzer. My mother has never dropped by to my apartment without notice. My mother has never dropped by, period.

Within moments she is at my door, grocery bags in hand. "I hope you don't mind my coming here unexpectedly," she says loudly, trying to talk above the screaming. "I thought it might help you if I cooked a few meals and tucked them into your freezer." She pauses, looking from me to Kate. "May I take her?" She asks.

I nod. "Please wash your hands first," I say.

My mother puts down her groceries and heads to the sink, her movements purposeful. Then she reaches out her arms to relieve me of my flailing daughter.

"She won't stop crying," I say, collapsing in a chair. "It's been like this every afternoon and night for the last few weeks. I talked to the doctor but he just said that it's colic and that there isn't much I can do."

"You were colicky," my mother says, looking around the apartment until she spots the bedroom door. She gestures with her chin and I nod. She walks into Kate's room and I follow. I watch as she carefully wraps Kate in a receiving blanket until she resembles an overstuffed burrito. "She reminds me of you."

"She does?" I ask. "Really?"

"Absolutely," she says, patting a calmer Kate on the back as she walks around the apartment. "Swaddling used to work for you too…at least some of the time. I'll teach you the different tricks you can try." My mother looks at me, a maternal smile. "Don't worry, honey, colic doesn't usually last past three months."

"So I have weeks and weeks more of this?" I ask, sitting back down in the chair. I lean back my head and close my eyes. *I'm so tired.* "Mom?" I ask slowly. "Does Kate really resemble me?"

"She's your mirror image," she says. "Why?"

"I just…I worry that if she's too much like me she might also get depressed."

"I don't see why that would happen," my mother says quickly.

"Well, depression often runs in families, Mom."

"No one else in your family has ever been depressed, Beth. Heart disease and Diabetes, yes. Depression, no." Her words seem clipped. *End of conversation.*

"But," my voice reaches down into all that is unspoken and pulls out a question, the question. "What about Dad?"

"Jacob?"

"No. My dad-dad, my biological dad."

"I've never said that Henry was depressed." My mother's rocking slows, and Kate begins to wail anew.

"I know you never *said* it. No one ever said it, but I still know." I pause. *Please don't make me say it.* "Mom, why else would he have killed himself when I was two?"

"Henry was in a car accident. You know that." My mother's mouth forms a thin, hard line, her lips almost disappearing.

"Mom," I say, tears running down my face. "Please. I know. He was driving fifty kilometres over the speed limit during a rainstorm with no seat belt!" I press my hands against my chest in a feeble attempt to slow my racing heart. "I also know that he was seeing a psychiatrist before he died—Grandma told me when I was little. I know, Mom, okay? I know!"

My mother looks at me. She seems broken, unfixable. Her mouth opens and closes like a baby bird's. *Please answer me, please.* "I think Kate needs to be changed. That's another trick that often helps," she says, raising her voice above the screaming.

"Mom," I say.

"You were a perfect baby, Beth. And a perfect little girl, too!" She walks away from me, back into the bedroom.

"Mom," I call after her, "I don't blame you for Dad!" I hear the door of Kate's bedroom carefully being closed, shutting out my daughter's screaming and my words. *I just blame you for everything else. Even for the things that weren't your fault.*

CHAPTER NINETEEN

*T*hroughout the hell that is colic, Patrick bravely continues to come to my apartment a few afternoons a week in order to take Kate for a walk. Despite having screamed for hours, Kate instantly stops crying when Patrick bundles her up to go outside. *How does he do that?* Thin fingers of jealousy tickle around my ribs, but I nudge them away. Patrick typically does not come back from his walks until he's managed to put Kate to sleep, something I have yet to be able to do. While Kate dozes peacefully in her stroller, I usually offer Patrick a snack as payment for his magical powers.

"You know that I'm dating now," Patrick says suddenly one afternoon, as he dunks a piece of pita bread in hummus and then shoves it into his mouth. "I have been for three months." He continues carelessly munching, but his eyes stare at me intently.

"Oh," I say, trying to busy myself at the kitchen counter. "Do I know her?"

"No," he says. "She's in the Ph.D. program but she's new. Went to Western before. Her name is Greta." He rolls her name around in his mouth like a peppermint, all sweetness and bite. *Did he ever say my name like that?*

"Well, that's great," I say, wiping down the spotless counter. "You should be dating."

"Yeah. Well. I just wanted you to know," he says.

"I'm glad," I say.

"Nothing has to change," Patrick tells me, mopping up the last bit of hummus from the bowl. "I mean, Greta knows that I like spending time with Kate and with you and she's cool with that."

"That's good," I say, sitting down next to Patrick. "I kind of like things how they are. I don't want them to change."

But in the weeks that follow I find that they do change. How could that not? It's not that we all don't try and make things work, Greta included. It's more that no matter how much we try and stretch either twosome to form a threesome, it doesn't work. The fit is just too tight.

A week after Patrick tells me about their relationship, he persuades Greta to drop by my apartment with him one afternoon, so that we can meet. I instantly like Greta—she's a cheerful, affable woman with thick brown curls who puts out her hand to shake mine the moment we meet. Her touch is firm, welcoming. Greta chatters to me about people I know in the Sociology department and seems interested in my work as a research assistant. I find myself asking her questions in turn and truly listening as she answers. In different circumstances we would likely become friends, a twosome unto ourselves. But just as I feel myself relaxing around Greta and wondering what the three of us should do next, I overhear Patrick crooning to a wailing Kate. We both stop talking for a moment to watch Patrick as he walks back and forth my apartment, soothing my daughter. As I glance at Greta looking at Patrick, I know that this can never work. All three females in the room want Patrick for themselves and there just isn't enough of him to go around.

In the weeks that follow their visit to my apartment, Patrick continues to come over as often as before. But now something's different. Our conversations are no longer easy, fluid. There's a space between us and it's filled with someone else. I know that if I leave things alone Patrick will continue coming to see us as often as before—he's made an unspoken commitment to me and Kate and he intends to honour it, even at the cost of his new relationship. So I decide to change things myself, to step back a bit and let Patrick and Greta's relationship heat up, even if it means that our friendship will cool. I owe so much to Patrick, this is the one way I have of giving back. It's not that I do anything dramatic. I just make sure to be out with Kate a few afternoons a week when Patrick is most likely to come by. The fact that Patrick never comments on my absences tells me that he approves of the change. He continues to drop in every few weeks but it's clearly to see Kate, not her mother.

₨⇓ℓ

As Patrick fades into the background, I become consumed by Kate. With colic a thing of the past, I am able to bask in the wonder that is my daughter. What did I do to deserve having this amazing little person in my life? Kate is an easygoing baby who doesn't seem to mind spending time strapped in a snuggly as I meet with Dr. Shields on campus or search the stacks in the university library for research articles. Kate seems curious about the world and everything in it. Whether it's a barking dog or a falling leaf, everything fascinates her. When the weather is good, I take Kate to the campus park and spend hours lying with her on a blanket, people watching. I like how her very existence seems to make others smile. Kate seems to change by the day, first rolling over, then sitting up, then starting to crawl. Each new milestone is a major triumph, one in which I feel a sense of misplaced pride. *Look at what I made! Just look!*

Once I feel I've gotten my sea-legs as a parent and it's clear who is in charge, I become comfortable with the idea of sharing Kate again with Jacob. About one weekend a month Kate and I take the train to Toronto, where we're met at the station by an ecstatic Jacob, empty stroller in hand. On sunny days we take long walks around the city, Jacob pointing out places I never got the chance to know as a teenager. *How different would things have been if I'd at least partly grown up here?*

Once back to his house, we make dinner together, while Heather watches Kate in the other room. Heather seems pleased by her new role of aunt, but is more hesitant in her old role of sister. It's not that I blame her. How can she be expected to play Happily Families with me after years of neglect? I just wish I knew how to break through the wall that seems permanently erected between us.

Before I head back to the train station on Sundays, Jacob always encourages me to call my mother, knowing that I probably won't contact her otherwise. "She deserves to be a part of this too," he reminds me. In the face of such generosity, I find myself unable to refuse. I keep the conversations short, usually less than ten minutes, but make sure to fill her in on the changes of her granddaughter. My mother always seems grateful to hear from me and I find myself wondering why I have never been able to give her this before. Whenever she mentions Peter, however, I suddenly remember.

❧☙

During one of the Toronto weekends I corner Heather in the living room and ask her if she'll come out for a walk with me and Kate.

"I've got a lot of studying to do for mid-terms," she says. "I don't want to fall behind."

"Just a short walk," I say. "Please."

Heather puts down her books and follows me and the stroller outside. It's a cool autumn day, the kind with a taste of frost in the air. I've bundled Kate up well and covered her stroller with a wind guard.

"This has to be really brief," says Heather, stuffing her bare hands in her pockets. "I'm freezing!"

"Just a few blocks," I say. "I never get the chance to be alone with you." We walk in silence for a few minutes, listening to Kate blow spit-bubbles from the stroller.

"Is there something you wanted to talk to me about?" Heather finally asks as we cross the street, doing a loop of the neighbourhood.

"How did you know?"

"Call me Ms. Perceptive," she says, quickening her pace. The wind picks up and blows her hair across her face. She takes her right hand out of a pocket to move her hair out of the way, then shoves it back into her coat.

I take a deep breath. "I guess I've been wondering how you feel about me coming around so much to see your dad," I say.

"He's your dad too," Heather says, the words sounding automatic.

"He is but he's not, Heath," I say. "And I know you haven't had to share him in more than ten years."

"That's not exactly true," she says.

"What do you mean? I've barely even contacted him, only cards and the rare e-mail at Christmas."

"I've had to share him with a ghost," she says, holding her hair back with one hand against the wind. "That's been even worse."

"But do you feel okay about me being here so much? Does it seem weird to you?"

"I don't really have a choice, do I?" She asks, shrugging. "This is Dad's dream come true, having you back in his life, and now Kate."

She shrugs again. "And I'm happy about Kate too. I really like having the munchkin in my life."

"And me?" I ask, feeling foolish but asking anyway. "Do you like having me in your life more often too?"

"I can't answer that yet, Beth." She stops walking and looks at me. "To be honest, I don't know if I can ever forgive you."

I feel my stomach start to spasm, a vibrating knot. "I don't know if I ever apologized to you," I say. "I swear that I never thought you'd find me like that. I know a twelve year old shouldn't have to deal with such crap. It's just that I was sure you'd be in Toronto for at least another day!"

Heather shakes her head and resumes walking. "I forgive you for *that*, Beth. You were just messed up. I know you didn't try to kill yourself to screw me up."

"Then what?" Too soon, I see Jacob's house up ahead, the walk nearly over.

"I don't know if I can forgive you for abandoning me, for not making more than a token effort to stay in my life, just because it was difficult for you." She touches my arm, almost an apologetic touch, then moves toward the front steps.

"I've forgiven Jacob for basically the same thing!" I call after her.

"But you should have known better," she says, and walks back into the house.

I stand in front of the house with the stroller, letting the wind numb me. I reach inside my coat and fiddle with my necklace, its small stone cold in my fingers. I think about the first time I met Heather, twenty years ago. My grandmother drove me to the hospital, where I was met by Jacob outside of the Labour and Delivery wing. When Jacob saw me walking down the hall in my best dress, his entire face lit up. Once I reached him, he thrust a small package towards me.

"I bought this for you," he said, watching as I opened the crinkly paper. Inside was a small jewelry box, which held a silver necklace. On the chain was a small green-blue jewel. I looked up at his face, questioningly. "That's your birth stone and Heather's too. An opal, for October."

"Thanks, Jacob!" I said, rubbing my thumb against the smooth, green surface. "But why did you get me a present?"

"Because it's an important day for you. Today you became a big sister for the very first time!"

I nodded. That made sense. "Can you put it on me?"

"I'll try," he answered. I lifted up my ponytail and waited patiently as he fumbled behind my neck with the delicate clasp. "There."

"How does it look?" I asked, turning to face him.

"Beautiful," he said. "Let's go show your Mom and little sister."

I took Jacob's hand and began walking towards the room. "Do you think the baby will be jealous?" I asked.

"No, bear-cub," he answered. "I got a necklace for her, too, for becoming a little sister today. I'm just going to save it until she's bigger."

I nodded. We walked quietly into a sunny room, where my mother lay against two pillows on a bed. Around her were vases of flowers and a few helium balloons. I ignored everything but what lay in her arms. A baby, sound asleep, wrapped tightly in a yellow and white blanket.

"Hi sweetie," my mother said, smiling. "Come and meet Heather."

Very, very carefully I climbed onto the bed and sat cross-legged near the sleeping bundle. I peered closely at my sister's face, my necklace tangling above her cheek. *Two necklaces for two sisters. Both born in October, together forever.*

CHAPTER TWENTY

It has been twenty-three months with no episodes, almost the longest interval ever. Kate has settled happily into the daycare on campus, where I was able to secure a subsidized spot. Now in the throes of toddler-hood, Kate's natural personality begins to shine through, and I breathe a sigh of relief. My daughter is all sun and boldness, laughter and light. Her joy at life has a fierceness to it, a don't-mess-with-me vibe. I'm certain that if depression ever dares to come knocking for her, she won't hesitate to slam the door in its face.

On a daily basis I practice the self-care that I've promised Dr. Green to follow. Proper sleep habits, good diet, medication, regular exercise, social activities, monthly visits to see my stepfather and sister. Heather hasn't moved much closer to me in our relationship with each other, but she hasn't moved farther away, either. To me, that's something. It *has* to be. On a weekly basis I make a point to e-mail her, filling her in on the latest accomplishments of Kate and asking her more about her life. I want the gap between ages twelve and twenty to be filled with more than anger or regret. I email my mother too, reminding myself that as a grandmother, she still has a clean slate.

Just as I'm beginning to believe that motherhood has served as a miracle cure for depression, it hits—the blackness. Its onset seems sudden, although if I'm honest I have to admit that it's been creeping through the curtains for weeks—just a sliver of a shadow, not enough to eclipse the sun. Then one afternoon, it all comes crashing down. I'm sitting on the carpet in my living room, still in my pajamas (what's the point in changing?), watching Kate as she explores her new world. I know that we should probably go for a walk to the park or at least around the block, but I can barely summon the energy to stay awake until Kate's bedtime, let alone follow my daughter around outside as she pushes her stroller. I keep checking the clock above the sofa. I wonder if Kate will notice if I put her to bed an hour early tonight. It's two o'clock and the day has stopped moving forward. I've called in sick to work every day for the last week and know that I'm running out of excuses for not going in. Neither of us have had lunch, but that's not such a big deal. I'm not hungry and Kate seems content to let me keep filling her snack bowl with Cheerios. No one can accuse me of being a negligent mother.

In slow motion I watch as Kate toddles over to the overfull bookcase, tries to climb on it, and pulls the whole thing down in one large boom. Kate stumbles backwards and hits her head against the carpet, somehow avoiding getting pinned against the floor. Startled by a surge of adrenaline, I leap into action, scooping up my wailing daughter and rocking her in my arms. Although I know the bookcase missed her, I can't stop from checking her body parts over and over for injury. I clutch her to my chest, as my heart threatens to leap out of my skin.

"It's okay, it's okay, baby, everything's going to be okay," I croon, all too aware that the opposite is true. My heart can't stop racing, my limbs trembling. How could I not have noticed my own fall, my plunge back down? Once Kate is calmer, I put on a Dora DVD and plop her in front of the TV. I've already proved myself to be neglectful, why not go all out? As Kate happily watches the images on the screen, I pick up my phone and call him. Patrick. Despite all of my previous bravado, I know the truth. I need him. He's the one who stops the depression, not me. I can't do this without him.

૬૭૦૮૨

This time it takes about seven weeks for my mood to stabilize. Not long in the grand scheme of things, but when each minute feels like a death sentence, it's an eternity. This time my biggest symptom is complete exhaustion, physically and emotionally. Everything seems slowed—my movements, my thoughts, my feelings. Even trying to contemplate performing routine tasks seems beyond me. I try and think about lifting a piece of toast to my mouth, chewing it repeatedly, and then swallowing, as the bread turns cold on a plate, uneaten. It's like I'm lying under a blanket of snow as a storm howls around me, trying to remain conscious as I succumb to the elements. *First my fingers, then my toes.* My Effexor dosage is increased twice and I'm started on a second medication as well. I start to see Dr. Green again on a weekly basis and take a brief leave of absence from my research assistantship. Hospitalization is considered, should my mood not begin to improve.

Through it all, Patrick is there for Kate, being the solid presence while I collapse. I beg Patrick to not call Jacob, letting him contact my mother for help instead. The balance I've achieved in my relationship with my stepfather is too fragile to be tested. If he comes to my rescue again and takes over, everything will become off-kilter. So instead I let Patrick take control. And why not? His presence is the only thing that feels right. It's agreed that my mother will stay for a few weeks, watching Kate while I force myself to eat and go for daily walks. Just going around the block twice feels like a marathon, but I do it, spurred by a tepid, barely perceptible desire to prove to myself and to my mother that I am not a failure. In her role as grandmother, my mother begins to shine. As I lie on the sofa watching her build block towers with Kate, long-forgotten memories of my mother getting down on her hands and knees to play with me and Heather come flooding back. I try to hoard these memories, hoping they'll melt some of the ice that's been built up inside of me.

After three weeks, I'm deemed reliable enough to be left alone with Kate in the mornings and to take her and pick her up from daycare. After my mother leaves, Patrick arrives on deck around suppertime each day, bringing takeout and journal articles with him. Most nights he sleeps on my sofa, keeping vigil. Whether or not this upsets Greta (and how could it not?), I'm not told and I find myself still too lethargic to care.

One night during the seventh week I wake up to the sound of someone weeping. I open my eyes and see Patrick sitting by my feet, crying. When he sees me looking at him he wipes his eyes with his sleeve.

"I dreamed that you killed yourself and that I found you," he says, his voice sounding like someone choking. "There was blood everywhere and I couldn't find where the wound was. The blood kept on coming and coming!" He stops, his shoulders heaving.

"Come here," I whisper, my arms open. "Come here and see that I'm okay."

Patrick stumbles over and clutches at me as if I might disappear. Without saying a word, without carefully analyzing the merits of the situation, my usually cautious, careful ex-boyfriend begins to kiss me hard on the mouth and pull off my T-shirt.

Patrick spends the night in my bed, then the next and the next. Greta is forgotten in a tangle of bed sheets. Without truly discussing it, we cross over from friendship into couple-hood. In a belated attempt to spare Greta's feelings as much as possible, and in order to ensure that my mood is truly stable, we wait a few months before telling others. When we let people know about our relationship, they claim that it was inevitable, that we have always been meant to be together, and that Kate is the glue that binds us all. Most people in our lives approve of the relationship—Jacob, Sarah, my mother, Patrick's friends and colleagues. Everyone is effusive in their pleasure about us finally getting our act together and being with each other. Everyone, that is, but Dr. Green. It's not that she vocalizes disapproval exactly. No. But the fact that my frequently smiling psychologist remains expressionless as I chatter on about Patrick says it all. I figure that she's concerned about the newness of my stabilized mood and decide that it isn't her approval that I seek. I have Patrick.

ॐ

My relationship with Patrick develops its own structure. During our first month together I talk to Patrick about the importance of not confusing Kate. We agree that now that I am feeling better once more, he can spend as much time as he likes with us, but that sleepovers are not an option. By unspoken agreement, Patrick comes over for supper a few times a week and stays to put Kate to bed and relax on the sofa with me. When I've got work to do, Patrick sits at the kitchen table next to me, helping to score surveys from my pile instead of working on his own research. Every other weekend we spent an evening out together, using cash-starved undergraduates as babysitters. Most Sundays the three of us do something for the afternoon, whether it's going to the zoo, walking in the campus park, or buying dipped cones at a nearby Dairy Queen. It's not much different than how my life was before and that suits me fine. During the first several months of our relationship we both feel like we're holding our breath. It's good now, but what happens when depression next strikes? How will we cope with me plunged into despair and an increasingly inquisitive Kate asking what's wrong with Mommy? We agree to be careful, very, very careful, and to take baby steps. Any sudden changes could make me tumble down like Humpty Dumpty and have my cheerful veneer shatter.

After ten months together, we go to Sarah's wedding. We rent a room in a small hotel for two nights, Kate and me in one bed, Patrick in the other. It's the first time we've gone away for a weekend. Staying in a hotel room with Patrick and witnessing each other brush our teeth or get dressed for the wedding feels different somehow, and I like it. The wedding is small and takes place in Peterborough, where Sarah and Alex moved two years ago, after she finished her teaching degree. I haven't seen Sarah often since her move, but we've stayed close through e-mail and telephone calls, so close that she makes Kate her flower girl. Given my continued distrust in the long-term stability of my mood, I turn down the option of bridesmaid, and instead watch the ceremony from the sidelines with Patrick.

I've never thought of myself as a die-hard romantic; I've never had the luxury of thinking in such forever-and-ever terms. Despite this, or maybe because of it, I find tears spilling down my face as I watch my dear friend take the leap and pledge a future together with the man she loves.

"Do you think that might be us some day?" I ask, squeezing Patrick's hand. He doesn't say anything in return, but instead squeezes back. I take that to be a good sign.

CHAPTER TWENTY-ONE

It's a sticky summer day outside, but I find myself shivering within the artificially cool confines of the train. I cross my arms against my chest, wishing I'd brought a sweater for the ride. The trip to Ottawa is several hours long, with a transfer in Toronto. I pick up the magazine that's in my lap and attempt to read it for the third time. I should have brought a sweater and a book, but I was so focused on getting Kate ready for her weekend with Jacob that I left my packing until the last minute.

Kate. It's the first time I've left my daughter for more than one night and my mind isn't ready to relinquish her. Did I give Jacob her health card? Does she have allergy medicine in case her hay fever comes back? Did she take her stuffed hippo? Did I remind Jacob not to let her stay up past nine no matter what, because she'll be cranky the next day?

I put the magazine on the empty seat beside me and try and close my eyes, hoping to lose a few of the hours that remain until I see my daughter again. The trip to meet Patrick's parents in Ottawa was his idea, not mine. Patrick had been away for the last month, conducting research while staying at his childhood home. After mentioning on the telephone that I missed him one time too many, he suggested that if I could find someone to take care of Kate, then maybe I could come visit him for a weekend. As I try and sleep on the train, the thought that Patrick never actually believed I'd ever accept his offer needles at me, but I push it away. The main point is that *he* suggested this visit, not me.

I'm jolted awake by the train's arrival into the Ottawa station. I wipe the drool that's been collecting at the side of my mouth and slowly get out of my seat, trying to ignore the cramp that's developed in the back of my neck. I had intended to make a quick stop in the train bathroom before seeing Patrick, but now there's no time. I grab my bag and eventually make my way outside. A wall of humidity greets me and I stumble backwards, before getting my bearings. I look around at the milling crowd, hoping to see Patrick's familiar face. There's something about being in the midst of a throng of strangers that makes my anxiety rev up. I walk over to a nearby bench and sit down. *Where is he?*

Ten minutes pass, then twenty. As time passes, I notice my anxiety being replaced by something less frightening and more manageable—frustration. *Where the hell is he?* I start to consider my options, when I notice a tall man in his early sixties approaching my bench and giving a small wave.

"Are you Beth?" He asks, standing in front of me. I nod, but remain sitting. "Of course it's you! You look exactly like your picture! I'm Frank, Patrick's father." His voice is low and friendly. He extends a large hand towards me.

"Oh! Hello!" I say, reaching out my hand to shake his. "Nice to meet you. But where is Patrick?" I ask, looking from side to side.

"Couldn't make it, I'm afraid. He's tied up at the university library. He said to tell you that he'll be waiting for us by the time we get home." Frank smiles at me, an affable smile, and I attempt one in return. I continue smiling for a moment, then two, not certain of what to do next. "So!" Frank lifts up the bag that's lying on the ground next to me. "If you're ready?"

"Of course!" I answer, then stand up. We walk in silence to the parking lot, Frank's loping steps requiring me to jog a bit in order to catch up. When I first met him, I didn't see any resemblance to Patrick, but as I watch his walk I instantly do—long, confident steps, his movement forward purposeful and resolute.

Frank stops in front of a new looking Toyota Corolla and puts my bag neatly in the trunk. Then he walks over to the car's passenger side and opens my door. Again, just like Patrick.

"So, Beth," Frank says, once we are safely buckled within the car and the air conditioner has been set on high. "Patrick tells me that you are also doing your degree in Sociology?" He patiently allows other cars to go in front of him before trying to drive out of the parking lot.

"Well, not exactly," I say, almost apologetically. This is not a man I feel comfortable with proving wrong. "I mean, I *was* in the same program as Patrick when I was doing my Master's degree, but I'm not registered in school right now."

"No?" Frank asks, his eyes on the road. "Are you working?"

"Yes I am. In the Sociology department actually, as a research assistant."

"What's the research about?"

"It's in the area of social inequality," I say, as if by rote. "The politics and the institutional structures involved that help keep it in place. Mainly in Canada, but also on a global scale."

"That sounds…commendable. What would you like to do in

terms of a career?" Frank heads toward the highway, always keeping five kilometres above the posted speed limit.

"I haven't really considered a career, to be honest. I've been too focused on working and taking care of my daughter." At the mention of Kate, I feel my chest muscles tighten. Being so far away from her makes me feel unsettled.

"A daughter, that's right! Patrick has spoken often about your little girl—how bright she is! How old is she now?"

"She's almost four," I say. I look out the window, hoping to find another topic to talk about in the scenery that flashes by.

"Four. That's a good age, isn't it?" Frank says. He chuckles to himself, an inside joke.

"Yes," I say, still looking out the window.

The rest of the ride passes in silence. With each minute, I become increasingly aware of my full bladder. By the time we pull into the driveway of a large suburban home, I am almost doubled over in pain. I start to open my car door, but Frank rushes to my side and insists on doing it for me. I grab my purse and head for their front door, not waiting for Frank as he opens the trunk and retrieves my bag. I do a little jig in place as Frank walks towards me and then rings the doorbell.

"I forgot the house key," he says, in way of explanation.

A few moments pass and then the door opens. Instead of being greeted by Patrick's familiar face, I find myself looking up to meet the gaze of a tall middle-aged woman.

"Hello, Beth," she says. "Welcome to our home! I'm Angela." She also extends her hand and I shake it quickly.

"Nice to meet you. Do you mind if I…use your bathroom?" I ask.

"Why, of course," she says. "It's just down the hall, to your left."

I rush inside, jostling her arm in the process. I open a closet door, then the pantry door, before finally finding what I'm looking for. Afterwards, I look at myself in the mirror. I'm a mess. Hair stuck to my forehead, my cheeks greasy with sweat, eyeliner beginning to run below my eyes. I grab a few tissues to try and remedy the situation, but it's pointless. I need a cool shower and a long nap before I will look human again.

"Everything alright in there?" Patrick's mother calls from outside the door.

"Everything's great," I answer, swiping on more time at my forehead. "I'll be right out." I flush the toilet a second time, then open the door. Angela and Frank stand waiting in the hall, their faces open and expectant.

"We're so glad that you're here," Angela says, gesturing for me to follow her down the hall. "We've been wanting to meet you for so long, but I guess the timing just hasn't been right for you." I nod, feeling bewildered. *Timing?* Patrick never suggested I meet his parents before last week and when he finally did, I jumped at the chance.

"Um, where is Patrick?" I ask, sitting down on a couch in their living room. I try to keep the bottom of my legs slightly above the white fabric, for fear that my sweaty self will somehow stain the pristine furniture.

"Would you care for a beverage?" Angela asks. "Perhaps a lemonade?"

"That would be great, thank you," I say, offering her a smile. She nods, then heads back down the hallway, where I hear Angela's alto voice mingling with Frank's lower baritone. *Where the hell is Patrick?* I look around the room, trying to make myself relax. The walls are painted a pale yellow and most of the furniture is white. There are subtle yellow touches placed here and there around the room— yellow throw pillows, a yellow jug holding fresh flowers, a painting of a golden meadow. In the corner sits a piano, a few sheets of music lining its top. I like this room—tastefully decorated, yet warm and inviting.

Angela and Frank return with three glasses of lemonade between them and my heart starts to flutter.

"Is Patrick not here?" I ask, accepting my glass.

"I'm afraid not. He called just before you arrived, to say that he's running a little late and for us to get you settled in without him." Angela sits down in a loveseat across from me and smiles encouragingly.

"Okay, great," I say, gulping my lemonade. I set my glass down on a coaster, then clasp my hands on my knees. "This is a beautiful room," I say.

"Why, thank you," Angela answers, still smiling. "Interior decorating actually is a little hobby of mine, something to pass the time when Frank's practice keeps him long hours."

"My practice?" Frank says, chuckling at his wife. "Don't let her fool you, Beth. Her work as a pharmacist keeps her just as busy as any court has ever kept me!" I watch as they exchange an affectionate glance at one another, wishing I was anywhere but here.

"Um, do you like being a pharmacist?" I ask, lifting my glass and taking another gulp.

"Why yes I do, Beth. I quite enjoy it, actually. I work in a small pharmacy, which allows me to get to know my customers. Some have been coming to me for twenty years. It's a nice community feeling, which can be unusual in such a large city."

"That sounds nice," I say, nodding inanely. "And, ah, Frank, do you enjoy working as a lawyer?"

"That I do, that I do. Especially in the last few years, since I've cut down the hours I actually spend working!" Again a chuckle.

I clasp my hands tighter and try to ignore how warm and slippery they've become. *At least all the handshakes are over.*

"So, Beth, do you and Patrick have any plans for while you're here?" Angela asks, her warm voice reaching across the room.

"Not that I know of. I mean, I've kind of left it up to him.

Hopefully he'll show me around the neighbourhood, so I can see what it was like for him growing up here."

Both Angela and Frank smile again at me and I smile back, the sides of my mouth starting to ache.

"Um, do you mind if I go to my room and freshen up a bit?" I ask. "It was kind of a long trip."

"Why of course! How silly of me not to think of this before! You must be exhausted from that train ride!" Angela says cheerily, abruptly standing. Frank stands too and I follow. Again we smile. "Your room for the weekend is just up the stairs, second door to the right." She says. "Frank has already put your bag on the bed for you."

"That's great," I say, heading towards the staircase. I quickly walk up the stairs and find my room. The door is slightly ajar and I can see my bag sitting in the middle of a brightly coloured patchwork quilt. To the left of the bed is a small table upon which sits a china lamp, a few magazines, and an empty water glass. Fresh flowers decorate an antique chest of drawers. Below a large window is a cushioned seat, with a throw blanket folded neatly on top. I walk in and shut the door, then dive backwards onto the bed. Despite being so warmly welcomed into this inviting house, I've never felt so out-of-place before. *If I click my heels three times will it take me back to Kate?*

ℰᴏᴄℛ

Despite feeling unbalanced, or perhaps because of it, I fall into a deep sleep and don't awaken until there is a knock on my door one hour later.

"Are you decent?" a voice asks me from outside the door. Patrick's voice.

"Come in," I say, struggling to sit up. Patrick opens the door, poking his head in first.

"Sorry I'm so late," he says. "You know how it is with research." He comes and sits down next to me. "Nice room, huh? Hard to believe that this once belonged to my bratty little sister and was filled with unicorn posters!"

"Unicorns, really?" I say, stretching. I suddenly remember Patrick's recent absence and the feelings of frustration return. "You know, you could have at least *tried* to get here on time," I say, crossing my arms. "It was pretty awkward for me to be here without you."

"Awkward? Really? You didn't feel comfortable with my parents?"

"No, no, it's not that. They're wonderful people. I really like them both. It's just that I can feel a bit shy at first and it would have helped if you were here."

"Look, I said I was sorry. I would have much rather have been here with you than stuck at the library trying to dig up more journal articles." He touches my arm. "Friends?"

"Yes, fine," I say, but fingers of irritability remain, tickling at my ribs.

"My mother wanted me to tell you that supper will be in about forty-five minutes. Just enough time for us to get frisky," he teases, pushing me back against the bedspread.

"Just enough time for me to have a shower, you mean," I answer, pushing him away and standing up.

It turns out that forty-five minutes is barely enough time to shower, dry my hair, and change before heading down to the dining room hand in hand with Patrick. Angela and Frank are waiting for us at either end of a long oak table. The light is turned low, with several candles elegantly lit. Cloth napkins are neatly folded at each place setting, with silverware lying in their assigned places. As soon as I see the table, I let go of Patrick's hand.

"Why don't you sit here, Beth," Angela says, gesturing to her right side. "And Patrick, you can sit in your normal place."

I sit down and make sure to hold myself erect. I look down at the tablecloth and take a deep breath. *Everything will be fine. These are just Patrick's parents. Calm down.*

"So, Beth," Angela says, sitting down herself and passing me a steaming platter of sliced roast beef, "I hear that you had a little nap. I hope the bed was comfortable."

"It was great, thank you," I say, reaching for the dish and then handing it to Frank without taking any meat. "I'm a vegetarian," I explain.

"You are?" Angela asks, looking momentarily flustered. "Patrick, why didn't you tell me?"

"Sorry," he says, shrugging. "It's been a fairly new thing, so I guess I forgot." He reaches for the bowl of new potatoes in front of him and spoons several onto his plate.

"Please excuse me for a moment," Angela says, heading for the kitchen. I look down at the tablecloth once more.

"A vegetarian, eh? Now there's an interesting choice," says Frank, using a giant fork to spear a few pieces of meat. "I don't think I'd last a week myself eating nothing but tofu! How long have you been not eating meat?"

"It's been a few years now, actually," I say, darting a look at Patrick. "Since my daughter was born, I think." *How could you forget to tell them?*

Angela comes back into the dining room, her arms laden with food. "I brought you some havarti cheese and some hummus. The hummus should go well with the dinner rolls, I think. We also have pistachios somewhere in the cupboard that I could find if you'd like."

"Oh no! But thank you! This is more than enough," I say. I reach across the table for the bread basket, grab a roll, then dip it into the hummus. "Delicious," I say, still chewing.

"Sit, Angela. Eat," says Frank and she obeys. For the remainder of the meal I make sure to take seconds of everything else that is offered to me. Midway through dinner, Frank pours himself another glass of white wine from a decanter and gestures to me.

"Another glass would be great, thank you," I say. Just as I'm about to take a sip, something in Angela's stare stops me. "Is…is something wrong?" I ask, putting down my glass.

"Would you mind seeing me in the kitchen?" She asks, getting up once more from the table.

"Sure," I answer, pushing back my chair. I follow her tall figure into the darkened room and stand in front of her.

"I don't want to make you feel uncomfortable, Beth, but I feel I need to say something." Angela speaks in a low whisper and I find myself having to lean closer in order to hear.

"No, no, it's fine," I say.

"Well, the thing is that Patrick mentioned to me that you are taking antidepressant medication." She holds up her hand. "Why you are taking it or exactly what you are taking is, of course, none of my business. My concern tonight is that you might not be aware of the potential side effects that can occur when mixing certain antidepressants with alcohol. The pharmacist in me felt that I couldn't let this go without saying something." She looks straight at me, her gaze so steady and earnest that I feel I must give the best response possible to match her concern.

"Um, I did know that I shouldn't drink excessive amounts of alcohol. I guess I thought two glasses of wine were okay. Thanks for letting me know."

"Two glasses *might* be okay, but I wasn't sure what your plans after supper with Patrick were, whether perhaps you were going to a place where more alcohol would be served." She takes a step backwards and then smiles. "Enough about this. What are your thoughts on apple crisp for dessert?" She asks and leads me back to the dining room.

ഇരു

The rest of the evening goes smoothly. Patrick and I do not head to a bar to fritter the night away, but instead take a long walk around his old neighbourhood. It's a warm evening, but pleasant, the humidity pushed down by the darkness. I walk holding Patrick's hand, his grip seeming so strong and sure in my own. I stare down at our feet as we move forward, the pace of our legs synchronized effortlessly. We head to Patrick's former elementary school and sit next to each other on the swings.

"Your parents are really nice," I say, moving back and forth.

"I think they like you," Patrick says, pumping his legs so high that they seem to reach the tops of the trees. "And that isn't always the case."

"What do you mean?"

"Nothing, really. It's just that they were kind of tough on my undergrad girlfriend and also the ones I had in high school." He swings higher. "They also met Greta and gave me mixed reviews about her." He chuckles to himself. *Just like his father.*

"Is that why you didn't have me meet them sooner?" I ask, slowing my swing down. I let my sandals push through the ground, the sand cool against my toes. "I thought maybe it was because you were ashamed of me." I can only speak these words now because it's dark, because it's night, and because my face can get lost within the shadows. In the unflinching light of day, such honesty would have to remain hidden, unsaid.

Patrick jumps off his swing, lands in a crouch, then comes to sit down on the ground next to my feet. "I could never be ashamed of you," he says, his voice gruff and un-Patrick-like. "Please never think that."

I get off my swing and settle down next to him. A light breeze moves through my hair. "I guess I wondered why you didn't want me to bring Kate," I say. "I know how much you care about her."

"I didn't want you to bring Kate because I wanted you to have a weekend where you could just focus on being you, not also have the pressure of being a mom. Just for a weekend," Patrick says. He reaches for my hand and takes it in his lap. He turns it over and gently rubs my palm with his index finger, tracing invisible life lines across my skin. "Just know that I love you, Beth," he says. "I need you to always know that." We sit still for a few minutes and then Patrick stands up, pulling me up with him. Still holding my hand, he leads me behind the jungle gym, then lowers me onto the grass. He begins kissing my cheek, then my neck, then my stomach. Together we move closer, all warm skin and soft touch. In the moments that follow, Angela is forgotten, Frank is forgotten, and Kate is placed temporarily into a safe corner in my brain. All that exists is now, by the jungle gym with Patrick, our movements synchronized perfectly once more.

❧

I sleep soundly that night, which is unusual for me in a strange bed. When I awaken it's still dark. I pull back my curtain and see that the summer sun has just begun its early rise. Careful not to make any noise, I head downstairs, hoping to grab a quick cup of coffee before anyone else gets up. I stumble into the kitchen and am startled out of my sleepiness by Angela's presence by the counter.

"Good morning, Beth," she says, turning away from the kettle to look at me. Her face is naked of makeup and she is wearing a thin blue robe that ties at the waist. For a moment, I feel disoriented by the dramatic change in her appearance. "I was just making a cup of herbal tea. Would you care to join me?"

"Oh! Thanks a lot, but do you have any coffee?"

"I'm afraid we don't have any beverage that's caffeinated, Beth. Ever since Frank's heart trouble we've tried to keep stimulants out of the household." She smiles at me and holds up a tea bag. "I know it won't wake you up, but this raspberry leaf is truly delicious."

"Okay," I say, trying to still the panic that's arisen at the thought of getting through a morning in this house without a jolt of caffeine running through my veins. "Thanks." I sit down at the kitchen table and begin smoothing the plastic tablecloth with my hands. *Why do I feel so nervous?*

Within moments Angela places a steaming mug in front of me. "Enjoy," she says, moving back to the counter.

"Oh, are you not sitting, too?" I ask, taking a sip of the tea and burning my tongue.

"No, I'm going to get a head start on the cinnamon buns. Patrick's favourite, you know," she says, her back to me.

"Would you like some help?" I ask, gingerly attempting another sip of the boiling liquid.

"No, no, Beth, please just relax. This kitchen isn't big enough for two."

A few minutes pass in silence and I notice my muscles start to loosen. It's peaceful here, sitting under an overhead light while the rest of the house sleeps in darkness. I notice my eyes start to close, but open once more as I feel a seat being pulled out next to me.

"The buns are in the oven," Angela says, sitting down with her tea.

"That's great," I say. "I love the smell of things baking!" I smile shyly at her, suddenly pleased that we are both still in our pajamas. I allow myself the momentary image of Angela as my mother-in-law and find that the thought grounds me. She smiles back at me and I feel myself relax more.

"Beth," she says suddenly, glancing at me sideways. "Do you mind if I ask you a few personal questions?" She pauses. "I know I already asked you a few last night, but to be honest, I still have a few more." Another smile.

"Um, sure!" I say. Involuntarily I feel my shoulders raise.

"I guess I was wondering how often Kate sees her father?"

"She doesn't. He's...he's not involved," I say. I start to notice the forgotten cramp in my neck from yesterday's train ride.

"When you say not involved, do you mean that he doesn't see her or do you also mean that he doesn't contribute financially and keep up with his support payments? There are laws in place to protect you and Kate, you know."

"I know. Um, he…" I look helplessly at my hands as they open and close on the table, hoping that they'll reveal an appropriate answer. "He's not really in the picture anymore."

"Not in the picture anymore? What do you mean? Was he previously in the picture?"

"He," I pause. "He never was in the picture, actually. I don't really know him. It's just me raising Kate. Since she was born."

"I see," Angela says, her tone implying that she clearly does not. "I'm sorry if I seem overly intrusive, Beth, but I still don't completely understand. Do you know where the father is and does he even know that he is a father?" Her voice takes on a shrill tone that I never noticed before. *Mother-in-law, my ass.*

"I explained this all before, Mom," Patrick interrupts from behind, walking into the kitchen and standing behind my chair like a personal security guard. "Has this suddenly become the Spanish Inquisition?"

I sneak a glance at Angela and notice that her cheeks have begun to flush. "Having an interest in my son's girlfriend and her child hardly counts as an inquisition," she says. She stands up rapidly and knocks over what remains of her tea. In silence we all watch as the ruby-red liquid spills across the table and onto the pristine floor.

∞∞

After breakfast, I go to my room and pack my bag, then ask Patrick to drive me to the train station. While avoiding eye contact with Patrick, I explain to his parents that my stepfather has left me a message on my cell phone and that he needs me to pick up my daughter who has suddenly fallen ill. Whether or not Angela and Frank believe my lie, I no longer care. I thank them profusely for their hospitality and ignore their vague offers to provide assistance in some way. Instead, I accept two neatly wrapped cinnamon buns for the long trip home.

The car ride to the station is long and silent. Once we arrive in the parking lot, Patrick turns to look at me.

"Beth, I'm sorry."

"It's not your fault," I say. My voice sounds false and flat.

"Do you really have to go like this? I won't see you again for three more weeks."

"You know I can't stay," I say, turning to look at Patrick's pale face. "I know your mother means well…"

"My mother is a really caring person," he blurts out.

I reach over and pat his arm. "I know your mother means well," I repeat, "but the truth is that ever since dinner last night all I could think about was the fact that I am a depressed person. Not that I'm your girlfriend, not that I'm their guest, but that I'm this walking, talking diagnosis!"

Patrick looks back at me, a baffled expression on his face. "Beth, I realize that some of her questions were…intrusive, but come on, you *are* depressed. And she's a pharmacist. She has legitimate concerns." As I look at Patrick I have the sudden realization that this morning may have been the first time he stood up against his mother and that the experience was far from a triumph for him.

"She has concerns because she's your mother and she wants to protect you, not because she's a pharmacist!" I grab my bag from the floor of the car and then open the door. "She may be nice, she may be wonderful, but the way she looked at me," I pause, trying to find the right words. *This is important.* "The way she looked at me, Patrick, is the same way my mother's husband looks at me. Like I'm not a full person, like I'm somehow *defective.* That wasn't okay when I was a teenager and it isn't okay now." I gently shut the door behind me and stand on the pavement, waiting for Patrick to follow me into the station. He remains sitting in the car, moving the car keys between both hands. I watch him for a few moments longer, then walk away. *He is his mother's son.*

CHAPTER TWENTY-TWO

In the months that follow, things between me and Patrick stabilize once more. He remains a steady presence in my life, someone who can be counted on. By unspoken agreement, the doomed visit to Ottawa isn't mentioned. When Patrick's parents come down to take him out to dinner he mentions it offhandedly, after the fact, as if two old acquaintances had happened to drop by. Time passes and my mood also remains stable. I continue to meet Dr. Green on a monthly basis, but more as a check-in then anything else. For a while I avoid talking about Patrick, but eventually I stop worrying about the psychologist's possible reaction to my relationship and begin to share more and more with her. After all, shouldn't she be pleased that things are finally going so well in my life?

"Beth," Dr. Green says one day, as I start prattling on about all that I get from being with Patrick. She leans forward, her hands clasped between her knees. "We've talked at length about current events in your life, as well as about negative thought patterns and dysfunctional beliefs. In some ways we've made such progress."

"In what ways?" I interrupt, feelings of anxiety inexplicably triggered by her blatant eagerness. *Is she about to dump me?*

"In your confidence in yourself, Beth. In your awareness of what you have to offer others and the world around you. In your ability to maintain lasting, close relationships."

"Oh, thanks."

"Wait," Dr. Green says, holding up her hand. "Patience is not one of your virtues." She smiles at me. "You need to wait for the 'but'." I stare at her palm, then look down, my cheeks reddening. *Why am I so quick to jump at even the slightest compliment?*

"Beth, look at me," she says. I raise my eyes. "The but isn't so bad, trust me. The but is what will help you to continue to moving forward in your life and what will hopefully fuel our future sessions, if you'll let it."

"Okay," I say, pulled in. "What's the but?"

"The but is this. You've come so far in dealing with your depression and your thought processes, *but* you remain somewhat stuck when it comes to thinking about certain relationships."

"I just told you that things are good with Patrick!" I blurt out.

"I don't mean Patrick, per se, although I have a feeling that things may be more complex there than they seem. I mean relationships in general. Interacting with your mother, with your stepfather, with new people who enter your life. My point is that I think some of the ways you continue to perceive yourself and your world may be stemming from the early interactions you had with others when you were a child. And these perceptions may be preventing you from fully realizing the rich life you deserve."

"But we've already talked about that," I say. "How I relate to my mother has taken up at least two months of sessions!"

"Yes, we have talked about the events that happened, but perhaps we need to look more into how these events have shaped you and continue to shape you." She looks intently into my eyes. "We need to figure out how these past events and old hurts trigger emotions in the present, how to recognize these triggers, and how to respond to them differently." She pauses. "What I'm suggesting is that we next do what is called schema work."

"But why now, when things are going so well? When I haven't been depressed in almost two years!" I feel a sudden wave of frustration towards the psychologist, as if she's changed the rules on me near the end of a game.

"Beth, it's precisely because things are going so well and you are so stable that I'd like to do some work in this area. I didn't think that you were ready before and now I do." She pauses. "What we've been doing lately is more maintenance, checking up on your mood and reviewing strategies for managing it. What I'm suggesting is delving into an area that might help prevent you from getting so low in the future. Obviously anything we do won't address biological components of your depression, but we might be able to help you recognize more of the psychological triggers. Isn't this what you want?"

Mutely, I shrug. Life has been going so smoothly. I'm not sure if I'm ready to start rocking the boat.

⁊)⅌

By the next session, I'm on board. After years of therapy under my belt, what's the harm in trying something new? I announce to Dr. Green my agreement and I'm glad I did—her enthusiasm is contagious. She hands me two large questionnaires to fill out before we next meet and I finish them that night at home. In the weeks that follow, I learn that the themes of abandonment, emotional deprivation, and defectiveness permeate most relationships in my life like the smell of rotting meat. Dr. Green initially focuses on the death of Henry, my biological father, a topic that I've always tossed aside as irrelevant.

"I don't even remember him," I tell the psychologist as she mentions his name. "I mean, no offense at your theories on stuff, but I was only two when he died!"

"Exactly," Dr. Green says, as if I've just agreed with everything she's been saying. "You were *two*, Beth, two. You were barely more than a baby." She looks at me. "At two-years-old, who are the people that a child is most typically attached to?"

I look back at her. "Probably the mother," I answer.

"And who else?"

"I don't know," I say. "I guess the father, too."

"That's right! The father, too. Let's assume that your family was fairly typical in the sense that you were most attached to your mother as a toddler, but were also quite bonded to your father as well." She looks at me again. "How do you think a toddler would react if the father is suddenly gone?"

"Be upset, I guess." I cross my arms against my chest. "As I told you, I don't *remember*. I remember nothing about my father!" I can tell that my voice is getting sharper, but I'm not sure why.

"I totally understand that you don't remember. But Beth, not remembering is different than not being affected by something, particularly a traumatic event. And I would argue that the death of one of your primary attachments when you are a young child would count as a traumatic event."

"Okay, I agree. I was probably upset when my father died."

"Good, good. What I'd like to add is that you were probably more than upset. You were likely devastated and undoubtedly didn't understand why he was gone or if he was coming back. You likely tried to express your feelings in some way, but of course you didn't have the language to truly say how you felt."

"No kidding! I was *two*!" I notice my leg has started to jiggle up and down and I try to still it.

"Beth, let's imagine that you are that toddler. Let's imagine that you are noticing that someone very important to you, someone that you love, is now missing. Maybe you toddle around the house, looking for this person. Maybe you wait by the window for him to come home after work. But he doesn't come home. He's not there to tuck you in at night, he's not there to read your favourite book to you, he's not there to go for walks with you outside. This important person has gone and left you and you have no way of understanding why."

I notice my eyes start to fill with tears and angrily wipe them away. "Yeah, that likely sucked! What's the point of all of this?" I ask. An image suddenly enters my mind of Kate when she was two, at her daycare's Christmas party. She was the only toddler who willingly went to sit on Santa's lap, while the other children hung back in terror. While perched on Santa's red knee, Kate alternated between pulling on his beard and waving at me, content in what she was doing and safe in the knowledge that I was nearby.

"Beth, I need you to stay with me here. I know this is painful to talk about, to really think about for possibly the first time. But I'm going somewhere that will hopefully help you."

"Okay," I say.

"Okay. So imagine that you are that toddler, confused and so incredibly sad. You feel abandoned in the most primary way. What do you think you do next?"

"I...I don't know."

"Let's put it another way. Who do you think you turn to for support?" She looks at me, the expression in her eyes warm and kind.

"My mom, I guess."

"That's right! You would turn to your mom for support! Let's imagine that your mother was your primary caregiver, which is usually the case. You would undoubtedly become even more attached to her. You would likely cling to her, cry for her, never want to leave her side." She stops. "If anything, you would need *more* from her than she'd ever given you before."

"Yeah, probably," I say.

"But let's imagine that your mother has been plunged into deep grief by the sudden death of your father. One minute she had a partner she could depend on and the next minute she was alone. She's been blindsided by this. If she's like most people, she's struggling to get through each day, struggling to remember to feed herself and to take a shower every morning. She's in the middle of grieving for her husband and feeling whatever she needs to feel." She pauses again. "Knowing your mother as you do, how much emotional energy do you think she had available to give to you, her confused and sad toddler, while coping with her own tragedy?" She stops. "To put it simply, do you think that, for however long it took your mother to get through her grief, whether that period was short or long, that your two-year-old self might have felt abandoned by her, too?"

I look up at the psychologist, about to respond with protests, but instead burst into sobs. Rough, ugly sobs that rip through my body and fill the room. Sobs that seem to be coming from a wordless place that I never even knew existed. Dr. Green reaches across the space between us and takes my hand.

"You will get through this," she says quietly. "You are no longer alone."

സായര

Still shaken from the session, I head home before picking up Kate from day care. I can't have her see me like this. Without taking off my coat, I sit down at my computer and e-mail my mother. I ask her to send me a few pictures of Henry and to finally tell me about what happened in the weeks and months after he died. Until today I hadn't realized that I have no concrete evidence of my own that my biological father even existed. Throughout my childhood his name was said in hushed tones by my relatives and only when my mother was out of the room. Without being told, I knew that asking too much about Henry was not appropriate and bordered on unseemly. Just mentioning his name as a small child could make certain lines appear between my mother's eyes, lines that made my stomach tighten with panic. Once Jacob entered my life, it felt like there was finally an adult who was safe enough to ask questions about Henry, but it also felt potentially hurtful. Jacob was the one who now mattered. What did I need that other father for?

In the days that follow, I check my e-mail several times a day to see if there's a message from my mother. There never is. *Typical.* One week later, however, a manila envelope arrives in the mail. With Kate sitting next to me on the floor, I open it up. Inside is a note and three photographs. I put the piece of paper into my pocket to read later, and then spread the photographs on the carpet between me and my daughter. The first picture is of my mother and father on their wedding day, both looking solemn and ridiculously young. The second photograph is of Henry standing in front of an old-fashioned looking car, his hand up on his forehead, as if shielding his eyes from the glare of the sun. I have a sudden urge to pull his hand down, in order to get a better look at his face. The third picture is of Henry asleep on a sofa, a baby napping against his chest. I hold the picture out in front of me, staring at it.

"Is that me?" Kate asks, pointing at the infant. "I sure was small!"

"No, sweetie, that's me as a baby," I answer. I put two of the photographs back in the envelope, but use an old frame for the one of me and Henry. I'm hoping that with time, looking at the picture will bring me pleasure, rather than a sudden ache in my chest.

Later that evening, after I've tucked Kate into bed, I sit down at the kitchen table and open the note. It is brief but informative. In a few short lines my mother tells me that after my father's accident, she found it difficult to cope with a small child, and sent me a few blocks away to live with Adam and his parents for several months. My mother emphasizes that she visited me regularly and adds that everyone persuaded her that this arrangement was in my best interests. My mother points out that it was during my extended stay that everyone started noticing that Adam and I were becoming a twosome, more like siblings than like cousins.

Could this be the reason why I always felt so at home at my aunt's house? Could my closeness to Adam be more about the fact that he was a part of that house, rather than having anything to do with Adam himself? I read the note a few times, then stare out the nearby kitchen window. The sky is black and empty of stars. I try to dig up a memory that will make everything I'm learning fit neatly together like pieces of a puzzle, but have none.

CHAPTER TWENTY-THREE

*I*n the therapy sessions that follow, Dr. Green focuses upon other relationships from my past and the themes which keep popping up in them. She encourages me to write letters to people in my life who I have felt wronged by in some way. She assures me that the letters are for my benefit and will only get sent if I choose to do so. I start the letter to my mother right away but find myself drifting away from the paper whenever possible to do chores. Two days later, my apartment looks cleaner than ever, but the letter remains half-finished. Finally I give myself permission to stop and promise to get back to it eventually. She can wait. Besides, my relationship with my mother seems too complicated and confusing to summarize on a sheet or two of foolscap. My letter to Jacob is brief, the few lines I've written seeming somewhat redundant. Since reconciling, I've pretty well said everything to him that I've wanted to say. He knows how I feel about our past. He *knows*. Why repeat myself with a letter?

The letters to Adam and to Peter come easily. The letter to my cousin is filled with the sadness and loss I've felt since he left me for good and how I'll do anything to have him come back. Without thinking it through too deeply, I mail Adam's letter. *What do I have to lose?* But I keep Peter's with me and bring it to my next session. The letter to Peter is lengthy, full of venom and bite. Dr. Green asks me to sit facing an empty chair and to imagine that Peter is across from me as I read the letter. At first I protest, the whole idea of speaking to furniture seeming like an exercise in embarrassment. What I find is that quickly my anger overtakes any awkwardness I have and soon I'm standing and pointing at the chair as I speak.

"How could you see me with cuts on my arm and then pretend nothing ever happened?" I ask loudly, gesturing at the empty air. "How could you watch me as my mood got worse and chalk it up to being a tormented teen? And how could you ship me back to university after I tried to kill myself? I was still a kid. I needed my mother, I needed some semblance of a father. How could you be so cruel?"

My letter finished, I turn and look towards the psychologist, suddenly tired and spent.

"How did that feel, Beth?" She asks me as I sit back in my chair.

"It felt good as I read it," I say. "But now I feel kind of…dejected." I shrug. "Maybe there's more that I need to tell him."

"That could be," she says, nodding. "But maybe there's more to it than that. Could it be that part of your anger, part of your *rage* against Peter comes from somewhere else?"

"What do you mean? The guy is an asshole! He was horrible to me!" I feel my anger reigniting and sit taller in my seat.

"I totally agree with you, Beth. In fact, I would argue that the behaviour you've described was emotionally abusive."

"Then what are you saying?"

"I'm saying that maybe some of your intense feelings towards Peter also stem from other sources, from other triggers. The life schemas we've been discussing, for example." She pauses and I feel my shoulders tense up. "I would like to suggest that some of this anger against Peter is due to the fact that he is the one male in your life who has consistently refused to try and rescue you."

"But I needed to be rescued!" I say, feeling the heat of indignation fill my face. "I was still a kid!"

"That's right," she nods again. "You *were* a kid. But you're not a kid anymore." She smiles slightly. "I would also argue that once you are able to recognize that you don't need rescuing anymore, the intensity of your anger towards Peter might diminish somewhat." I open my mouth in protest and she holds up her hand, now a familiar gesture. "I'm not saying that you would forgive Peter, necessarily, or that you *should* forgive him. And I'm definitely not saying that your anger over how he treated you in the past wouldn't still be justified. What I'm saying is that you might be better able to move forward in your life if you truly began to see that you don't need anyone, whether it's Adam, Peter, Jacob, or Patrick, to rescue you. You now have the tools to rescue yourself."

"Patrick doesn't rescue me," I say quickly. I watch as Dr. Green raises an eyebrow. "Alright, he *has* rescued me in the past, probably several times. But not lately. Not in the last few years. Now the relationship we have is very good. If anything, his stability helps me."

"Does it, Beth? Does Patrick's stability actually anchor you or does it reinforce the belief that you are somehow an unstable creature who will become unmoored without him?"

"As I said, things between us are good," I repeat.

"Beth, do you not find it at all meaningful that you wrote letters to almost everyone who has been important in your life *except* Patrick?" *Checkmate.*

"The reason I didn't write a letter to him is because I don't think I need too! I mean, come on, I didn't write a letter to my friend Sarah, either! My relationship with Patrick is actually the way it's meant to be and that's fine for me!" I've never felt such frustration towards the psychologist before. *I can't believe I'm paying her for this!*

"But is it?"

"Is it what?"

"Is it fine?" She stops. "Beth, you've told me that ever since you were a child you asked too much of Adam. And now, as an adult, beyond needing him to rescue you when depressed, you seem to ask so little of Patrick." She pauses. "What I'm trying to say is that in a fundamental way, these relationships are mirror images of one another." She looks at me. "What would it mean if you asked Patrick for what you really wanted?"

"And how do you know what I really want?"

"I don't, Beth. But I think you do." She looks at her clock. *Time's up.*

℘℃℞

I cancel my next session with Dr. Green, my frustration building anew as I recount the last appointment in my head. How dare she criticize what's finally good in my life? The morning after my cancelled appointment, I'm trying to put a wiggling Kate into her jacket for daycare when the telephone rings. I almost ignore it, but realize that it could be Patrick phoning about our weekend plans, and finally pick up. It's Adam, his first real contact since Kate's birth.

"You've got to be kidding me," Adam says, as soon as I answer the phone. "You think that I abandoned you?"

"Um, what?" I ask. *Can this really be Adam?*

"Your letter! The one that's in my hand right now. The one that I'm thinking must be a joke because no one in their right mind would ever write something like this. You think I abandoned you?"

"You haven't exactly spoken to me in years!" I say angrily into the phone. Kate turns to me, startled, and I lower my voice. "I tried calling you after my daughter was born, but you couldn't be bothered to even meet her!"

"And you think that's me abandoning you?"

My heart starts to race and the hand holding the receiver becomes sweaty. Suddenly I feel less certain of my position, whatever it is. "Well, how would you describe it?" I ask.

"How would I describe it? I would describe it as finally standing up for myself after being pulled into your…into your self-destructive spiral one time too many!"

I look at the floor, at my socks. What can I say? What can I truly say? Once again, my frenzied self is stopped short by Adam's truth. Images of my cousin tumble through my mind. Adam as a nine-year-old, covering up for one of my many pranks; Adam at fifteen, holding me while I cried after my parents separated; Adam sitting next to me for hours in the psychiatric unit, following my first overdose; Adam, standing next to my hospital bed instead of with his new bride, his eyes large with confusion and hurt. Solid, steady Adam, who stood up for me and forgave me time and time again until he just couldn't do it anymore. The realization that none of my memories of Adam involve me taking care of him suddenly hits me and I feel nauseated with guilt.

"Adam," I say, holding the phone closer. "Forget what I just said. I'm sorry. For the letter, for your wedding, for everything. I'm so damn sorry."

I hear him take a deep breath, then another. "I know," he says quietly. "But thank you for saying it."

I stay silent, listening to him inhale and exhale.

"Take care of yourself, okay?" He says finally. "Maybe someday… just take care of yourself."

I hold the telephone for a few moments after he hangs up, my connection to him gone, take a deep breath, then go back to my daughter and her zipper.

CHAPTER TWENTY-FOUR

In the weeks after receiving the photos from my mother, I feel the slight flicker of hope nudge against my ribs. My mother could have ignored my request, but she actually made the effort to find the photographs and send them to me. I imagine her rooting through old boxes in the attic, checking her watch repeatedly to make sure that Peter didn't come home midway through her search. That couldn't have been easy for her and yet she did it, she came through for me. I take the gesture as a possible indication that my mother is becoming more open to sharing the past with me, to guiding me through the dark confusion of my adolescence and pointing out all that I don't understand. While I realize that nothing she says will ever change what has happened to me and what I've put myself through, I remain convinced that some clarity from her about Jacob and Peter could only help. I decide not to finish her letter but to instead invite her into town. By e-mail I suggest that she come mid-afternoon to meet for coffee and then come with me to pick up Kate and have dinner as a family. To my relief, she immediately accepts.

I choose a coffee shop that's three blocks from campus. It's my favourite, a little place that I used to meet Sarah at when I was pregnant, our friendship growing over bottomless cups of coffee and shared pieces of strudel. It is one small room, stuffed with mismatching, comfortable chairs and sofas, the walls adorned with paintings by local artists. My mother and I order our drinks off a blackboard by the counter, then head over to two seats by a large window.

"This is a great place for people watching," I say, as we settle in. "You can really get a good sense of the city just from sitting by this window."

"Well, it certainty seems popular," my mother says, looking around at the filled chairs nearby. She turns to me and smiles politely. I smile back. Now that I've finally gotten her here and have her full attention, how do I begin? *Ready, set, go!*

"Mom, I asked you here today so that we could talk about some stuff that's been on my mind," I say, pouring milk into my coffee from a tiny china pitcher. "Stuff that I've been talking to my therapist about."

"What kind of stuff?" she asks, taking a sip of her cappuccino. She puts down her mug and I notice a white foam mustache lingering on the top of her upper lip.

"Mom, your lip," I say, gesturing.

"My lip?" Her two hands flutter in front of her face like lost hummingbirds. "What's wrong with my lip?"

"Nothing's wrong, you just have some foam on it," I say. "Here, let me." I reach across the table with a napkin and dab at her face. My mother puts down her hands, closes her eyes, and leans toward my touch. As I wipe her lip, I feel instantly uncomfortable by this sudden moment of intimacy. *When did I last touch you, even accidentally?*

"All gone," I say.

My mother opens her eyes and smiles. "Thank you," she says. "Now, what was it that you wanted to talk to me about?"

I pick up my spoon and keep stirring my coffee. Now that I have her attention, I want time to leap forward so that I am safely back home once more, analyzing the conversation piece by piece over hot chocolate tonight with Patrick.

"Well, first I wanted to say thanks for sending me those photos of Henry." I pause. "When you come back to my apartment you'll see that I put one in a frame. It's the one of me with him when I was a baby."

"Oh?" she says, her voice not betraying any emotion. "That's nice."

"Yeah, it *is* kind of nice. Nice for me and for Kate, too, I think. A link to the past, you know?" I take a sip of my coffee too soon and feel the hot liquid scald the top layer of my tongue. "I guess the reason I asked you here is because I want to understand better what happened between you and Jacob," I say, finally. "You separating had such a big effect on me. And it all happened so fast. I want to *get* why you decided to leave him and be with Peter." I purposely try and keep my voice neutral like Dr. Green does, to not let even a drop of sarcasm colour Peter's name.

"Relationships aren't always simple, Beth. You must know that. Jacob and I had a lot of problems that we tried to keep from you children. We were always good parents together, but not always the best as a couple." She looks at me, her eyes seeming to be waiting for me to accept her explanation as a gift and to be done with it.

"I realize that you must have had problems," I say, pushing on. "But I also know that you often really got along. I mean, I have memories, Mom, of the two of you. Don't you remember those picnics on the lawn or all of us building snow forts in the backyard every winter? Or what about decorating the Christmas tree? Remember how you and Jacob would always kind of joke-argue about who would put the star on top, but then he'd always let you do it even though you needed a stool to reach?" I smile at her, hoping to break through her defenses with happy memories and an encouraging gaze.

My mother sighs, a heavy sigh. "Those are family moments you're remembering, Beth. And they *are* special to me. But they have little to do with us as a couple."

"Okay. But you always seemed so happy together." I crack my knuckles. "I remember having friends whose parents got divorced and the decision to divorce was so *obvious*. Like, finally you guys are separating! But you and Jacob were different." I stop. "You always looked so happy," I repeat.

"Looks can be deceiving," she says, staring at her fingernails.

"Okay, I agree. But what I don't get is why you didn't even have a trial separation? Why was it all so rushed? Why didn't you go to counseling together or something and try and make it work? And why did you run to Peter?" I take a deep breath. "I mean, come on, you had two children together to think of."

"We had *one* child together, Beth." She looks at me and shakes her head.

"That's not true and you know it," I say, my voice shifting from neutral and becoming angry and shrill. "Convince yourself that Jacob wasn't important to me if that's what helps you sleep at night, but don't you ever try and convince me!" *Why can't you for once acknowledge that you made a mistake?*

My mother straightens in her chair, her spine rigid with resolve. "You know what, Beth? I'm not sure I feel comfortable talking to you about this any longer. Some things are private and should remain that way." I watch as the relaxed look leaves my mother's face, to be replaced by one of a cornered animal, vigilant to danger and ready to pounce.

"I know that your marriages are private to you, Mom," I say, lowering my voice once more, "but they really impacted me." I notice my heart start to race and attempt to ignore it. I take a big sip of my coffee, then put down my mug, my tongue still throbbing. Perhaps caffeine isn't the best idea right now.

"Is this conversation going to be about you blaming me for the mistakes you've made in your life, Beth? Did you ask me here just to rehash what happened in the past ad nauseam?" My mother pushes her mug away from her and crosses her arms. "Peter warned me that this could happen." She takes in a deep breath. "Did Jacob put you up to this?"

"Jacob? No! Of course not! If anything, he'd probably be your defender if I mentioned anything to him!"

"And God forbid anyone ever try and defend me, right Beth? God forbid that the truth be anything other than what you say it is. Do you even remember how often you'd push me away when I tried to help you get better in the beginning?" Her lips almost disappear into her pinched face. "I have had enough...interrogation for one day, Beth. Now if you'll excuse me, I think it's time to go." My mother reaches for her purse and pulls out five dollars. "For the coffees," she says primly, then stands up. "Please give my love to my granddaughter and apologize to her that I can't come visit this time."

I remain sitting, staring into my coffee mug as the liquid cools and congeals. My heart is no longer racing, but instead feels heavy in my chest. This conversation piles neatly on top of all previous conversations with my mother since I was sixteen. While the exact content might be somewhat new, the way it ended is identical. Why did I think that it would be any different? I now know that I won't be sitting with Patrick tonight analyzing this conversation with my mother. I want to move away from it as quickly as possible, before I get sucked back in. I am done.

୧୬ଓଷ

I cancel two more sessions with Dr. Green, not willing to have one of the few truly stable relationships in my life picked apart. My mother might not be there for me, but Patrick definitely is. Eventually I decide to face the psychologist directly and force myself to head back to therapy.

"Here's the deal," I say, starting to talk as soon as she opens her office door. "I'm willing to continue looking at themes in my life and relationships, but I'm not comfortable focusing on me and Patrick. Whether you agree with me or not, whether you think I'm wrecking my life or not, I'm happy with how things are." I stay standing in the doorway, knowing that my certainty may diminish once I walk into her space. "You asked me what I really want from Patrick and I'll tell you. I want what he gives me right now!"

"Alright, Beth, that's fine with me," she says, gesturing for me to enter the room.

"It is?" I ask, walking over to my regular chair and sitting down.

"Yes, of course it is. This is your therapy, Beth. You are meant to be a full collaborator and participant in anything we do. I'm just throwing out ideas to help you think about some things differently. If there is ever an area you don't wish to explore further, then all you need to do is express it." She smiles. "Like you just did!"

"Okay, that's good to know." Now that I've said my piece, I'm not sure what comes next.

"So, maybe we could start today with you giving me feedback about the letter-writing process. Did that exercise go as you expected?"

"Sort of," I say. "Not totally." I stop. Now I know what I want to talk about. "Adam called me after he got my letter. It didn't go very well but it made me realize something," I say.

"Yes?"

"It made me realize that I've always thought of myself as a victim, as someone who had things done to her and who has maybe behaved badly because of that." Dr. Green nods encouragingly. "I mean, I think I *was* a victim as a child, lots of times. But even when I got older, I would sometimes go into new relationships thinking of myself in that way. It was like being a victim gave me a get-out-of-jail-free card, you know? Like what I then did to other people wasn't important, because of what had been done to me."

"That's quite an insight," Dr. Green says. I can see by the expression on her face that her enthusiasm is building quickly. I want to slow her down somehow, to warn her that my pockets are empty, that I have no other great insights to give.

"I guess so," I nod slowly. "Um, anyway, thinking about that made me also think about the other people I've hurt in my life. People like Heather and Adam, but also people who never mattered that much to me."

"Can you give me an example?"

"Yes, I can. There was this guy, Scott, who I dated for a long time in university. I started seeing him right after my first suicide attempt. He's someone I kind of used to try and forget that I was depressed." I look up at Dr. Green. "I didn't intentionally try and use him. It's more that I was kind of cavalier, that I didn't really consider how he felt, until it was too late." I sigh. "I guess you could say that he became like collateral damage."

"Do you want to tell me more about what happened?"

"I could, if you think it might help. I mean, it was a while ago." I look at Dr. Green again and force a smile. "To be honest, I'm probably making this to be bigger than it was, like I usually do. I mean, Scott's probably forgotten all about me and what happened by now."

"But it's clear that you haven't forgotten all about him," Dr. Green says. "And in this room, it's what you remember and are affected by that counts."

CHAPTER TWENTY-FIVE

In a valiant attempt at normalcy following my first suicide attempt, I started dating Scott a few weeks after my return to school. He was my first real boyfriend, and he was a nice boy, the kind of guy any grandmother would approve of. He was a year younger than me due to skipping grade two in school and was in several of my Sociology classes. He lived off-campus in the house he had grown up in, with his two loving, professional parents who would have foot the bill for any university of his choice, but he chose to remain in town. He was cute but in an unthreatening kind of way. Tall and strong looking but not muscle-bound, with longish, tousled brown hair and a line of light freckles across his nose. He liked to go on dates at the movies and to talk on the phone. He wasn't opposed to partying, but would never do anything that he'd regret the next day. He liked to write me notes during class like someone in junior high, fold them into interesting shapes, and then save them for me to read at the end of our next date. In these notes he liked to write our initials in a huge heart with an arrow through it. From his shy smile when I opened these notes, I could tell that this was meant to be both ironic and sincere. He was the bass player in a band called Bite Me, a name which caused him to blush whenever he mentioned it. He didn't let band practices ever interfere with schoolwork or seeing me. He liked to fool around but knew I had very little experience and never pressured me to take it further than I wanted. *A nice boy.* With Scott I could have fun without risking anything. Except maybe his feelings.

I started to spend every Friday and Saturday night with Scott. Sometimes we doubled with my roommate, Ella and her boyfriend, John and sometimes we'd go off on our own. When in a group, we often checked out campus parties that were going on but left if they became too crazy. No togas for this boy. Scott was smart and funny and had the ability to make anyone feel comfortable. My favourite thing to do with him was to just hang out in his parents' den and rent a video. It made me feel like I was fifteen again, like the future that was spread out before me was still unsullied and full of promise. Scott loved comedies—*Airplane, Animal House, National Lampoon's Vacation, Revenge of the Nerds*, that kind of thing. I usually ended up watching Scott while he watched the movie, not wanting to miss the moment when his whole face lit up with the pleasure of slap-stick. I liked the fact that Scott could be so completely satisfied by such movies, that he didn't always have to crave for something more. I liked to sit next to him on the sofa, snuggled under his arm. This was exactly the amount of physical affection that I craved from Scott, although I was willing to compromise on occasion. With Scott I felt normal and that made me happy. This was different from saying that Scott himself made me happy. It was more the fact that Scott viewed me as a typical girl that brought on the happiness. I avoided letting him see my scars and never told him about my recent hospitalization or about the darkness that continued to dog me. When I ran out of counseling sessions on campus I didn't try and seek therapy elsewhere, for fear that a new counselor would turn my focus onto Scott and what I was doing. At all costs, I tried not to evaluate my feelings for Scott too closely, because that could mean that I'd have to change the direction that things were moving in and I was comfortable just drifting.

Our relationship continued easily throughout the summer between first and second year. In early May, Ella and I searched around the city for a house to sublet rooms in, with the understanding that we would continue staying there once the fall semester began. We found a house nearby campus that was occupied by three friendly third year guys, all members of the university's rugby team. I was ostensibly at the university that summer to retake a course I had failed during my doomed winter term, but the truth was that I never intended to set foot in Peter's house again. Whether or not my mother wondered why I didn't return home and take a correspondence course instead, I didn't know and didn't care. The fact that she continued to send me cheques to cover my summer rent rather than protesting about the cost seemed to give me my answer. The image of Heather's face occasionally entered my mind, but the intense shame I felt over wounding my baby sister so deeply would leave me breathless and I would push the thoughts far away from me, desperate for oxygen again.

After about six months of dating, Scott invited me to his parents' home for a romantic dinner. When I arrived at the house, I noticed that the lights were turned low. A small table sat in the large kitchen, covered with a white tablecloth. On top were lit candles and two place settings. A small glass bowl of forget-me-nots provided the centerpiece. Classical music played in the background.

"Wow," I said, walking over to the table. "This looks beautiful, Scott."

"Thanks," he said, placing two wooden bowls of salad onto the table. "I have to admit that my mom made most of the food for us, but I did the table!"

"You remembered that I love forget-me-nots!"

"Yeah," he smiled, then pulled out a chair for me. "Your seat, mademoiselle?"

"Is this an anniversary or something?" I asked, spearing lettuce with my fork. "I thought that we celebrated our six months last Saturday."

"No anniversary," Scott said. "I just wanted to show you what you mean to me." He cleared his throat. Despite the low light, I could make out the freckles on his nose. He looked so young, too young. "In fact, I wanted to tell you that..."

"This salad dressing is delicious!" I interrupted. "If you don't mind, I'd like to get the recipe from your mom! Yummy!" I stuffed more salad into my mouth, then kept talking as I chewed. "How did the band practice go last night, anyway?"

"It was just jamming," Scott shrugged. "You know."

"Still, you guys are great! And I love your band's name! How did you come up with it again? Bite Me—that's catchy!"

"I dunno," he shrugged again, his cheeks reddening. "I guess we thought it up for a talent show during the last year of high school, when we had no name. It was actually just supposed to be temporary, but it kind of stuck. I know it's sort of lame."

"No, it's cool!" I said. "Hey! You know what you guys need to do? You need to get a gig somewhere, get noticed!"

"You think so?"

"Absolutely!" I kept on chewing. "I mentioned your group to that guy who lives in my house. You know, Charlie? He said he also has a group with some of the rugby guys and that he'd love to hear you sometime," I said, overemphasizing my house-mate's enthusiasm.

Anything to get the conversation away from the serious direction that it was going in.

"No way," Scott said.

"Seriously!" I said, chewing vigorously. "Maybe I could convince the guys at my house to let us use the basement sometime for a show. I'm sure Ella would be into it. I mean, her boyfriend's in your band, right?"

"Beth, that would be amazing," he said, smiling at me. I smiled back.

The rest of the dinner went well, with Scott serving linguine and strawberry cheesecake and me bulldozing my way through the food and through every discussion. By the end of the evening, I felt nauseous and wiped out.

"I am *so* full!" I told Scott, lying down on the sofa and rubbing my bloated stomach. "I don't think I can ever move again!"

"Beth," Scott said, sitting down next to me, "I think that I love you. Like, really love you."

"What? Wow! Thanks!" I replied. I suddenly sat up. "I'm actually incredibly tired and I've still got to finish that essay if I want to hand it in on time. If I don't pass the course this time around I'm in trouble. Can you take me home? I also want to make sure that I get to talk to Charlie tonight about the gig, before he goes to bed." I patted Scott's hand then quickly headed toward the front door.

"Beth…"

"No, really! This was all great! And thank you for, for that." I pointed to the sofa. "I just really need to go now." I stuffed my feet into my sandals and then headed to the car, Scott following slowly behind. On the drive home I popped a CD of his band in and turned up the volume. I pretended to nod my head in appreciation of the great music. *Shit, shit, shit.*

The next day, I woke up with a migraine, although I didn't know what the nausea-inducing explosion in my head was called until Dr.

Nelson gave it a name. He also gave me a prescription for Tylenol with codeine. The bottle was filled with little pills that not only took away the headache pain but had the added benefit of softening the world around me. No more sharp edges. The first time I popped one of these pills I just wanted the throbbing in my head to go away. Within an hour, I was higher than I'd ever been in my life. My mood jumped from zero to one hundred in a matter of minutes, and I felt a euphoric joy in just existing. Much better than antidepressants! Two hours after taking my first pill, I insisted on sitting on the sofa in the TV room between Charlie and Ella, chattering incessantly about how amazing the kids on *Degrassi* were.

The next morning I woke up migraine-free. Despite this, I instantly popped another little pill. I decided not to waste my high on classes and headed to a nearby park instead, a camera and lunch in tow. Before the medicine kicked in, I felt a little foolish, walking around the park so early in the morning.

"This is a short-cut to campus," I announced loudly to an old man as he walked by with his dog. He looked at me, nodded, then continued down the path.

Impatient to get that feel-good feeling again, I took two more pills, washing them down with the coffee I'd brought in Ella's thermos. *Hurry up, already!* The next thing I knew, I was lying under a huge fir tree, my camera on my chest. Every few minutes I summoned up the energy to lift up the camera and snap a few pictures of the branches above me. I started to feel warm all over. The ground below me had become soft, Jell-o-like. I could see the occasional bottoms of legs walk by me, as well as the wheels of various baby strollers.

"I'm inside a tree. Inside a friggin' tree!" I started to giggle. After about ten more minutes, I gathered up the strength to sit up, hitting my head on a limb above me. I was so stoned that I didn't feel a thing. I sat hunched over and cross-legged, taking swigs of cold coffee and letting my body vibrate. *Why didn't I know about these pills before? They're friggin' amazing! And maybe I actually do love Scott! I think that I may even love this tree!* I wished I had a megaphone, to announce my joy and caring to the world around me. By mid-afternoon, my buzz started to fade, and I popped two more pills before heading back home. I knew that my camera was filled with the most amazing pictures ever. Who else had come up with the idea of taking photos *inside* a tree? I was absolutely brilliant! When I got home no one else was around. I called Scott's phone number, shouted "I feel the same!" into the answering machine, then called right back and said, "That was a message for Scott. From Beth." As I hung up the phone I realized that I needed to lie down. I headed to bed, letting myself float away on the mattress. I couldn't wait to tell everyone I knew about this medication.

Several hours later, I was awakened by the sound of groaning. It was me. I was clutching my knees up to my stomach. My entire middle was one huge cramp. I was pain. I heard a knock on my door and my doorknob being rattled.

"Hey, are you okay? Do you still have the migraine?" Ella's voice asked from the hallway.

"My stomach! It...hurts!" I thrashed around on my bed, hoping that movement would at least shift the pain to somewhere else in my body. My stomach couldn't take it anymore.

"Your stomach?" Ella asked, opening my door and heading to my bedside. "Is it serious? Should I call a doctor or something?" She knelt down next to me and started to rub my back.

"No," I gasped, rolling from side to side. "I think it's from the medicine I took!" I groaned again.

"And what was that?" She asked.

"They're over there," I moaned, gesturing to my bureau. "That bottle!"

"This bottle is half empty," she said, shaking it a few times. She looked at the label. "I had to take those after having my wisdom teeth removed," she said. "I remember being told not to take too many at once because the codeine can be hard on your stomach," she said. "Do you want a heating pad?"

"No, thanks. I'm just going to try and sleep," I whispered.

The rest of the night passed in slow motion. The next morning, still pale and shaky, I dumped the rest of my pills down the toilet. I'd have to survive through any future migraines on my own. During the next week, I tried to avoid Scott's phone calls but let him know that I couldn't wait to hear his gig at my house, which I had managed to set up with Charlie for Saturday night.

The next weekend the basement of our rented house became transformed into some sort of studio. Drums, electric guitars, and amps covered the floor. After giving my house-mates money for a few cases of Molson Canadian, they agreed to stay and be an audience for Bite Me and even invited a few of their buddies over for the gig. I spent most of the time rushing around and trying to avoid Scott as much as possible.

"I got your message last week," Scott whispered in my ear before the band started playing, giving me a one-armed hug. "Do you really feel the same?"

"What? Of course! For sure!" I smiled, moving away from him. "I'm going to help set up the mikes. Talk to you later!"

As the band played, I sat on a couch with Ella, who was cheering on her boyfriend. I watched her watching him and attempted to imitate the caring. I mean, how hard could it really be? The four members of the band played mostly old covers from the Seventies and Eighties, like *The Rolling Stones* and *The Clash*, as well as a few *Journey* songs for the girls' benefit. The music was so loud in the basement that the sofa began to vibrate. I started to put my hands on my ears, but realized that might not be construed as supportive girlfriend behaviour. Ella's boyfriend was the lead singer, with Scott mostly playing base and singing back-up. The one solo Scott did he dedicated to me. *Foolish Heart*. When he put his mouth to the mike, I had to look away.

After a few sets, we all sat around drinking beer and listening to *The Who*. I started to loosen up and enjoy myself. Hanging out with the band wasn't so bad after all. Maybe I could become some sort of professional groupie, without the associated benefits. My house-mates also seemed to be having a good time and one suggested to Scott that he come over and jam sometime.

"Beth, can you help me get some more beer from upstairs?" Scott gestured to me.

"Are you sure that you need help?" I asked, reluctant to be alone with him.

"Beth!"

"Sorry," I said, heading for the stairs. I walked into the kitchen and opened up the fridge. "It looks like there's only two bottles left, Scott. I think that you could have managed that on your own, don't you?"

"Baby," he said into my hair, holding me from behind. "I just wanted to get you alone."

"Alone?" I spun around to create some distance between us. "Why?"

"I got you something," Scott said, reaching into his jeans pocket. "I wanted to give this to you at that dinner but then you were in such a rush to get home that…"

"I had to get back to talk to Charlie, remember? I wanted to set up this gig for you."

"I'm not mad. I'm just saying that there wasn't time to give you this," Scott pulled out a small jewelry box and put it in my hand.

"What's this?"

"Just open it, okay?"

"But," I said. I stared at the box as if it might explode. I sat down on the floor and put the box in front of me. Then I slowly opened it. Inside was a ring, a simple, pretty ring with a blue stone in the middle of it. "Scott!" I looked at the ring and then up at his face. He looked so open, so hopeful. *I'm such a shit.*

"It's not an engagement ring or anything crazy like that," he said quickly, gesturing with his hands. "It's just a ring to symbolize how I feel about you, how I, you know, love you." He stopped and looked at my face. "Is that okay?"

"Of course it's okay!" I quickly took the ring out of the box and shoved it on my finger. "It's beautiful! Thank you! No one has ever bought me a ring before."

"And hopefully no one else ever will," Scott said, pulling me up from the floor. "Are you sure you like it? Are you sure that it's not... too much? I asked Ella and she said that it might be too much."

"Ella knows?"

"Of course. I mean, come on. I needed a female to come and help me pick it out." Scott smiled. "I wanted it to be perfect, for you." I smiled back, trying to ignore the stones that had started to fill my stomach. *He gave you a ring, Beth, a ring. He's a great guy. You can make yourself love him, you can.* I gave him a full-body hug, then headed downstairs to show off the ring. I ignored Ella's quizzical look and sat back down on the couch. I took huge gulps of my beer as the band played another set. *I can do this.*

CHAPTER TWENTY-SIX

*I*n the weeks that followed, I started canceling plans with Scott, claiming that I had to keep up with my new fall classes. I couldn't afford to almost fail any courses ever again, if I had a hope in hell of getting into the Honour's Sociology program. Despite this, I ended up seeing Scott more often than before. He suddenly kept showing up to jam with my male house-mates, who seemed to have lots of time on their hands. Despite my best intentions, my feelings didn't grow. I hid the ring that Scott gave me in my desk drawer and only wore it when I knew that I'd be seeing him. Even then, I often forgot. I put my focus into my courses and pulled off my best grades yet at university. Trying to find another excuse to avoid Scott and realizing that I might not always be able to depend on my mother financially, I started looking for a part-time job. After two weeks of looking, I was offered a position at a used book store around the corner from the university. While sitting behind the cash register I was safe in the knowledge that no one knew anything about me or cared to know. I was in heaven. Scott liked to drop by after my shift on Saturdays, and take me out for something to eat. Sometimes we went to a movie afterwards or to play pool in my basement. After getting all A's on my finals I let him take me out to dinner after work to celebrate. Otherwise I would feign fatigue and ask to be driven home.

I spent a lot of time planning how to make it *seem* like I wanted to be with Scott without actually being alone with him. Everything changed when his parents, in a burst of holiday cheer, spontaneously invited me to come with them to their cottage for a week during Christmas break. The plan was to leave on Boxing Day, before sunrise. Scott and his parents were all so happy with this idea that I didn't know how to say no. I mean, hadn't I just been complaining to Scott about my plan to stay all alone over the holidays, as my house-mates went back to their respective homes, one by one? What girl wouldn't be thrilled with the idea of having a full week with her boyfriend instead of all by herself in a decrepit rental house? It just wasn't in me to be honest.

We drove down in his parents' car to their cottage on a small lake in the Muskokas. The place was large but simple and made of horizontal logs which seemed to fit together seamlessly, like a child's construction toy. The main attraction was the lake, which stretched out for miles in front of their property and was blanketed with a thick layer of pure white snow. The other three sides of the cottage were surrounded by a forest that you could lose yourself in, without even trying. His parents were to sleep in a spacious upstairs loft, while Scott and I were each assigned a small, cozy bedroom off of the main room. There was no TV, no radio, no distractions. After we arrived and unpacked, we headed into town for dinner. The restaurant they took me to was paneled in dark wood, with a fireplace in the middle. While eating, his parents informed Scott and me that they planned to spend most of the next day driving to nearby little towns.

"In other words, you kids will be free to spend the day at your leisure," his mother said at the end of supper, smiling across the table. "I know that you haven't been able to spend much time together lately, with you both working so hard at school. Tomorrow you'll have the day to yourselves. You can ski, snowshoe, play board games, just spend time together, and we'll meet up again for supper."

"Great!" Scott said, squeezing my hand under the table.

"Yeah, sounds fabulous," I said, counting to five before I pulled my hand away.

After supper I suggested that we all take a walk down by the lake to look at the stars. I spent my time pointing out any constellations that I could remember from the two years I spent at a Girl Guides camp. Luckily, Scott seemed even more into the stars than me and quickly turned his attention to the sky. After about thirty minutes outside, I started to shiver and we all headed back to the cottage for an early night.

The next morning came too soon. Scott's parents made a point of leaving the cottage as loudly as possible, announcing that we were free to enjoy the surroundings for the next eight hours. How was I going to distract Scott for eight hours? I stood at the door of the cottage in front of Scott, waving to his parents' departing car. Why couldn't his parents be overly conservative, straight-laced people who wouldn't dare leave their young adult son alone in the clutches of his girlfriend? Why did they have to be so *normal*? I kept waving at the empty road, trying to delay the inevitable.

"So," Scott said, shutting the door and then pulling me into a hug from behind. "We've got the place to ourselves."

"Yeah," I answered, starting to hop from one foot to the other. I spun around, to face Scott. "You know what would be totally fabulous and amazing? A picnic in the snow!"

"We just had breakfast, Beth," Scott said.

"I know, but I love this weather!" I started to hop again. "We could cross-country ski into the forest and then maybe have hot chocolate or sandwiches before coming back." I did a little jig. "Did I ever tell you how much I love skiing? When I was a kid, my stepfather used to take me out to this conservation area in the winter and we'd spend the day skiing on the paths. I used to pretend that the little hills were these huge mountains I had to go down!" I paused, caught off guard by my memories of Jacob. "Anyway," I said, my voice suddenly subdued, "It was fun."

"Didn't you tell me that you got frostbite once from being outside?"

"Well, yeah, nearly, but that was in high school, when I'd refuse to wear gloves. That's beside the point. Let's make a picnic and go!"

"Your wish is my command," Scott said. He took my hand and led me further into the main room "But first, I want us to spend a little quiet time here, okay?"

"What do you mean by quiet time? Can't we get quiet time out in nature?"

"That's not the kind of quiet time I mean," Scott said, leading me over to the couch. "Let's just hang out here for a while, okay?" He pushed the hair out of my face and gently stroked my cheek. "You know, quiet time." He moved closer and kissed me, once, twice. I tried to stop staring at the freckles on his nose.

I felt the muscles in my back tighten, my hands clench. *Relax, relax, you can enjoy this.* I tried to will my body to loosen, to remind myself that a boy, a kind, gentle boy was caressing me, loving me. I forced my mouth to open and kissed him back. I concentrated on making my mind turn blank, with no image to distract me from what I needed to do. The memory of making out with several random guys last year suddenly entered my mind and I felt revolted. *Shit.* My lips closed and my head pulled back.

"Your lips are so soft," Scott whispered, moving his face closer to mine again. I lifted my hand to play with his hair, my arm feeling wooden. Why couldn't I feel anything? What was the matter with me? Was I not only depressed but frigid too? Most girls my age had been having sex for years! In frustration, I suddenly pushed Scott down on the sofa and moved on top of him. I started to kiss his face, his neck, his sweater.

"That's nice," he whispered. "Kiss me more." *I can do this.* I pushed his sweater up to his shoulders and started to kiss his stomach. I moved my face lower to the top of his jeans. "I love you so much," he said.

"Shhhh," I said, moving back to kiss his lips and stop the words. "Shhhh." Suddenly, I noticed my skin start to warm, an energy begin to fill my body. I started to kiss him harder, more urgently. *It's working!*

"You're beautiful," Scott said and gently reached under my turtleneck with his hand. "Your skin, your body. You're just so beautiful to me."

"Don't!" I abruptly sat up, and pulled my sweater down over my chest.

"Beth? What's wrong?"

"Just don't!" I stood up and headed to the bathroom. I shut the door and turned on the water. I sat on the toilet lid with my knees under my chin, stone-still.

"Beth, what's wrong?" Scott knocked on the door. Slowly, he opened it. "Beth?" I turned my face away, to avoid the concern I saw on his.

"Nothing's wrong. I just stopped being in the mood, okay? Is that a problem?"

"No. I'm just confused, I thought that you were into it." Scott came and sat down next to the toilet, looking up at me. "Weren't you?"

"Yeah, I was. But then things changed."

"Why? Because I touched your breasts?" Scott's look of confusion slowly changed into one of understanding. "Did some guy ever do anything to hurt you?" He asked, searching my face for some answers. "Oh my god! Is that it?"

"Um, yeah, that's it," I said, looking at him. "Sorry for freaking out."

"No, I'm sorry for not getting it." Scott reached out his hand, and I took it. "Let's make that picnic, okay?"

"Sure," I said, smiling. "Just let me pee first."

After Scott left the bathroom, I walked over to the sink and stared at myself in the mirror. *Liar.* But it *was* about guys, sort of. Just not in the way that Scott assumed. *Liar.* But how could I tell the truth? How could I tell this caring, gentle boy that having someone I liked but didn't love touch me is almost as sickening as drunkenly making out with random strangers? And how the hell could I tell him that I didn't love him? *Liar. Ugly bitch.* I reached into the medicine cabinet and pulled out a razor. I turned it over and looked at the blade. It was rusty and dull. Roughly I pulled it across my upper arm, pressing harder and harder until bubbles of red appeared. *Bingo.*

❧

The rest of the week passed in a blur. I spent most of my time planning activities for us to all do as a foursome. During the daytime I gathered everybody together for snowshoeing, cross-country skiing, and tobogganing. Evenings were spent around the fireplace with rounds of poker, charades, and even a seemingly endless singsong. I was the camp director that no one had bargained for. Scott's parents initially gave me quizzical glances, but then began to participate wholeheartedly, once I hinted to his mother that I wished I could have such close relationships with my parents. Scott willingly gave everything a try, and kept looking at me as if I was a wounded bird that he needed to rescue. I got worn out by my own enthusiasm and false cheer and almost welcomed back my black mood.

By the end of the week, I knew what I would have to do. There was no way that I could keep pretending forever that I wanted to be with Scott. I was just not that good an actress. Back home in my room I practiced what I needed to say over and over. I had never been in this situation before. I had no idea what true romantic love felt like, just the intense feelings of desire that had flamed up briefly for Adam and then had thankfully went out. My closest experience to being broken up with was what had happened with my stepfather Jacob. From him I knew what it felt like to throw your love at someone and have them move out of the way, rather than catch it. I knew what it felt like to be left behind, diminished. I just never knew that having to do the leaving could feel this bad. That it could make you feel like shit. I was a shit.

In the weeks that followed, I kept putting off the break-up. I needed to make sure that I did it right. As long as I ended things before Reading Week, it would be okay. Such a permanent decision couldn't be rushed. I kept reducing the amount of time I spent with Scott and announced that I had been neglecting my friendship with Ella and needed to have more weekends just with her. Soon after I informed Scott that I needed to start taking on double-shifts at the used book store in order to have enough money to pay rent for the summer. I didn't have amazing parents I could count on like he did, after all. The worst of it was that Scott was so damn agreeable through it all. Why couldn't he tell me to go to hell or make some demands on my time? And why couldn't the boy get a bloody backbone? Becoming pissed off at Scott felt infinitely better than my own guilt.

Over time, however, Scott quietly started to assert himself. The more I avoided him, the more he kept appearing at my house for impromptu gigs with Charlie. If I didn't go out with him one week, he'd be over at the house at least twice. I gave up trying to reason with my house-mate about this and just pretended that it wasn't happening.

I started to reconcile myself to the possibility that thanks to my cowardice, Scott and I would still be together after graduation and into our senility. I tried to convince myself that getting married to him someday wouldn't be *that* bad. Besides, I already had a ring. I started to see him more again and I pushed us to have sex. Maybe that had been the missing piece. I quickly discovered that it wasn't. Final exams loomed and I plunged into studying, head-first. I figured that if I could put my focus and attention onto school, then I could forget about what I was doing to Scott, at least for a little while. I spent long evenings in the library and once again obtained straight A's, thus maintaining my place within the Honour's program.

When it became clear that focusing on school wasn't enough of a distraction, I decided to return to therapy. Having used up all of my on-campus sessions long ago, I eventually found a psychologist within the community who was willing to charge me on a sliding scale. I sent all bills to my mother and let her insurance company deal with the cost of my treatment. When I scheduled my first session, my goal was to have the psychologist help me find the courage to end things with Scott. Unfortunately, unlike the Social Work and Psychology interns I'd often been assigned to at the university clinic, Dr. Miller intimidated me. He wasn't a struggling graduate student, he didn't become flustered in session and need to pause to look things up in textbooks written by experts. He was an expert. Dr. Miller seemed so polished and sure of himself, so certain that his techniques would glue together my broken self. Instead of starting each session telling him what was on my mind like I had at the university clinic, I became cowed and deferential and let him take the lead. Distorted thinking, mistaken beliefs, and lack of behavioural rewards all became the focus of our work together, while my continued betrayal of Scott took a backseat. I became fixated on becoming the perfect client and made sure to complete all of the homework exercises that Dr. Miller gave me as soon as I got home from our sessions. My goal became trying to please the psychologist, rather than to actually get better.

A few weeks after finals, Scott's twentieth birthday arrived. Feeling generous, I suggested that we celebrate by going to any restaurant of his choosing. Scott chose a small Italian place downtown, my favourite restaurant. The sweetness of his dinner choice made me feel nauseous. Sitting in the back of a taxi, I grabbed Scott's hand and squeezed it to cover up my guilt. Scott had nice hands, with a safe, comforting grip. His hands were bigger than mine, stronger. I liked how his fingers covered mine so completely. I could disappear in his hands. Holding onto Scott reminded me that my staying with him was due to more than pure cowardice. If we broke up, I'd lose the security, the warm certainty of Scott. I'd lose one of my best friends. I realized that what I'd most miss about Scott was the way that he always seemed to notice me when I was in a room. Everyone else might be oblivious to where I was, but not Scott. I'd watched him keep scanning a room for me, until he'd gotten me in his gaze. Scott saw the good in me, no matter how shitty I felt. I held his hand tighter and willed myself to surrender already. As we got to the restaurant, Scott gave my hand one quick squeeze, and then loosened his grip. I didn't want him to let go first.

After dinner we took a taxi over to my house to hang out with Ella and the members of Scott's band. We spent a few hours in the kitchen, playing drinking games. Eventually we all settled in the den, drinking beer and watching old John Hughes movies on TV.

"This one's my favourite," I said, as the opening credits of *Sixteen Candles* filled the screen. I put my feet up on the coffee table and burped loudly.

"Beth, can you come here?" Scott asked from the top of the stairs. I looked up, suddenly realizing that he was not in the den and hadn't been since the last movie ended.

"What?"

"Just come here," he said, walking down a few steps and putting out his hand.

"For what?"

"You know, come on. Please, Beth." He held out his hand further in the air. Ella elbowed me in the side and I reluctantly stood up and walked over to the stairs. I tripped a few times before reaching him, suddenly aware of how drunk I was. "Just please come," Scott said again. While holding onto the banister for balance I followed him slowly as he led me up to my bedroom.

"Why are we here? Is it bedtime already?" I laughed, trying to make a joke.

"I thought that we could use some private time together," Scott said. "I want this birthday to be special. I thought it would be good to be alone with you without worrying about someone coming in."

"Why would we worry about…oh!" I started to laugh again, and tried to sit up.

"Stay down," Scott said, switching off the overhead light and turning on a lamp. He walked over to the bed and quietly undressed.

"Let's go back down, okay?" I asked, as he lied down next to me. "The movie!"

"Shhh," Scott whispered, stroking my shoulder. "I love you and want to celebrate my birthday with you." He placed his hand under my chin and gently kissed me. "Is that okay?"

"Yeah! Sure! Happy birthday!" I said loudly, sitting up and moving my back against the wall. The ceiling was tilting. "Want to sing show tunes?" I started laughing loudly, the sound of my voice falling hard against the floor.

"Shhhhh honey," Scott said, unbuttoning my shirt.

"Yeah, okay. This is good, too!" I lay back on the bed. The room had started spinning.

"You want to, right?" Scott asked, caressing my face. "We don't have to have sex if you don't want to. I just thought that…"

"No! Great! Go for it!" I moved closer and kissed him back. "Perfect! Why the hell not?" For the next half-hour, I turned off everything, and let myself float.

Afterwards, we lay next to each other on our backs, me with my hands in fists on my chest. I wasn't floating anymore. I noticed tears start to slide down the sides of my face, onto the pillow. I didn't know why I was crying. I just knew that I couldn't stop. Scott turned to look at me, then sighed.

"Why are you crying?"

"No reason," I said.

"Did I hurt you?"

"No. Nothing's wrong. Don't worry about it!" I rubbed my fists roughly against my face. I heard Scott inhale deeply.

"Why are you with me, Beth? Can you just answer me that?"

"You know," I said.

"No I don't. I need you to tell me."

"Well, because."

"Because what?"

"Because you're such a good guy. You're this amazing guy, and you care about me so much!" I felt my face get wetter.

"And that's it?"

"What do you mean?"

"That's the only reason why you've stayed with me for over a year? Because I care about you?"

"Of course not! Or not the way that you're saying it."

"Then what way do you mean exactly?"

"I mean, I don't know! That you *get* me, that you love me despite myself. That's good, isn't it?"

"But how do you feel about *me?*"

"You know how I feel!"

"No Beth, I don't. Tell me."

"I, well, you're a lot of fun to be with and I really, really like you."

"And that's all? I'm *fun* to be with? A fucking clown is fun to be with!"

"Why do you have to ask so many questions? Why can't you just enjoy this?"

"Enjoy this? Enjoy that my girlfriend can barely stand to make love to me?" He looked at me. "I'm not an idiot you know!" Scott's voice came out high-pitched, strained. He abruptly sat up in bed, and put his face in his hands. A few moments later, I noticed his body start to shake.

"I know you're not an idiot," I whispered into the sheets. "And you caring about me so much *is* a good thing, I swear!"

"Yeah? And what about me, huh? During the last year did you ever give a flying fuck about me or were you too busy getting cared about?" I placed my hand on Scott's arm but he jerked it away.

"No! I don't, I didn't mean to, I do care! I really do care!"

"But do you love me? Can you answer me that? Do you? Or am I just someone to fill in the time until you graduate?" Scott lifted his head and stared at me. I'd never seen that look from him before. I suddenly felt shut out, cold.

"I," I started to cry. "I want to love you! I do! I've tried to make myself, but I can't! I don't know what the hell is wrong with me! I'm a messed up person! I'm sorry! I'm so, so sorry!" I covered my face with my arm. I felt the bed move and heard Scott walk toward the door.

"I can't let that be good enough anymore," he said. "I deserve to be loved back. I fucking deserve it!" Scott walked out of the room and slammed the door. In the silence that followed, I breathed in the empty air and felt myself get suffocated by my guilt.

ᏚᎧᏟᎧ

A week after the break up, Scott wrote me a song. He handed me a CD after I answered the doorbell one afternoon, then walked back to his car.

"It's all about you!" He shouted from the driveway. "There's no lyrics, just music. I did all the instrumentals. It's about how I felt about you, about all of it!"

Later in my room, I put the CD in my ghetto blaster and listened. The song went on and on and sounded like one long hurt. When it was over I sat still, staring off into space. And that's when I knew. That's when I really knew about what it meant to love. Not from the whole Adam experience. Not from watching my mother and Peter. And definitely not from anything that I'd ever done. It was only after listening to the tape that this good boy had made for me that I understood how love could be used to strengthen or to weaken, to diminish or to grow. This sudden knowing was too late for Scott, but I hoped it wouldn't be too late for me.

CHAPTER TWENTY-SEVEN

After telling Dr. Green about Scott, I feel lighter. We continue examining ongoing life themes but eventually agree that our work in that area is pretty well complete. I have the sneaky suspicion that Dr. Green would jump at the opportunity of dissecting my relationship with Patrick into its component parts, but I'm pleased to see that she truly does seem to respect the boundaries I've set. Several months pass and my mood still remains stable. I've come to accept that I will be taking antidepressant medication for the rest of my life and feel reassured, rather than threatened, by this reality. Having completed schema work, I stop having regular therapy sessions and instead meet Dr. Green for a mental health check-up every six months or so at my request. Instead of focusing upon life schemas or upon other cognitive-behavioural techniques, I spend the sessions filling in the psychologist on what's been happening between appointments, reassuring both her and myself that I'm now living as a person with depression, rather than as a Depressed Person. These sessions are about thirty minutes long, just enough to make me to feel inoculated for the next several months.

The psychologist is pleased with my mood's stability, Patrick is pleased, Jacob, and even my sister are pleased. But while it is *good* news, even great news, there are some unexpected drawbacks to ongoing mental health that I hadn't exactly anticipated. Although I won't admit this to anyone, I've come to realize that there were some benefits to experiencing recurring episodes of depression. Getting regularly depressed forced me to become highly productive when in remission. Like a squirrel gathering nuts for the long winter ahead, between episodes I worked hard, in anticipation for the darkness that was just over the horizon. Getting depressed regularly also meant that I could give myself permission to just focus on the here-and-now; I didn't have to plan too far ahead. This present focus was encouraged by most therapists I met. How could I seriously prepare for a future when in a month or two I could be lying near-comatose on my bedspread? True, in the past I did plan enough to apply for a Master's degree, but that was mainly to avoid having to think about what I might really like to do in the real world.

What I've come to realize is that living contract to contract as a research assistant made sense when the most I could count on was a few months of stability. But now that three years have gone by without a relapse, I'm faced with possibilities that were never in my reach before. And with possibilities come responsibilities. If I'm to live a full life for myself and model a full life for my daughter, then maybe I need to actually aspire to more than living pay cheque to pay cheque as an assistant to Dr. Shields or date to date as a girlfriend to Patrick.

To my surprise, through my years as an assistant I've grown to be interested in the research I'm doing in ways that were non-existent when previously in graduate school. Dr. Shields' interest in social and institutional inequality has led me to start investigating the possible marginalized role of mental health in politics and society. For the first time, I feel excited about the idea of pursuing ideas of my own, ideas that actually matter to me. With that in mind, I apply for and am accepted into the Ph.D. program. I'm assured that I can complete coursework on a part-time basis and that if depression strikes I can take a leave of absence. The funding given to Ph.D. students is enough to allow me to start paying for my two-bedroom apartment myself, which makes my relationship with Jacob feel more balanced. Through repeated teaching assistantships, I manage to save enough to buy myself a used car and Kate a pet cat. The car is a beater really, but something that can take my daughter and me from point A to point B. At the age of thirty-two I finally feel like a grown-up.

Having made such a seismic shift in the direction my life will take, I try and convince myself that no other major changes are needed. When feelings of dissatisfaction about Patrick and me bubble to the surface, I try to push them down with my morning glass of water and Effexor pill. What we have is good, it's good enough. I'd rather keep things at status quo than risk rocking the boat and losing Patrick forever. At least that's what I tell myself.

But then the daydreams start happening, the ones in which I'm with someone else. It's not that I want to replace Patrick with another man; I can't imagine a life without Patrick in it. It's more that I want him to want what I want, to need what I need, to have this dam finally break so that our life together can stop stagnating and begin to flow forward once more. As the daydreams start to come more frequently, I find it more and more difficult to push things down, to forget.

ഇറ

It's an overcast April morning, the kind of morning that in the past would have added a layer of damp heaviness to my already depressed self. It seems strange to look out the window at a bleak and rainy day and actually feel light inside. I'm aware that part of my improved mood is associated to my brain chemistry being duped by high doses of Effexor, but I don't care. If that's what it takes to feel normal, so be it. My bags all packed, I head out with Kate and her booster seat to a waiting taxi. A soft rain mists my skin and I turn my face towards it.

"Mommy! You're going to get all wet!" Kate says, pulling at my coat.

I follow her into the backseat of the taxi, then buckle us both in. The ride to the station is uneventful and soon we're on a train headed to Peterborough and Sarah. While Kate colours in the seat beside me, I close my eyes, content. The last several hours have been a mad rush to get everything organized, but through it all, I've felt calm. Alex's phone call last night was unexpected and occurred less than an hour after I had called Sarah to check-in. It had been two weeks since she had given birth to a healthy, nine-pound baby boy, via an emergency C-section. *I'm fine*, she had said. *The baby is great.* In a hesitant, almost apologetic tone, Alex explained that Sarah was in fact *not* fine, that her recovery from her emergency C-section was slower than either of them had anticipated, and that Sarah's mother—their primary helper since the birth—had to return home that morning or risk losing her job. Sarah would kill him for asking me, but was there any possibility, even if only for a day, that I could come and help out? My answer was quick and certain—I would be there the next day and would stay for a week. Kate would have to come with me, but if anything, she could be a little helper.

"Are you sure this is a good idea?" Patrick asked a few hours later, when I told him about the phone call. He sat on my bed as I packed a bag for Kate and me.

"What do you mean?" I asked, holding up two shirts. I'd bring the stain-resistant one.

"I just mean…what if you get over-tired?" Patrick reached over and touched my leg. "I think it's wonderful that you want to help Sarah, I just don't know if going there and staying up all hours with a screaming baby is really the greatest thing for you."

"I'll be fine," I said, swatting away his hand and turning back to my packing.

"Okay," he said. "I just wanted to put it out there."

"I know, but I'm a big girl, remember?" I folded a sweater carefully before setting it in the suitcase. "Just remember to come by regularly to feed Butterscotch and scoop out her litter and I'll be happy." I smiled at him, secure in the knowledge that he was concerned about me, that he did care. His concern and caring didn't affect my decision to go help Sarah, however. Whether or not I helped my best friend did not even feel like a choice to me, the decision was so obvious. The very fact that Sarah, or at least her husband, had reached out to me, that she actually *needed* me, filled me with a strength and sense of purpose that had remained hidden for years. After feeling ineffectual for so long, I was ready to bring positive change to someone else's life.

Our train arrives in Peterborough just after lunch. As the train enters the station, Kate kneels on her seat and bounces up and down.

"We're here! We're here! We're here!" She says, her nose pressed against the window. "Do you think Alex will have brought Addy to meet us?"

"I think the dog is staying with a neighbour right now," I say, pushing my daughter's squirming arms into her jacket and zipping it up. "New babies and big dogs don't always mix well. Addy will be back with them in a few weeks."

"There's Alex!" Kate shouts, pointing at the glass. "Right there! See? See?"

I look out the window and see my best friend's husband standing by himself, a look of bewildered fatigue on his face. We take time getting off the train, our exit slowed down by two bags and an overly excited Kate. As soon as Alex notices us, I see relief soften the lines on his face.

"I'm so glad you're here!" he says, reaching over to take my bags from me. "Thanks so much for doing this. My boss isn't the most understanding type and after Sarah's mom left, we kind of ran out of options."

"It's no problem," I say, grabbing Kate's hand as we head to his car. "I was planning on visiting in a few weeks anyway. Besides, I *want* to do this."

Within ten minutes we arrive at their house. It's small and one-story, with a kitchen, a tiny den, and a living room in the front and two bedrooms and a bathroom in the back. The living room is my favourite place to be in the house. It's a generous size, with large, bay windows making it seem brighter than would seem possible on this rainy afternoon. The walls are decorated with a few mounted quilts that Sarah's mother has made over the years, filled with colour and light. All over the house, the tops of bookcases and shelves are adorned with small glass sculptures of animals and people, Alex's hobby. I suggest to Alex that he show Kate the sculptures while I go see Sarah. I find her in her bedroom lying against a stack of pillows, her normally rosy face pallid.

"You're here!" she says as I enter the room and sit down next to her. "I told Alex not to call you."

"You needed me!" I exclaim. "Of course I'm here!"

"You didn't let me finish," Sarah says, putting up a hand. "What I was going to say is that I told Alex not to call you, but I'm so glad that he did." She reaches out and squeezes my arm. "Have you seen Thomas yet?" she asks, pointing to the crib. "He's finally sleeping!"

I get off the bed and creep over to the other side of the room. There he is in a crib which seems monstrously large for such a tiny being, wrapped tightly in a blanket.

"So you learned how to swaddle?" I ask in a whisper, turning back to Sarah. "I never could catch on to doing that."

"Alex learned," she says. "I think I slept through that prenatal class!"

"How are you feeling?" I ask.

"Tired," she says. "Mostly sore, especially around my middle. I never expected a C-section to be so painful." Sarah attempts to sit up, winces, then settles back into the pillows. "I don't know why so many celebrities actually choose to do this. Are they all insane?"

"Undoubtedly," I say, turning back to look at Thomas. I gently touch his cheek with my finger, barely stroking the surface. I'd forgotten how soft a baby's skin can be. I stare at him sleeping, amazed at how such a little person could have already figured out the basics of breathing, sleeping, eating, and pooping. How is this possible? How can he know? I look over at Sarah to share my thoughts, but see that she's asleep. Quietly I tiptoe out of the room and shut the door.

The days that follow are more exhausting than I had expected, but also more exhilarating than I could have hoped. Each morning and afternoon is both structured and chaotic. Everything revolves around Thomas—when he needs to be fed, when he needs to be changed, when he needs to be rocked. I spend what seems like hours walking him back and forth across the length of the small house, my footsteps making a slight indentation in the beige carpet between the living room and the bathroom. Kate follows me step by step, mesmerized by the wailing infant. While Thomas sleeps, I do loads of laundry and make as many meals as can fit into their small freezer. Casseroles, spaghetti sauces, muffins. I've never been the greatest cook before, but I find it easier than expected to follow basic recipes in Sarah's batter-stained copy of the *Good Housekeeping Cookbook*. Kate insists on helping with whatever I'm making and stands next to me on a chair, stirring various items with a giant spoon. While Sarah nurses her baby, Alex, Kate, and I sit down to eat at their kitchen table. Usually our meals are simple, my more elaborate attempts at cooking saved for the future freezer meals. We often dine on canned soup and sandwiches or make-your-own pizzas, Alex filling the room with tales from his own childhood in England.

Each afternoon if it's not raining, Sarah and I go for a walk with the stroller, Kate running ahead of us. As if tied to me by an invisible string, Kate inevitably stops moving in her trajectory before she is out of my sight and then patiently waits until my nearness causes her to run ahead again. Sarah holds onto my arm or grips the bar of the baby's stroller, taking careful, tiny steps along the sidewalk. On our first venture outside Sarah only makes it to the end of the driveway before doubling over in pain. By the week's end, however, she is walking up and down the street. Her steps, while still slow, seem less timid. It's as if her pain is more tolerable now, something to be managed, rather than stoically endured.

As the days pass I realize that I've completely forgotten what it is like to take care of a newborn, or maybe it's that I never truly had that experience in the first place. My memories of Kate as an infant are blurred by the fog of depression. My goal during those first several weeks after Kate was born was to just survive. Kate was ever present, but always in the background, safe and secure in someone else's arms. Moments of sadness nip at me, but I brush them away. After all, were my experiences after Kate's birth really all that different from what Sarah is going through now? Doesn't she also need help to take care of her child? Isn't she also feeling helpless and dependent on others? Maybe this is part of what becoming a mother is all about—not only having someone totally dependent upon you, but also learning how to push down one's own need at absolute independence—perhaps for the very first time—in order to accept those offers of help when they come along. What I do remember is the smell of a freshly washed baby, the smell of pure bliss. As Thomas lies slumped and boneless against my shoulder following each feeding, I breathe in memories of my daughter through the scent of his skin.

On the night before I'm to head back home, I call Patrick to arrange for him to pick Kate and me up at the station.

As soon as he answers the phone, my elation at the week's success bursts out of me. "Patrick, he's amazing! Thomas is amazing! All the things he can do already! He's such a little person!" I smile into the phone.

"That's great, Beth," he says. "It sounds like you're enjoying yourself."

"I am! I mean, don't get me wrong, I'm so tired I could sleep for two weeks and probably will. But it's been great and I feel good knowing that Sarah is now getting back on her feet. She was so wiped out before, but can now walk around the block." I pause. "Do you ever think of us someday having a baby?" The question comes out suddenly and unexpectedly, my joy elbowing past a normal tendency to self-censor.

"Beth, come on," Patrick answers, cutting off my giddiness at the knees. "I'm totally overwhelmed by the changes I need to make in my dissertation right now. Having a baby is the last thing on my mind."

"I don't mean right now!" I say, feeling my cheeks flush. I suddenly feel foolish, but can't pin-point exactly why. "I just meant, do you ever think about it as a someday kind of thing?"

Patrick sighs, the noise a reprimand that reaches me across

the distance and puts me in my place. *Settle down, Beth.* "Have you forgotten everything that happened when you had Kate? The postpartum depression and all the help you needed?" He stops. "You had help for months, not just for a week or two like Sarah. Don't you remember?"

"I know," I say.

"And don't forget how high a dose of Effexor you're now on. I can't imagine any doctor allowing you to stay on your meds if you wanted to get pregnant. I don't know about you, but I don't really relish the idea of a two-headed baby!" His attempt at humour hits me sharply, like a quick slap.

"You're right," I say, quietly, staring down at my stained shirt. Was it really only thirty minutes ago that a milk-drunk Thomas had laid heavily against my shoulder as I confidently rocked him back to sleep?

"And how would you ever get a career together if you had a baby right now?" Patrick asks.

"I said you're right, okay?" My voice sounds loud and shrill. I attempt to soften it somehow, to round its edges. "I wasn't speaking about having a baby right now anyway, Patrick. That wasn't what I meant." *What did I mean?* "I was just kind of fantasizing. It's no big deal."

"Okay," he says. "Let's not fight, alright? I miss you and can't wait to see you tomorrow."

"Me too," I say, switching gears and turning my focus onto our plans for the upcoming weekend, plans that don't include burping, diapering, or rocking anyone. My time here is done.

∞

It's a few days after our trip to Peterborough and I'm tucking Kate into bed. I pull the covers up to her chin, just as she likes, then gently put her stuffed hippo in bed next to her and kiss her on the forehead.

"Good night, sweetie," I say, standing up and heading for the door. I leave it open halfway, then start to walk back to the living room.

"Mommy?" Kate calls out, her voice high and clear. "You know Alex?"

I move back towards her door and open it fully once again. "Yes?" I ask.

"Why don't I have one of those?"

"One of what?"

"You know, an Alex? Like Thomas has!"

"Do you mean a dad?" I ask, walking over to her bed and sitting down once more.

"Yeah, one of those!" Kate pushes her covers down to her chest and leans over on her elbow. "I have a mommy, but I don't have a dad. And Thomas is just a baby, but he has both!"

I can feel my heart start to race but will myself to remain calm. Since Kate's birth, I have always promised myself that my daughter would not grow up like me, afraid to ask questions about her natural father. Unlike my mother, I would be open with Kate and would never convey that she should be ashamed of who she is. I would keep the information flowing between us, always cognizant of her level of understanding. This had been my plan, my genuine intention. It had made me feel slightly smug and superior just to think about it. But now that the moment has arrived, I don't feel quite ready yet.

"Well, sweetie, you had a dad before you were born, but he had to go away."

"Why?"

"Well, he had to go away for work. He moved far away and I never found out where he went. And the truth is that he had to go away before he even knew that you were coming." I look into my daughter's brown eyes, searching for a part of this forgotten man in her face. Is he in her smile? Her chin? "He would have really liked you if he had met you," I say.

"Do you think I would have liked him, too?" She asks. I smile at her, my chest aching, and push a few strands of hair off her face.

"I know you would have. He was a really nice guy. He was polite and very handsome too. You would have had a lot of fun together." I try to stretch the few facts I remember about the man as far as they'll go, without turning them into absolute lies. For so long I've thought about him as a mistake, as a screw-up, as a sign that my depression had returned. My interaction with the flesh-and-blood person he had been was so fleeting and insubstantial that no lasting image remained in my mind. I wait for more questions about him, but for now there are none. *Please don't ask me to tell you his name.*

"He sounds good," Kate says, snuggling back under her covers. "And you know what else is good? I have a Jacob!"

"You do have a Jacob," I say, relief flooding my voice. "And you also have a Grandma and an Auntie Heather," I pause. "You have lots of people who love you so much, Kate. And don't forget Patrick!"

"Yeah," she says, closing her eyes. "I've got him too. But he's no Alex."

"What do you mean?" I ask.

Kate opens her eyes once more, a look of patience on her face. "Patrick is my *friend*, he plays games with me and he sometimes reads to me and he paints with me, but Alex is a *dad*, mommy, remember?" She says, then rolls to her other side, already half asleep. "A daddy and a friend are *not* the same thing!"

"You're right, sweetie, you're right," I say softly.

I stay sitting next to my daughter, watching her back as it rises and falls. Kate's words mix with comments from Dr. Green in my mind and I feel off-balance. Could my five-year-old daughter have become wiser than me?

ജ)ൽ

Heather calls unexpectedly one night to ask if she and a friend can come visit for the weekend. The times that Heather has reached out to contact me in the last few years are few and far between; while we now communicate fairly often, the pattern tends to be me calling or emailing and her responding. I mostly see her when visiting Jacob, our interactions cushioned by his affable presence. Our relationship as sisters has grown warmer and closer, but only to a point. Heather's request to visit seems so spontaneous that I can't help but say yes. In the days that follow, Heather emails to let me know that the friend who is accompanying her is a *male* named Caleb, that they've been dating seriously for over a year, and that they intend to move in together once they both finish their Master's degrees. In an attempt to show what a hip older sister I am, I decide to have Kate bunk in with me and give my sister and her boyfriend the second bedroom for privacy. I borrow a double air mattress and sheets from a neighbour and try to make the room as welcoming as possible. I put fresh flowers on the dresser and a few magazines for them to read, hoping that such touches will offset the Cinderella decals on the walls.

Kate and I head over in my car on Friday night to pick them up from the bus station. As I'm turning off the ignition, I notice Heather and a man standing together, their hips and shoulders touching. I watch as my sister's boyfriend lifts up her hair to whisper something in her ear. I see my sister smile and turn to touch his cheek with her hand. There's such an ease and familiarity in their movements that I want to keep watching, to somehow grab the moment for myself.

"Auntie Heather!" Kate shouts from the car. She opens her door and shouts again. "We're over here!"

I watch as my sister's face lights up. She turns her head again to her boyfriend to tell him something and together they head over to the car.

"Hi Beth, hi Kate," Heather says, ducking down and climbing into the backseat next to my daughter. "It's great to see you guys!" She gestures to her boyfriend to take the front seat. "This is Caleb."

"Nice to meet you," I say shyly.

"Good to meet you, too," he says. He turns his head back towards Kate. "And you must be Kate! Your aunt won't stop talking about you!"

Kate giggles loudly. "That's 'cause I'm her only niece!"

We drive back to the apartment, the short trip filled with Kate's tales of daycare and play dates with friends. Heather remembers the names of each important person in Kate's day-to-day life, as if she had just spoken to her the day before. Once back at my apartment, we quickly settle in. Caleb offers to play a board game with Kate and is soon involved in an intense match of Candy Land. While they face off in the living room, Heather and I decide to make pizzas for dinner in the kitchen.

"I'm so glad you came," I say as we start to pull ingredients out of the fridge. "What made you decide to visit?"

"Well, I wanted to see you and have you meet Caleb," she says, "but there was another reason I wanted to visit, too."

"Please tell me this has nothing to do with Mom," I say, taking out the cutting board from a drawer. "Please, Heather."

My sister shrugs and starts grating cheese. "What can I say? I'm a sucker, okay?"

"So what happened?" I ask, sitting down on a stool. Suddenly the prospect of making supper seems like too much effort.

"Mom called me after she came to visit you. She's called me every week since."

"What is she calling about?"

"She's calling about you, Beth. About how much you blame her for everything that happened between her and Dad and about how she's sick of it." Heather lifts up the grater and a mountain of mozzarella tumbles onto the cutting board. Heather grabs some of the cheese and pops it in her mouth.

"She's sick of it?" I ask, laughing bitterly. "Join the club!" I watch Heather as she pulls a red pepper out of a bag, washes it, then begins to expertly chop. "I mean, what does she expect?"

"She says that you need to respect her marriage with Peter, that they've been married for almost fifteen years and that he makes her happy."

"Do you really believe that, Heath?" I ask.

"I dunno, maybe." Heather puts the pepper pieces into a neat pile, then reaches for the package of mushrooms. "Don't get me wrong, I think the guy's a prick. But he's mainly a prick to you and me, not to Mom. I think he makes her happy."

"He tells her what she can and can't do! She's become his puppet!"

Heather stops chopping to look at me. "If that was completely true, do you think she would have come and visited you? Give her a little credit."

I get up off the stool and reach into the cupboard to get a can of tomato sauce and a packaged pizza crust. Deep dish, Kate's favourite.

"So you don't think I should blame her for anything? Is that what you're saying?"

"Beth, that's not what I'm saying. I agree that Mom didn't stand up for you enough when Peter got in your face and you were... going through everything. But she did learn from it."

"How did she learn from it exactly?" I ask.

"She stood up for me sometimes when I was a teenager," she says. "She didn't just let Peter walk all over her. She got...stronger."

"Well, I'm glad for you about that. But it doesn't change anything that happened. And it doesn't change how crappy she was to Jacob."

"Mom said you'd say something like that," Heather says, spreading tomato sauce all over the crust before sprinkling on the toppings. She pauses, holding up the spatula. "You know what I think one of your problems is?"

"No, I don't. Please enlighten me."

"I think you're too much of a dreamer. I think you've built this fantasy about Mom and Dad in your head and it's blocked you from seeing what really was."

"What are you talking about?"

"Well, you always say how great things were between them."

"Things were great!" I say. "And besides, what would you even remember? They separated when you were only eight!"

"I know. I was kind of glad," she says. I stare at my sister, this young woman who I'm only now starting to really know and I have no idea how to respond.

"But things were happy!" I finally say inanely.

"Beth," Heather slips the pizza into the oven then walks over to me and touches my arm. "I also remember the happy times. But near the end what I remember most is all the arguing, late at night."

"I never saw any arguments!" I start to feel something valuable slipping away from me and I try and reach for it before it's gone.

"I didn't *see* any either, Beth. Mom and Dad were great at hiding problems. Which I suppose was a whole other problem. But I heard arguments, lots of them. They usually happened late at night. Not loud, no yelling or name-calling, but loud enough to keep me up at night. Their bedroom was next to mine, remember?" She looks at me. "Let's just say that the walls are pretty thin in that house."

I sit back down on the stool. I don't want to let go to all the happy memories I have of childhood with my family. I'm not ready too.

"I'm not saying the good times didn't happen," Heather says again, sitting on a stool next to me. "I'm just saying that you might want to give Mom some slack about the break-up. Theirs was *not* a perfect marriage."

"I'll think about it," I say softly.

Heather looks at me and smiles. "As I said, the problem with you is that you're a dreamer. I'm more of a realist. I think I take after Mom in that way."

"So who do I take after?"

"Dad, obviously!" Heather rolls her eyes. "You two are dead ringers for each other in terms of being die-hard romantics! Sometimes it's sickening!" She smiles at me, an olive branch extended.

"How did you get to be so brilliant?" I ask. "One minute you're ten and wanting a bra and the next you're spouting theories at me!" I shake my head, but smile back.

"I am in psychology, after all," Heather grins, then stands up and stretches. "And you still owe me that bra," she adds.

The rest of the weekend goes smoothly, with Caleb slipping easily into our small family dynamic. He's an instant hit with Kate, who flirts shamelessly with him as only a small child can. I ponder what Heather has said to me, grateful of her honesty. I realize that while what my sister has told me is likely right, much of what my mother has said remains wrong. While I should not blame my mother for choosing not to stay with one husband for the sake of her children, in my mind she is at least somewhat culpable for deciding to remain with another husband at their expense.

CHAPTER TWENTY-EIGHT

On a Sunday afternoon in mid-August, we drive through two rows of trees, the windows rolled down as far as they will go. My hair has come loose from its ponytail, the strands whipping against my face. I push at them with my right hand while holding a bottle of water with my left. Behind me Kate sits on top of a towel that's wedged into her booster seat, the frayed fabric buffering her legs from the burn of hot plastic. Kate plays with a box of Lego on her lap, seemingly oblivious to the sweat that's begun trickling down her neck.

I turn to offer Patrick some water, then hesitate. He's staring straight ahead, his body barricaded by fists tight on the steering wheel and a clenched jaw. Is this about forgetting to get the air conditioner fixed or is this about something else, something too heavy perhaps to push through with an offer of water? I sigh, then listen to the sound as it sinks through the air. I sigh again, this time more deliberately, and turn my gaze back to the road.

The two rows of trees that flank the highway seem never-ending. To me they are winter trees, the kind that are meant to be covered with a thick white snow. Now in mid-August they seem clumsy and overgrown, standing as they do so brown and naked between fields of dead grass and the road. I let myself drift into the familiar daydream.

It's early on a Saturday morning in January. The rented cottage is supposed to be winterized, but the electric heater in the bedroom can't work hard enough to snuff out the cold of the new year. When I open my eyes I notice my breath in front of my face, each exhale a quick cloud. I burrow under the quilt for a moment longer, stretching like a cat. There's pure luxury in that stretch. I spot a sweatshirt on a nearby chair and reach out an arm to grab at it. As I pull it over my head, I inhale a familiar scent, his scent. A mix of wood, sweat, and peppermint, plus something I instantly recognize but can't yet name. I sit up in bed and pull the sweatshirt over my knees. It looks ridiculous on me, the sleeves hanging past my fingertips, giving me the appearance of an ape. Still, it's warm. Still, it's his. I push down the quilt and step out in my socked feet onto the wooden floor. I pad out into the empty main room, a kitchen and living room all in one.

I spot the sofa next to the wood stove and make a run for it. Sitting cross-legged, I push my hands out of my sleeves and hold them toward the warmth. Another cat stretch. I turn to look at the wide windows above the kitchen sink and watch as pink-orange fills up the sky. All I can see is colour and trees, winter trees, a mix of white and green.

I feel the cottage door open suddenly behind me, a rush of frost icing my back. My hands dart into the sleeves and I again pull the sweatshirt over my knees. While my body shivers, my face and smile turn to meet the cold, to welcome it, to welcome him.

"Good morning," I say, as he stamps his boots.

"Good morning," he answers, pushing the door shut with a shoulder. He

walks toward the stove and dumps an armload of cut wood nearby. He unzips his jacket, takes off his hat and gloves, then walks over to the coffee maker. Under his breath he's humming. I've never heard the tune before, but the sound warms me. Soon he's in front of me, holding out a chipped green mug.

"For you," he says, "two creams". Instead of going back to get his own mug he sits down before me on the ottoman, his hands clasped loosely on his knees.

"Beth," he says, then ducks his head and smiles. I reach out to him with my socked foot and nudge his leg.

Now that he's directly in front of me, I can take a good look. He's wearing a red and blue plaid flannel shirt with a grey T-shirt underneath. His sleeves are unbuttoned and rolled partway up each arm. The shirt hangs over an old pair of Levis, grey woolen socks covering his feet. His hair is a thick brown, just starting to recede, his face freshly shaved and smooth.

"Beth," he says again, reaching out to touch my cheek. Another smile.

I know what's coming next. I've been here many times before. Next he'll say he wants to talk about our relationship, about our future together. In this same moment, Kate will come stumbling out of the other bedroom, a Barbie in her hand, and slump right into his lap. Then, with the room so full, we'll decide to get engaged.

It's not this moment I want to focus on, however, but the one that comes just before, the one when I know what he's about to do, what he wants to do, what nothing will stop him from doing. The moment when I can truly feel that he shares my want, that his want is so huge mine doesn't seem quite as monstrous or shameful anymore. I want to hoard this moment, this not-Patrick moment, as my imaginary lover watches me from the ottoman, the chipped mug warming my hands.

"Beth." A quick nudge on my bare knee. "Water?" Patrick taps me again. "Hey, Beth?"

"Oh, sorry—here you go," I say, handing him the opened bottle.

He puts the bottle to his lips, takes a deep sip, then hands the water back. "Thanks," he says.

I nod, tightening the lid back on the bottle.

"You looked happy just now," Patrick says softly, glancing at me.

"I was," I answer, my eyes on the endless rows of brown trees.

ഓരു

By the time we reach the lake, Kate is cross and sticky, the Lego box deliberately overturned on the seat beside her. At five, she's too old to allow herself the indignity of a nap but too young to successfully fight the pull of sleep without her temper suffering in the process.

"I want to go home!" She shouts from behind, kicking the back of my seat with both feet.

"We can't go home, silly, we're here! Just up this road is Aunt Sarah and Uncle Alex's cottage and then we're here!" I turn around in my seat and smile brightly at my daughter.

"I don't want to go to Aunt Sarah's cottage! I want to go home!"

"Now sweetie," I say, reaching towards the back of the car with a juice box. "You're just hot and you're thirsty, too. Drink this and you'll feel better." I hold the juice box out in the air for a few more seconds then place it in the cup holder.

"No!" Kate shouts, all sweaty outrage. "I-want-to-go-home!" Her feet kick against the seat in unison. Thud, thud.

"Sweetie…"

"ENOUGH!" Patrick says loudly from the driver's seat. "Just stop it!"

Kate's feet stop in mid-air. She reaches over to her cup holder and opens up her juice. With loud sucks she pulls at her straw. I turn to face the front.

"You didn't have to yell at her, Patrick," I say quietly. "She's just cranky from the heat. She's just a little girl."

"First, I wasn't yelling. Second, I wasn't speaking to her, I was speaking to you." Patrick's jaw has clenched again, his shirt wet with sweat.

250

"What?" I say. "You told *me* to 'stop it'?" I blink.

"I was just frustrated, Beth," he says, his eyes on the road. "You shouldn't have to reason with a five-year-old. She should do what you ask the first time you ask it."

"She's hot and tired, Patrick. We all are. It's been a long drive in such heat."

"And that's an excuse for obnoxious behaviour?" He asks. "You know I think you're a great mother and you know I think Kate's a terrific kid, but…"

"But we're here!" I say loudly, turning once again to the back. The little girl's face has lost its furious redness, an empty juice box lying on her lap.

"Hey! Can we go for a swim?" Kate asks, her eyes wide and hopeful.

"Of course!"

"The dog, too?"

"The dog too, if Sarah says it's okay to take him swimming."

"I *know* she will," Kate answers authoritatively. "Last year she let me because I was so gentle with him. Sarah said I'm a dog person!"

"Don't let Butterscotch hear you say that," Patrick says. He turns and smiles at Kate, who sticks her tongue out at him. He pauses, then sticks his tongue out back at her. Kate giggles and peace is procured.

Patrick indicates right and turns down a long, gravel driveway. Kate moves her face towards the open window and listens to the *ping, ping, ping* of small stones jumping up against the car doors. The air seems cooler, the promise of water moving in the breeze.

Patrick clears his throat once, twice. "Now we're here," he says. The car stops in front of a small, one-story building. Before Kate opens her door, an adolescent golden retriever lopes across the lawn to the car.

"Addy!" Kate yells, unbuckling herself and tumbling out of her booster seat and onto the grass. "Do you want to go swimming?"

"Kate! Let's get settled in first," I call after my daughter, watching the little girl and the dog leap at each other.

"Who needs to get settled in when there's swimming to be done?" asks Sarah, moving across the lawn to the car in a few quick strides. "Beth, Patrick, you guys made great time!" She combs her short, blonde hair away from her forehead with her left hand, then reaches out to hug Kate to her hip with the other.

"We had to make great time," says Patrick, as he gets out of the car. "We would have boiled to death if I hadn't sped a bit."

"I forgot to get the air conditioner fixed on my car," I explain to Sarah, shrugging. "I don't really have the money for repairs right now."

"Well, enough about that. Who needs air conditioning when you can jump into a freezing cold lake, right Kate?" Sarah asks.

"That's right!" Kate shouts and reaches into the trunk to grab her pink swimming bag. "I'm going to get changed right now!" She says, racing towards the cottage.

Patrick turns to look at me. "I'll take her in the water," he says, picking up his own bag. "I have a feeling she's not going to wait." He takes a small step toward me and kisses me on the forehead. "Sound good?"

"Yeah, thanks," I answer. I watch him follow my daughter into the cottage, then sink onto the grass, feeling the blades tickle against my bare legs.

"Where's Thomas?" I ask, looking around, as if I'll find the baby hiding behind a tree.

"He's in the cottage, having a nap with Alex," Sarah answers, looking at me closely. "Everything okay?" She asks. "Really okay, I mean?"

"Yeah," I answer, tossing a piece of gravel onto the driveway. "You know."

"I know what?"

"Well, my mood's fine. I haven't been depressed in several years now, actually. I mean, sometimes I get a bit down, but it's not depression. I haven't had an episode since that time when Kate was two. I'm just tired from the drive."

"Then let's go watch them swim," says Sarah, reaching out her hand to pull me back to standing.

ഇ)രു

We have supper on the back deck at a round table, looking out over the lake. The back door of the cottage is open and Thomas's bassinet is in sight. Kate is playing with the dog on the side lawn, her half-eaten meal forgotten. A warm breeze is blowing and I watch as Sarah's husband gently tucks her hair behind an ear. The intimacy of the gesture embarrasses me and I look away. *What's that like?*

"It's beautiful here," I say, looking out on the water.

"I know. This place has been in my family for two generations," says Sarah, reaching across the table for the carafe and refilling her wine glass. "I used to take coming here for granted, until I became a teacher and realized how much I needed a place to come escape to!" She pauses, taking a sip of wine.

"I wish I had a place like this," I say.

"As I always tell you, you're welcome anytime, Beth," Sarah says, putting down her glass. "Not to change the subject, guys, but did you hear that Claire is getting married in the fall?"

"Yeah, someone in the Department mentioned that," says Patrick, spearing a cherry tomato onto his fork. "I have a feeling we won't be invited."

"I doubt we will be, either," says Sarah, dipping her finger into her wine and rubbing the top of her glass. The sound that emanates is low, mournful. "Now that I'm kind of tipsy, do you mind if I ask you a totally inappropriate question?"

"Go for it," says Patrick, grinning. I feel my stomach tighten.

"Should we expect an invitation anytime in the future from the two of you?"

"Sarah!" says Alex, shaking his head at his wife.

I feel the skin on my face start to burn, beginning at my chin and spreading up to my forehead. What happened to my quiet, gentle friend? I turn slightly to look at Patrick's face, which remains pale and relaxed.

"*Of course* I know that I am being a complete ass in asking the question, Alex, but you have to admit, we're all curious. I mean, it has been three years." Sarah takes a gulp of her wine, then places the glass in front of her, swirling the liquid.

"Sarah!" Alex repeats, reaching out to touch her arm. "Come on."

"No, no, Alex, it's fine," says Patrick, cutting lettuce into small, neat pieces. "I'm not surprised that a close friend of Beth's would want to know." He pops the lettuce into his mouth and begins thoughtfully chewing. "The answer to your question, Sarah, would be that we are very happy with how things are right now and why make a change when the status quo is so good?" He smiles in my direction, but his grin does not reach me. I shiver in the candlelight, digging my nails into my palms.

"Am I right, Beth?" Patrick asks.

"I think it's time we head back," I say, standing and reaching for the salad bowl. "Let me first help clean up before I go and get Kate."

"I told you," Alex admonishes his wife.

Sarah stands up and follows me into the cottage. "I'm sorry if I embarrassed you," she says, as she carries plates into the kitchen. "I could blame the wine, but the truth is that I'm worried about you."

"Worried? Why would you be worried?"

"Come on, Kate, I know you, and I know that you must have that white picket fence all picked out for yourself, with the two point five kids running around outside."

"I don't need another one point five children when I have Kate," I answer, sponging off the counter. "And I don't waste time thinking about it."

"And why don't you?'

"Why don't I what?"

"Why don't you waste time thinking about it?" Sarah asks softly, touching my arm. "Beth. I know you. Maybe you don't care about an actual wedding, but I know that you do want a commitment from Patrick. Am I right?"

I look at my friend and try and give an honest answer. "I guess I've never thought I *deserved* those things before. My depression has been like this mine field between us. We spend our energy trying to tiptoe around possible triggers, you know? There hasn't been enough left over to really plan for a future."

"But Beth," Sarah says slowly. "Didn't you tell me earlier that you haven't been depressed for a few years?" I look at her kind face and nod. "So if you can't plan for a future now, then when?"

I shrug, not able to answer, not wanting to answer, for fear that what will come out of my mouth can then not be unsaid.

CHAPTER TWENTY-NINE

I'm quiet on the drive home, which seems to suit Patrick fine. He prefers silence on a car ride. As I sit in the darkness I think about how close Sarah was to the truth. During the last few months I had begun going to open houses near the campus, to see if there were any small homes that we could afford once Patrick finished his Ph.D. and hopefully began teaching. I always told myself that if Patrick found out about these excursions into domesticity I would tell him that I had just looking for fun, that of course I wasn't serious. *Who had I been fooling?* Patrick pulls into my parking lot and turns off the car. He opens the back door and pulls Kate—heavy with sleep—into his arms.

"Thanks," I say, locking the car.

As Patrick puts Kate to bed, I sit down on my sofa. When he comes out to the living room, I beckon him to join me.

"Who ever knew that a five-year-old girl could gain fifty pounds while sleeping?" He jokes, sitting down next to me. "I should really get going, but I'm almost too tired to move!" Patrick reaches over and takes one of my feet in his hands. "Want a quick foot rub before I call it a night?"

"Thanks," I say. After a few moments, however, I pull my foot away from him and sit up. "I just realized something," I say. "You never ask to sleep over."

"Ask to sleep over?" Patrick snorts. "Beth! What are you talking about? You made it very clear when we started seeing each other that because of Kate that was a no-go."

"I know," I say, moving ever-so-slightly away from him on the sofa. "The point is that you never ask."

"What are you saying, Beth?" Patrick crosses his arms. "That I'm supposed to ask to do something you specifically told me not to?"

"No," I say, choosing my words carefully. *What do I mean?* "I realize that when we first started dating again I told you staying over would be too confusing for Kate. But that was over three years ago, Patrick. I mean, why haven't you pushed the issue by now?"

"You want me to push issues?"

"No! I want you to want to sleep over by now. I want you to not be so…accepting of this arrangement." I pause again, finding my words. "I want you to want more."

"Is this about what Sarah said tonight?" Patrick asks, shaking his head. "I knew it, I just knew it."

"It is, in a way. She just touched on something that's been on my mind for a while."

"Come on, Beth. We've talked about this before, about the house, marriage. I said maybe someday we'll take the leap. Just not now."

"Why not now?" I ask. "Why not at least talk about it now?"

"What's wrong with what we have?" Patrick asks. "We have more than most couples I know."

I stare straight ahead, the air between us suddenly as solid and impenetrable as a thick slab of stone. "It's not enough," I say. "Not anymore."

"You know I love you," Patrick says, reaching out to touch my foot. "You must know that."

I nod. "And I love you. And we both love Kate. That's why this is not enough."

"And why do you get to decide when things are not enough? Who appointed you to make decisions for us?"

"I'm not making decisions for us. I'm making decisions for me." I take a deep breath. "What I want," I start, then turn to look at Patrick. I see my worried face reflected in his eyes. Why am I always so eager to make sure that I'm still there? "What I *need* is for this to be something more, to be a true commitment to each other and to Kate. I want us to be a family." My voice has become high-pitched, tight.

"Beth, you shouldn't be getting yourself so worked up. Are you feeling okay?"

"This has nothing to do with my depression," I say, slowly, my throat taunt and aching. "This is the opposite of depression. This is about me wanting a life!"

"You know a life for you includes depression, Beth." Patrick says.

"Why are you telling me that? Don't you think I know that? But I also know that right now I feel fine and that I have been feeling fine for years but that we keep playing these roles of me as the patient and you as my savior and that's *not* fine!"

"And what if I say no?" Patrick asks. "What if I tell you I'm not ready to commit to more than I already have? Are you going to get depressed again?" His words slap me hard on the face.

"Why would you say that?" I whisper.

"Because for the last five years I've had to tiptoe around you for fear that if I upset you in some way, if I *disappointed* you, you'd crash." He pauses. "Do you know how much pressure that puts me under?"

"And do you know how much pressure it puts me under to always feel like I should be *grateful* to you for sticking around, that I shouldn't expect more than this because I don't deserve better?" I gesture with my hands.

"I'm sorry if you feel that way," Patrick says. "Because I like things how they are."

"Then I guess that's it," I say. *Did I really say it? Should I take it back before it's too late?* My words hang low between us, like overripe fruit.

Patrick takes a deep breath and then exhales. He stands up and heads for the door. "We're both tired right now, Beth. Please think about what you're saying," Patrick says, putting on his shoes. "*Please*, just think about it more. This doesn't have to be over." He pauses at the door. "We'll talk tomorrow, okay? Let's meet at the grad pub. Just don't make any final decisions until then."

"Alright," I answer, a lie. I know that the decision has already been made by him, by me, by fate. I think about my tendency to reach out to Patrick to save the day whenever I'm becoming depressed and his equal tendency to come charging in on his white steed. How did I get into such a dysfunctional dynamic? I suddenly think about Patrick driving us to and from Sarah's cottage. Why did we both assume that he would be the one driving my car? And when did I let him start to drive my life? With Patrick I'd willingly become obsequious and deferential. Somehow, when I wasn't looking, I had turned into my mother.

I stay sitting on the sofa for one hour, two. Now that I've made my decision, I'm afraid to go to sleep, afraid to have to face what's waiting for me tomorrow. Even imagining a life without Patrick makes me feel nauseous, gutted. I remember what it was like almost six years ago, when through my thoughtless, impulsive behaviour he left me. *I deserved that.* But this time it's different. This is not about being masochistic, about destroying what is so precious to me. This is about trying to build up, to create a life. This is about moving forward, not back. *So why does it feel the same?* I finally push myself off the sofa and head to my bedroom. Staying awake won't delay the inevitable.

CHAPTER THIRTY

On my way to the ending, I take a detour. Before it's all done, I decide to drive across the city. I park on one of the old streets, the kind that flows in a cement thread to the downtown. It's a street that demands walking, too narrow to navigate between the cars docked on each side. I'll walk, I have time. I step out of the cramped heat of my car and onto the curb. The street is lined with trees, huge maples that threaten to cut out time with their vast branches. No midday sun can penetrate this canopy, here it's always morning.

I start to walk down the sidewalk, searching for the house. I have never seen it before, yet I know it must exist. My gaze moves back and forth, counting the for-sale signs as I go by. One, two, three—not too many for such a long street. I'm half-way down the other side before I see it. *There.* How could I not have noticed it before? Red brick, two stories, with a peaked roof. The house sits at the top of a small hill, its front yard a gentle roll to the sidewalk. The eight steps that lead up to the front door are coloured a dark blue, the paint beginning to chip just a bit. It would be a minor fix-it project for Patrick and Kate, with Patrick doing most of the work yet letting the little girl take all of the credit. Driving down the street after getting groceries one day I would see Kate running to meet me, with Patrick smiling silently behind. Kate would rush to the side of the car before the door had even been opened, all quick, jumbled words and hot pride. *Look at what I did, mommy! See? See? I painted all of it! I did it! It was me! And I even let Patrick help a little!*

To the right of the house is a driveway but no garage. No matter, as we would only need one car. It would be close enough for Patrick to bike to campus; he always said he liked the exercise. And two blocks over I'd noticed a school for Kate. On a street like this there would be a pack of children who would walk together and wouldn't mind the addition of one more little girl.

I creep up the driveway, through the side gate, and into the backyard. The yard is generous, with a small tool shed in the right corner. Just like Patrick always wanted. Another large maple stands guard near the back fence, the perfect place for climbing or fort building. All along both sides of the yard runs a garden in full bloom. I don't know the names of what I see. I've never before had the need to know. But that would not matter. Patrick would take Kate on a hunting expedition to the public library and together they would return hand in hand with the biggest picture book in existence on flowers. I look at the back of the house, at the big kitchen window that faces the maple. This is where I would call to Patrick and Kate to please hurry up and finish naming the flowers already, that dinner was getting cold. Or maybe instead this is where I'd quietly watch as Patrick and Kate bent over the garden together, the meal suddenly not as important as what I saw growing before my eyes.

I peer into the window and see a small, simple kitchen opening up to a larger living space. There's a double sink that's squeezed between the countertop and the stove. This is where Patrick and I would do the dishes after supper, hips and arms bumping as he reached to put each plate up on the shelf. The window would be open to let in a breeze and the far-off drone of cars from outside would be mixed with Kate's high, sweet murmurings as she played in the next room.

In the kitchen would be a small functional table where we would eat most winter meals. In other seasons, weather permitting, we would move to the backyard, Kate leading the way with a handful of forks and spoons. The round outside table would be big enough to eat there with friends but we would often prefer it to be just the three of us, complete. On hot sticky evenings Patrick would light a few citronella candles before supper, while Kate would dance around him, counting her bug bites.

I look up at the second floor, a bit smaller than the bottom perhaps, but with enough room for two bedrooms and a study. Kate would get the room with the wide window, maybe with a cushioned seat just below it. There would be wood floors in each bedroom and oval rugs, thick and welcoming. The main bathroom would be downstairs, with a deep old bathtub and a hand-held shower. On summer nights I would leave the door slightly ajar as I lay in the tub, listening to Patrick and Kate at the piano, as he helped her to discover Middle C.

Kate would want to spend hours in the tub each night, often haggling about how high to run the water. She would bring in three or four of her plastic dolls and would meticulously wash their long blonde hair with a bar of pink soap and the shower head. She would even try and clean off her stuffed lamb as well, getting him soaked in the process. There would be many tears, until Patrick would come up with the idea of hanging the sodden toy by its ears on the clothes line.

On my walk earlier I'd noticed a small park down the road with an old metal slide and a set of swings with hard fabric seats. There's enough of a field to kick around a soccer ball or try to fly a kite. The park is close enough for an evening walk after supper, but far enough that Kate would inevitably clamor to be carried all of the way back. After many refusals Patrick would hoist her up, all elbows and knees, and she would snuggle in like a kitten, her five-year-old legs dangling at his sides.

I walk back through the side gate and stand in the driveway, looking at all that surrounds me. This is the house that has been building in my mind for the last three years. This is the place where Kate and I were meant to grow to three, the place where I could stop drifting and become anchored.

If I am honest—the kind of honest that makes my insides cramp up with cold shame—I will admit that this has only been my plan, just mine. All that led me to this street, to this house, was my dream, not his. For Patrick it was a pleasant story to muse about while sitting on my sofa after supper, in the hours before he headed back to his solitary life, fifteen minutes away. He'd companionably rub my feet while I chattered, spinning castles in the air. To Patrick it was much like the fairy tales Kate thrust at him when he arrived at bedtime, full of fancy and whimsy. A momentary pleasure, not something meant to huddle against on a never-ending night.

What makes this different—what makes this so *hard*—is that I now see that it could have happened, that it could have been real. I hadn't been searching for a kingdom far, far, away. No. What I'd wanted, what I'd needed, had only been three blocks up from the downtown core. Looking at the house I exhale a breath of warm regret. Although I have never been here before, I have come to say goodbye. I glance at the front steps, then at my watch. Patrick will be waiting to have that one last talk. Now it is time to go.

About the Author

$\mathcal{B}$orn in 1970, Alicia Hendley grew up in Waterloo, Ontario, Canada, and now lives in Guelph with her husband and four children. She is a psychologist in the counselling centre at the University of Waterloo, where she works primarily with young adults.

©2010, MEGHAN HENDLEY-LANGEWISCH

Alicia wrote the initial version of *A Subtle Thing* while on maternity leave with her third child, using stolen moments to write and create while her baby napped nearby. Alicia has found the busier and more chaotic life has become, the more vital writing. Whenever possible, wherever possible, and however possible, she writes.

Five Rivers Books

A Subtle Thing, Alicia Hendley, ISBN 9780986542701

Al Capone: Chicago's King of Crime, Nate Hendley, ISBN 9780986542725

Motivate to Create: a guide for writers, Nate Hendley. ISBN 978098654718

Crystal Death: Methamphetamine, North America's #1 Killer Drug, Nate Hendley, ISBN 9780973927832

Harness the Business Writing Process, (Workshop-in-a-book series) Paul Lima, ISBN 9780986563010

(re)Discover the Joy of Creative Writing, (Workshop-in-a-book series) Paul Lima, ISBN 9780986563003

How to Write a Non-fiction Book in 60 Days, (Workshop-in-a-book series), ISBN 9780973927849

Elephant's Breath & London Smoke, Deb Salisbury, ISBN 9780973927825

From Mountains of Ice, Lorina Stephens, ISBN 9780973927856

And the Angels Sang, Lorina Stephens, ISBN 9780973927801

Shadow Song, Lorina Stephens, ISBN 9780973927818

LaVergne, TN USA
20 October 2010
201630LV00001B/28/P